PENGUIN BOOKS

KINGDOM OF BLOOD AND GOLD

Joyce is the author of the young adult contemporary romance, *Lambs for Dinner* (Straits Times Press, 2013) and *Land of Sand and Song* (Penguin Random House SEA, 2021), the first of an Asian fantasy trilogy. She graduated from the National University of Singapore with a degree in English, and is now a finance editor by day and author by night. When not writing, she can be found on Instagram and TikTok at @joycechuawrites sharing her random poetry or fangirling over Asian dramas.

Praise for *Land of Sand and Song*

'An epic, riveting fantasy journey into lush and magical lands, with fast-paced action that will keep you at the edge of your seat until the very end.'

—June CL Tan, author of *Jade Fire Gold*

'With a heroine whose courage is sharper than her knives, and a lush Asian-inspired world stretching from desert dunes to imperial cities, Joyce Chua weaves an enchanting tale of political intrigue, ancient magic, and rebellion.'

—Amélie Wen Zhao, New York Times bestselling author of *Song of Silver, Flame Like Night*

' . . . one of those classic YA fantasies that is fast-paced and action packed and slips in all the fun tropes and character dynamics . . . a fantasy world filled with history and gorgeous mythology and culture.'

—C.G. Drews, author of *A Thousand Perfect Notes*

'Joyce Chua is a masterful wordsmith who understands the craft. Be prepared to lose yourself in her words, be sucked into her world, and find yourself a part of this epic journey.'

—Ning Cai, author of the *Savant trilogy*

'Joyce spins an enchanting tale of magic, vengeance and romance in this new Asian fantasy world. *Land of Sand and Song* is brilliantly written with compelling characters, and you'll find it hard to put down this book once you pick it up.'

—Leslie W., author of *The Night of Legends*

'*Land of Sand and Song* may be set in a desert, but it is full of life, colour and beauty.'

—Daryl Kho, author of *Mist-bound: How to Glue Back Grandpa*

'Fabulously written and multi-layered, this book has everything I love about a good wuxia drama. A must-read.'

—Audrey Chin, author of *The Ash House*

'Compelling and unpredictable.'

—Kopi Soh, author of *Looking After the Ashes*

' . . . a fantastic ride that immediately immerses you into its enchanted world from the very beginning.'

—Catherine Dellosa, author of *Of Myths and Men*

'. . . fast-paced fantasy infused with gorgeous Asian-inspired mythology.'

—Low Ying Ping, author of *Prophecy of the Underworld*

Kingdom of Blood and Gold

Joyce Chua

PENGUIN BOOKS
An imprint of Penguin Random House

PENGUIN BOOKS

USA | Canada | UK | Ireland | Australia
New Zealand | India | South Africa | China | Southeast Asia

Penguin Books is part of the Penguin Random House group of companies
whose addresses can be found at global.penguinrandomhouse.com

Published by Penguin Random House SEA Pte Ltd
9, Changi South Street 3, Level 08-01,
Singapore 486361

First published in Penguin Books by Penguin Random House SEA 2023

ISBN 9789815058789

Typeset in Garamond by MAP Systems, Bangalore, India

www.penguin.sg

To the ones forging their own fates

Contents

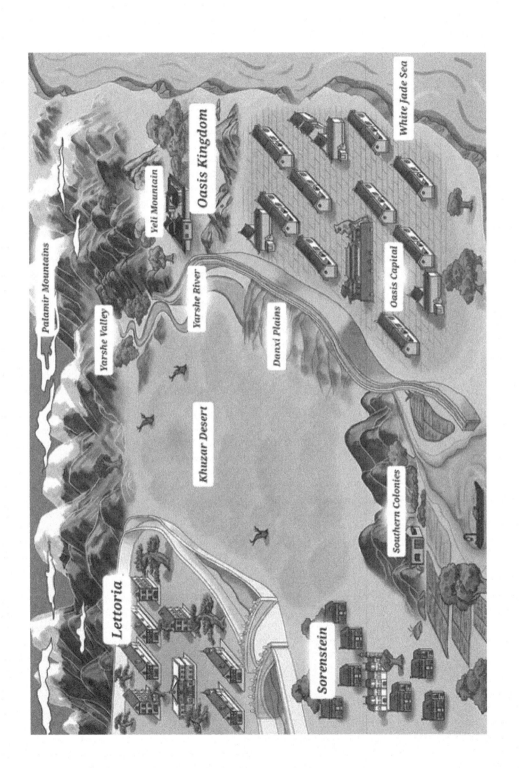

Damohai, Children of the Desert

The story begins with the Immortal Spring and is prophesized to end in the ancient Khuzar Desert, the last dying wilderness on earth where the world would be unmade and remade.

Once the secret meeting place of two celestial beings who defied the rules of heaven and fell in love, the Khuzar Desert is the birthplace of the Damohai—the children of the desert. Descended from the Earth Prince and the Sky Princess's illegitimate son, this race of half-human, half-immortals were once considered guardians of the desert and the Immortal Spring that lay within it.

But even these descendants of the gods were not spared from the greed of men. Built upon the shifting sands, the Hesui Empire—once the largest and mightiest empire in the world ruled by the Damohai—was decimated by an up-and-coming general by the name of Zhaoshun, who colluded with the western colonies to destabilize it.

With Hesui split up, Zhaoshun declared himself the First Emperor of Oasis Kingdom, the eastern part of the fallen empire. The north-western region was snatched up by the Lettorians, the south-western region by the Sorensteins, and the southern region by various colonies that remain in turmoil to date. The Khuzar Desert remains in the middle of these warring nations.

Centuries passed. History was rewritten, and the geography of power was reshaped. The Damohai remains scattered, a lost people practising their magic in the dry, dusty heart of the desert, waiting to be reunited by their prophesied leader one day. Meanwhile, *Oasis Kingdom flourished behind its walls, relying on global trade and the will of its people.*

But the desert's story does not end there, nor does the Damohai's. The story does not end until the Children of the Desert take back what belonged to them—the sacred land that they inherited from their celestial ancestors. It ends only when the five Elementals, chosen from amongst the Damohai, step into their full power and fulfil their destiny to find and unlock the Immortal Spring.

Many now consider this tale to be nothing more than wishful thinking, one that the scattered tribes of the desert, who were once a unified people of the most powerful kingdom in the world. They now cling to it in hopes of restoring their lost glory.

But there are those who believe that the last Elemental would lead the Damohai back into power so that they would, once again, reclaim the desert and their rightful role as guardians of the spring, restoring the balance of magic between heaven and earth.

What remains to be seen is how the Elementals find the spring—would they kill each other on their way to it or be destroyed by their own powers? The fate of the world—and the collective hope of a lost people—is a terrible burden to bear, but it is the fate of the five Elementals to one day restore the lost empire of Hesui to its former unparalleled glory.

Meanwhile, as magic falls in the wrong hands of corrupt rulers, the world continues to be plundered and ravaged by men.

—Excerpt from *Land of Sand and Song:*
Tales from the Khuzar Desert by Lu Ji Fang

ONE

Desert Rose

The desert felt like home.

The frigid wind that ripped across the expanse of sand through the deep, dark night felt like a welcome. Even the sting of the raw northern wind hit differently. Spring might have settled into Oasis Kingdom, but out here on the edge of the desert, they were still in the final grips of winter.

Desert Rose closed her eyes and turned her face to receive the wind, inhaling its sharp, cold scent. Even on the balcony of the small inn—still a two-week ride away from Oasis Kingdom—she thought she could distinctly taste the mulled rose wine, sarnakh. But it was impossible, of course, to smell it all the way from this desert town. There was still some way to go before they reached the Khuzar Desert, where the blood roses would be blooming, ready to be picked, their petals tossed into the mulled wine that would be served in warmed clay bowls to beat the cold.

Yet, they were so close. It had been two weeks of running and hiding from the Oasis Army, giving aliases under hooded cloaks at dodgy-looking inns. Two weeks since the assassination of the Oasis Emperor and their dramatic escape from the palace and the Capital.

Two weeks of travelling with the rogue prince Wei after he broke his mother out of prison.

Last season, when she was still safely home with her father and her tribe, had someone told her she would become a fugitive along with her best friend Qara, a wanted prince and his mother, a fallen queen, she would have laughed. Qara would have laughed with her, too.

But she couldn't appreciate the hilarity of the situation now. The thought that she was now on the run from the Oasis Army, which she had almost drowned with her strange, newfound magical ability to control water, was sobering enough. She was also no closer to finding her father, after being persecuted by her tribemates at the start of last winter.

Ex-tribemates, she corrected herself. They hadn't had an amicable parting the last time—not when they overthrew her father, and Blackstone declared himself the new chieftain of the Dugur tribe. And certainly not when Bataar, one of her best friends growing up, had shot her with a poisoned dart and betrayed her. There was no going back to the way they once were.

Her magic bubbled in her like a lively spring, eager to be released.

Months ago, she had fled from her tribe only to run straight into a capital that wanted her dead for her supernatural abilities, and now she was returning after failing to find her father and armed with a magic she didn't understand herself. What would be waiting for her back home? How would her tribespeople regard her powers? Would they be like Golsha, who saw her as an abomination, or like tribe matriarch Anar Zel, who believed with religious fervour in the five Elementals who would one day come to save them all?

Desert Rose raised a hand and felt the energy flow through the meridian points on her fingertips. Almost instantly, a puddle of water grew at her feet, staining the ground. She had never known anyone who could conjure and manipulate water like that, or like how Windshadow made the wind her weapon. Not even the highest shamans could wield the elements this way; Windshadow was the only other person she knew with an ability like hers.

But how could it be? The Elementals were a myth, a story made up by her ancestors who wanted to believe the Damohai would one day take back the desert and restore their kingdom to greatness. Anar Zel considered her scepticism blasphemy, but Desert Rose didn't care. She was no Elemental; she was just an orphan her father had picked up in the desert—a child with no name and no past. She would have died if not for him. But then how had she survived until he'd found her? What was her life like before he took her into the tribe?

A deep voice behind her made her jump.

'You know, whatever your worries are, you're not going to solve them by losing sleep over them.'

She turned to find Wei behind her, a wry smile on his face as he glanced at the puddle of water, then at her. She was getting accustomed to seeing that smile these days, especially when he looked at her, almost as though they were in on a secret that no one else was privy to.

But his face reflected the bone-deep exhaustion she had felt even before they fled Oasis Kingdom. On some nights when she was unable to sleep and went to check on everyone, she could hear him toss and turn in bed, murmuring in his sleep before he jolted awake, panting.

On one of those nights, she went over to his bed and heard the names he was calling out. He called for his Snow Wolf Sect friends, the ones who had met their end when they helped him charge into the imperial palace last winter. He had called for his brother, Crown Prince Yong, who had been a pawn in a political struggle and was assassinated within his chamber. He called for his mother, too, who was sound asleep in the next room but growing weaker by the day.

She understood Wei's nightmares; she had her fair share of them. They might have left the turmoil of the palace behind, but the demons continued to live inside them.

'I could say the same for you,' she replied.

He stared out at the swathe of snow-dotted sand before them. 'The desert feels restless. It makes me restless too.' His tone was light, but there was no hiding the tension in his voice.

'We can set out earlier today,' she suggested.

'My mother is too weak to travel further. She needs more time to rest.' A small sigh escaped his lips. 'But we don't have the luxury of that.'

Wei's mother had been imprisoned for a year, framed by the current Empress Dowager for attempted regicide. It was little surprise that her body was still struggling to adapt to the outside world, not just the one beyond the prison walls but outside, where magic—both light and dark—ran rampant. Out here, the air was keener, its scent almost feral in the dregs of winter, nothing like the tempered breezes within the confines of the staid Oasis Kingdom.

'There's a desert town three days away from here—two if we ride fast,' she said. 'You can stay there with her.'

'And leave you and Qara to fend for yourselves?'

'May I remind you that I've fended off the Imperial Army before— and a sand hound. Plus, Qara is a skilled rider and markswoman. We'll be fine.'

There was that wry smile again, almost indulgent. A hint of amusement brought temporary light to his onyx eyes. She was glad she wasn't the only one who recalled how they had first met, fighting off a feral desert demon that her tribe had sent to hunt her down.

'I wouldn't brag about the sand-hound incident, given that you were attacked and I had to help you purge out the venom,' he said.

She couldn't argue with that.

His expression sobered before she could find a retort. 'You saved my life, Rose. Mine and my mother's. We stick together from here on—at least until we get you both home.'

A wave of gratitude surged through her. To think they had started in this desert barely trusting each other. If the events of the past few months had taught her anything, it was that the people you trusted the most could turn out to have deceived you the longest, while those you had your guard up against could become the most unlikely allies.

'We'll have my tribe shamans heal your mother,' she promised. 'She'll get better in no time.'

He nodded, then peered at her face. 'Will *you*?'

He had noticed. In the days after their grand escape from Oasis Capital—where she had nearly expended herself by conjuring a water platform that propelled them through the streets, over the Capital walls, and into the relative safety of the outside world—she had been reeling in the aftermath of using her powers to such an unprecedented extent.

She lifted a shaking hand to summon an orb of water in her palm. The sensation of her soul filling up from within grew increasingly familiar each time she used her power, like a flame that became brighter the longer it burned. She was starting to understand its rhythm and gain control of it. Using it in short bursts no longer wore her out, though it left her body buzzing and restless, as though another creature lived inside her, demanding she use more of her magic.

Whatever this power was, wherever it came from, she would learn it, understand it, and wield it the way Windshadow did. It was hers to own now, and she would become its master before it made her its slave.

'I think I will,' she said at last.

TWO

Wei

Wei watched the spark of determination flare in Desert Rose's eyes, not unlike the first time when he had met her. She had been adamant about entering Oasis Capital to find her father then, despite having no connections there or an understanding of the Capital ways. It was partly her unshakeable resolve that had compelled him to offer her a ride to the Capital.

Her hands began to shake the longer she sustained the water orb between her cupped palms. Her brows pulled closer and she bit her lower lip hard. He wrapped his hands around her cold ones, not letting go until her palms met and the orb shrank and disappeared between her folded hands. She looked up at him, blinking as though she was snapping out of a trance.

'Take it easy,' he said. 'We need you at full strength for the journey ahead.'

Her expression settled as she looked him in the eye. A small smile flickered across her face. He felt the sudden urge to say something, but nothing sounded right in his head. He had already thanked her for rescuing him and his mother from the Capital. He had also thanked her for offering them a place of refuge among her people. But what he meant to say was more than just a thank you.

Before he could figure out what exactly it was, something else interrupted them—a raspy hiss that rattled through the desert. For nights now, ever since they came here, he had heard the noises coming from beneath the sands, the ghostly cries and chittering of beings cloaked by darkness. The desert was growing restless, and something stirred beneath the sands like a beast seeking its first meal after a long hibernation.

Could it have sensed Desert Rose's magic? Was it responding to it?

In the distance, a dark spot appeared among the steel-grey clouds. Wei squinted. The dark spot loomed closer until he could make out the shape of his pet hawk, Sunrise. He let go of Desert Rose's hands to receive the folded letter it brought to him.

Matron's script was as neat as ever. The head of all Houses in the imperial palace—also the emperor's court lady—had trained him in calligraphy when he was a boy; he could recognize her handwriting anywhere. Back when he was out in the desert searching for the mythical spring his father had desperately sought, it was her intel that had kept him apprised of all the goings-on in the palace.

And now, it seemed like things were happening at breakneck speed in Oasis Kingdom.

Fourth star rises, a castaway returns. Witch-hunt ensues, spring army heads northwest.

Wei read the note once, then showed it to Desert Rose. She took less than a moment to understand Matron's words.

Now that Wei's half-brother and Fourth Prince, Meng, had ascended the throne as interim emperor, the first thing Empress Wang Yi—now the Empress Dowager—did was to have her eldest son, Han, officially brought back from exile.

Meanwhile, a search party targeting Desert Rose was now on their trail, and the Imperial Army continued to scour the desert for the spring that his father had spent his last days fixated on finding.

Wei exchanged a grim look with Desert Rose. Nothing seemed to have changed since the last emperor's rule. The ripple of unease he had felt in his gut ever since they fled from the Capital now grew into a wave. He shouldn't be so attached to the kingdom that had shunned him and vilified his mother, a kingdom that was so steeped in the fear and hatred of magic that it drank up every lie fed by his father. He shouldn't still worry about the fate of the kingdom that he had long ago left behind.

Yet, as much as it had denounced him, it remained a place that held a handful of fond memories. He had grown up there; there were corners of the palace that once brought him solace.

There was much to fault with Oasis Kingdom, not least of all the centuries of lies and manipulation by the monarchy, which had created the current environment of fear, distrust, and hate among the people towards those who were different from them—the outsiders and the outcasts.

Yet, despite having turned his back on the imperial family, a part of him still hoped his kingdom could be salvaged.

Desert Rose's voice broke into his thoughts.

'So he got what he wanted,' she said, still staring at the note. Wei's attention drifted back to her. 'Prince Meng told me the only way he could restore the kingdom and help the people was by becoming emperor.'

'I don't doubt his intentions, only his execution,' said Wei. 'And his autonomy.'

She glanced up at him. 'You think Empress Wangyi will be controlling him from the back?'

'I've learnt not to underestimate that woman's ambition.' The fact that she had framed his mother for attempted regicide and had her imprisoned, and then plotted to have Meng take over the throne said it all. 'Meng will no doubt attempt to change the system and transform the kingdom. But his hands are tied, even as he sits on the throne.' He shook his head. 'In any case, that's out of our hands now. Our mission now is to get you home and find your father, then maybe we can catch a break at last.'

The smile she gave him was weary. 'Sounds like a plan.'

Wei could see the worry behind her troubled eyes. Before he could offer some feeble reassurance, Zeyan, his oldest and most loyal friend, appeared behind them on the balcony, looking more resigned than flustered this time. Wei guessed almost right away what he was about to say.

'The imperial scouts are here.'

* * *

There was no time to gather everyone and run. The scouts were already in the inn by the time everyone had packed up their belongings. No one else was up at this hour, save for the bleary-eyed innkeeper who seemed flustered by the sudden barrage of soldiers. Their conversation was low, but he could make out the words 'rogue prince', 'refugees', and 'traitors'.

Wei watched them from the stair-landing with Desert Rose as Zeyan hurried to gather everyone. He turned to Desert Rose. 'Ride hard. I'll catch up with you lot in the desert town.'

She frowned. 'What are you going to do?'

He nodded at the scouts downstairs. 'I'll distract them, buy you all some time.'

'By distract, you mean…'

'Trust me,' was all he said. She didn't need to know that he didn't exactly have a plan yet. What mattered most now was that they manage to put as much distance from the scouts as possible.

Wei clattered down the stairs, drawing his sword once he secured the soldiers' attention. A collective look of recognition dawned upon their faces, and they charged forward without hesitation. He was no longer a prince, just a wanted man, so there was no need for courtesy or ceremony.

Just like old times, Wei thought with a grim smile as he dodged past the scouts and slipped out the front door. He had crossed swords with the likes of them countless times in the years he had spent outside Oasis Kingdom until the news of his brother's death drove him home eventually.

Out in the stables, his steed was already raring to go before he freed it and hopped on. The remnant sting of winter remained in the air. The wind scraped his skin like fine sand as he rode.

Had Zeyan and Desert Rose managed to lead the rest out of the inn? There was no indication of a commotion anywhere in the inn, which Wei took to be a good sign.

Now for a plan.

His time with the Snow Wolf Sect had taught him that the best way to go unseen was to blend in. They had passed by a bazaar not too far from this inn, a day ago. It would be bustling at this hour with merchants and shoppers, traders and thieves. Perfect for hiding.

Wei rode into the breaking dawn, making no effort to conceal his movement. The scouts gave chase soon enough, with five of them jumping on his trail. Wei rode without a backward glance, relying on the sound of hooves and voices behind him to gauge the distance between them.

He had promised his mother a better future, away from what she suffered at the palace. But what future could he give her when he was being chased by imperial scouts every day when his feet could not even touch the ground long enough for him to build his mother a home?

A year of being locked up in a draughty prison cell had also worn down her already frail body, and Wei was desperate to find a quick fix for her. The water from the Immortal Spring was said to cure all mortal maladies, and even contain the elixir of life his dead father had been desperate to acquire for himself. But Wei had, like countless others, scoured almost the entire Khuzar Desert for the spring to no avail. To continue holding on to the foolish hope that he might succeed in finding it would be continuing to put his mother's life on the line.

In the distance, the bazaar came into view, already teeming with the morning rabble. The band of imperial scouts were still on his tail, though far behind enough for him to blend into the crowd. Wei slid off his horse and left it at the stables by the entrance of the bazaar; then, he entered the fray.

The bazaar was just large enough for him to get lost in for a while before sneaking out through the other end. Here, he could get some respite amongst the mix of weary travellers, eagle-eyed bargain hunters, and hopeful merchants from around the region.

The air was laced with the smell of sweetened fried buns and mare's milk, which made Wei aware of his growling stomach. He paid for a fried bun and let the crowd jostle him along as he absently observed the display of various cured meats, clay pottery from N'yong down south, nuts and dates from Iria on the south-western corner of the desert, silk scarves and porcelain wares from Oasis Kingdom, and ornately carved knives likely from the southern territories.

He paused to pick up a pair of double knives, momentarily forgetting about the scouts on his tail. Desert Rose's double knives were a gift from her father, and she always wore them close to her. Wei often caught her reaching for them at her belt, almost as if to reassure herself that she was protected by more than just her weapons.

'Impeccable taste, good sir,' the stall-keeper cooed, breaking into his thoughts. 'This is a rare find from Chinnai, absolutely one of its kind, with a mother-of-pearl hilt, and Katari steel blade.'

Wei found himself paying for them before he realized what he was doing. He stashed them away as quickly as he tried to put aside his thoughts of Desert Rose, but the familiar image of her fiddling with her knives made the corners of his lips rise.

A figure in the distance on his left made him pause.

Instincts heightened, he whipped around and scanned the crowd. Not twenty paces away, he caught sight of a familiar face. Matron's letter flashed across his mind.

A castaway returns.

Han. In the flesh. Half-obscured by the milling crowd, but it was him, no doubt.

The last time Wei had seen his eldest brother—*half-brother,* he corrected himself—was almost three years ago, before Han was exiled by their father for suspected treason and Wei left Oasis Kingdom in search of his own destiny.

Han was believed by many to have died in the wind-ravaged wilderness of Hobeska up north, but Wei knew Empress Wangyi had never given up hope of restoring him to his imperial position. Everything she had done—framing Wei's mother for regicide, arranging for the murder of the Crown Prince, orchestrating Meng's ascend to the throne, and the chaotic coup that happened during the Spring Ceremony—was ultimately to bring Han home again.

Everyone knew that Wangyi had always favoured Han. He shared her ambition, her hunger for power, and the same ruthlessness towards anything that stood in their way.

A memory surged to the surface, catching him off guard. They were children then, Wei ten and Han twelve, but his older brother already had a taste for cruelty. Yong, his second brother, would always try to stay out of Han's way and instructed Wei to do the same.

'We are not brothers to him,' Yong once told him. 'Don't expect him to treat us like we are.'

But Wei hadn't fully believed him. The four of them had grown up together. Surely no brother could be so heartless, even if they didn't share the same mother.

Wei had followed Han to his chamber one day after their lessons, armed with a list of topics to engage him in, as well as his bow and arrow, hoping that he and Han might practise together. Wasn't that how brothers bonded? But Han had ignored him all the way from the classroom to his chamber, taking great strides to throw Wei off.

Yet, Wei was determined to have his brother speak to him. If their handmaiden and servants thought him foolish, they showed no indication of it as they trailed a respectful distance behind them in silence.

It was a balmy summer's day, one that Wei would usually spend sneaking to the military courtyard to watch the Imperial Army train, or the archery square to practice his aim. But that day, he was on a different mission.

When they arrived at the Red Circle, the servants bowed and drifted away; only their nannies remained. Wei finally approached his elder brother, just as they stepped through the doors of the Han's chamber.

'Han,' Wei said, aware of how thin and reedy his voice sounded, very much like a boy's, while Han's was already starting to break. He cleared his throat and tried again. 'Han, do you want to play bow and arrow with me?'

Han paused, then spun around, a wolfish smile spreading slowly across his face. 'Sure. If you can help me retrieve a water lily from the pond for my mother, I'll even teach you my special archery trick. But it has to be a water lily from the middle of the pond.'

Wei had waded straight into the Seven Star Pond with nothing but a rope that he made his nanny hold on to, ignoring her pleas to abandon this mission.

He had barely gotten halfway across the pond before the cold, slimy water reached his neck. Another step forward, and his foot sank into the soft, muddy ground. The more he struggled, the deeper his feet drove into the mud.

'Han, help,' he cried, swallowing a mouthful of muddy water.

Han watched by the side with his hands behind his back. His nanny looked torn between her desire to help Wei and her loyalty to Han, eventually choosing to remain where she was.

'You'll have to try harder, Wei,' Han drawled.

It took four manservants to drag Wei out of the pond that afternoon, but not before he went under. When at last he managed to crawl to land, sopping wet, covered in mud, and choking on pond water, Han only shot him a stony glance.

'Shame,' he said. 'I was looking forward to beating you in archery.'

'But—I tried,' Wei spluttered as his brother started to walk away.

Han whirled around, all patience lost. 'Let me make this clear once and for all,' he snarled. 'I am not your brother or your friend. You are just an unwanted son, and I have no use for someone who is in no one's favour. Speak to me again and I will kill you.'

After that incident, Wei never spoke to Han again.

Even from afar in a crowded market now, he saw the same coldness in the older boy's gaze. In fact, it had become even more pronounced, as though he had brought the bitterness of Hobeska back with him. Years of being in exile had also hardened his features further and distorted his face into a perpetual sneer.

Han had always been a lone wolf, but this time he was not alone. Next to him traipsed a younger boy with a sharp gaze and a wiry frame that keened with restless energy. It was hard to figure out his origins—

he had the rosy flush of a Sorenstein city-dweller, the sun-weathered skin of a desert tribe member, the heavyset jaw of a northerner, and the lean frame of N'yongite.

Wei suddenly realized he had lingered here for too long. Caught between the imperial scouts and Han was the last place he wanted to be.

He was about to scurry off when Han turned in his direction. Wei found himself staring right into his brother's dark, pitiless eyes. He turned away, his heart racing. Had Han recognized him? He ducked behind a hawker who was balancing two woven baskets of spices on his shoulders and followed in his footsteps.

'Fire!' someone cried somewhere to his right.

The fire seemed to have ignited out of nowhere and was already ravaging a part of the market. In the time it took Wei to locate the source of the commotion, at least four stalls and two carts were already in flames. What kind of fire spread that quickly?

People began to scream and flee, abandoning their goods, carts, and purchases, as the fire tore through the market. Released from their stalls, horses, camels, and livestock trampled through the market, adding to the chaos.

Out of the commotion, Wei heard the snarl of Han's voice. 'Find him. I know Wei is here.'

Wei jostled through the stampeding crowd towards the stables, praying there was but one camel left for him. Behind him, Han and his younger companion stormed through the blazing market, eyes peeled and unbothered by the flames.

Had his brother set that fire? Had he done all this just to kill him, never mind the number of innocents here?

He reached the stables at last. His steed was gone and the remaining ones were stamping their hooves in panic. He released them all, then leapt onto a camel and took off into the desert again. Behind him, the market grew quieter and quieter, until nothing more could be heard but the hiss and crackle of flames.

He rode just far enough to leave the stench of smoke behind before looking back. All that remained were the charred remains of a once bustling market, now razed to the ground. Smoke spiralled into the azure sky, streaking it with sooty fingers. Pockets of contained fire riddled the grounds, but there was no more sign of life. No one else had escaped.

Wei found himself shaking, his fists clenched by his side. These people had died because of him. Because his brother had caught a mere glimpse of him and wanted to leave no stone unturned to ensure his death. Han had always been unscrupulous, but Wei had never expected him to go to this extent, or that he would make good on his promise to kill Wei the next time he saw him.

Now that he was returning to Oasis Kingdom, he would be after only one thing: the throne. And the only people standing in his way were his brothers.

Wei rode back into the desert, eager to catch up with Desert Rose and the rest. Han was back, and today's destruction was only the first sign of things to come.

THREE

Windshadow

As twilight crept upon the House of Night, a lone gust of wind whipped the stray leaves in the backyard into a frenzy. It whirled and whistled like a creature with a life of its own. Yet, on the cusp of spring, no one would find this breeze out of the ordinary. No one in Oasis Kingdom, which had been purged of all magic centuries ago, would suspect that something supernatural lived within the palace grounds.

In the dwindling light, Windshadow spun and twisted through the winding corridors, swerved around sharp corners, and trailed through the deserted gardens and cavernous halls. In her elemental form, she could stretch out her stiff, aching body and draw strength from her element. As the wind, she was infinite—near invincible. But this was nothing like what the natural arts had taught her, nothing like what she had learnt in her tribe. No, this was all her. Her power wasn't cultivated by the shaman mentors in her tribe; it had always been a part of her.

She was born with a destiny, and she was here to fulfil it through whatever means possible.

Following the events of recent weeks—the mayhem wreaked by the beast-people, the assassination of the Fifteenth Oasis Emperor, and

18

Prince Meng's ascension to the throne—the palace was near deserted at this hour. Save for the odd pair of maids and servants, everyone else had retired to the safety of their chambers after dinner.

At the House of Night, her fellow assassins-in-training—what remained of them, at least—had retreated to the dormitory and didn't pay much heed when Windshadow told them she was going for a walk.

Windshadow had no desire to remain in the dorm with them, but since she was involved in the assassination and everyone in the palace was still under investigation for the Spring Ceremony mayhem, her physical presence around Prince Meng—*the Sixteenth Oasis Emperor*, she corrected herself—now would bring about suspicion towards them both.

Rumours were already swirling around the palace. There was talk among servants and even court officials that he had joined hands with the shouren, the shapeshifting beast-people of the North, to stage the Spring Ceremony rebellion so he could finally seize the throne. 'How can we lay our faith in someone who murdered his own father?' she overheard one soldier say to another.

At one point, Windshadow almost acted on the urge to set the record straight. Prince Meng had never intended to murder his father. His plan had always been to overthrow him and take over the throne, which would have been easy for Prince Meng since the people had lost faith in his father long ago, thanks to the famine and border wars.

Killing the emperor was Windshadow's idea; so was framing Desert Rose for the murder. It was the only way the road before them could be properly cleared. She did what she had to do, and she would not apologize for it. Prince Meng was too sentimental. He would have let his father live and put a stop to what Empress Wangyi was orchestrating. Windshadow couldn't put her fate entirely in his hands. They had an agreement; they were a team. Neither of them could succeed if the other failed.

Spurred by renewed determination, she barrelled between a pair of court maids carrying empty trays of food back to the Hall of Virtuous

Happiness. They leapt apart at the sudden gust of wind, almost dropping their trays.

Closer to the Red Circle, the last vestiges of the emperor's death remained as a stark reminder of the unrest that had swept through the palace not too long ago. The mourning altar had been taken down that morning, now that it had been over a week since the emperor was killed, but the buildings remained swathed in white cloth that billowed in the breeze like ghosts in the night. A troubled air lingered in the palace. With both the Fifteenth Emperor and Crown Prince murdered in a matter of months, no one knew what to expect next.

Windshadow arrived at last at the Anqing Palace, home of the Empress Dowager. Low voices drifted out of her lit chamber, but Windshadow couldn't make out the words. She seeped through the window and settled in a corner, far enough so she wouldn't be detected but close enough to overhear Empress Dowager Wangyi and High Advisor Mian's conversation by the tea table.

'—all thanks to your superb planning, Your Majesty,' Mian was saying. 'I'm sure Emperor Meng harbours nothing but gratitude towards you now that he's on the throne.'

'Unfortunately, he's been too busy with his duties to express that gratitude to me,' the Empress Dowager said as she reclined in her seat. 'But at least Han is on his way home as we speak.'

Never mind that her husband had been murdered mere weeks ago or that Oasis Kingdom and the palace were in upheaval. The First Prince was all Wangyi could talk about ever since Prince Meng became emperor. The first thing she made Meng do was to bring her eldest son back from exile.

'This calls for a celebration, Your Majesty,' said Mian.

'Not until Han is safely back home. I want no mistakes this time. Everything must go according to plan.'

Mian bowed. 'Of course, Your Majesty. Be assured it will.'

'What news of the desert girl?'

Windshadow stilled. She didn't need the Empress Dowager keeping tabs on her; no one except Prince Meng was supposed to know about her alliance with him.

'You mean the one who escaped with Prince—' He flinched at the sharp look the Empress Dowager shot him. 'I mean, Wei and Luzhen? They're still at large, Your Majesty. Our scouts have been on their trail for almost a month.'

Windshadow felt a twinge of guilt at the mention of Desert Rose, her fellow desert girl whom she had called *azzi* more times than was genuine, but she shook it off almost instantly. She was never meant to befriend another Elemental, not if she wanted to be the last one standing.

The Empress Dowager narrowed her gaze. 'We need the girl captured or killed. The court will need someone to convict before the emperor's death can find closure. And I want Wei and Luzhen both dead. Even the thought of them roaming beyond our gates makes me uneasy.'

'Yes, Your Majesty. I will inform you once I receive any news about the refugees.'

'And what of the other desert girl?'

'Still training at the House of Night, Your Majesty.'

'Watch her closely. I don't want her getting too close to Meng. If she was part of what happened at the Spring Ceremony, then she knows too much.'

Windshadow gave her a mental sneer. *You wouldn't have become Empress Dowager if not for my help.*

The Empress Dowager glanced at the window. 'It's chilly in here. Make sure the windows are closed tight on your way out.'

Mian bowed again before retreating.

Windshadow slipped out through the windows before he shut them behind him. She thought about stopping by Prince Meng's chamber to update him on what she had overheard, but it was too risky. She had to return to the House of Night before anyone noticed her extended absence. Besides, being in wind form still made a dent in her energy, and she needed it for tomorrow's training.

She skirted around a pair of maids and ducked past Matron standing by the courtyard of the Hall of Virtuous Happiness. A sense of dread grew heavier in her by the moment. It wasn't until she arrived at the House of Night and joined the other assassins-in-training in the dormitory that she understood why.

The unsettling notion that something bigger was in store—something beyond what she and Meng had anticipated.

Those who aim for the throne cannot have it.
Those who seek power cannot wield it.

—'Tenets for the Heavenly Ruler'
by High Priest Gao Zong

FOUR

Meng

In the desolate quiet of his study chamber, the Sixteenth Oasis Emperor sat slumped in his seat.

It had been a full day of approving official documents, discussions with magistrates and sessions with the council members, meeting foreign ambassadors, and more approvals of documents. With everyone pressing close to him or wanting something from him, Meng barely had a moment to breathe.

He longed to sit with his knees drawn at the foot of a bookshelf in the imperial library like he used to, but that sort of behaviour wouldn't befit an Oasis Emperor. He had expected to have more autonomy once he ascended the throne but he was wrong. More eyes were on him now than ever before. One wrong move and he would be deemed incompetent, or worse, treasonous. The rumours about his involvement in his father's death hadn't died down yet, and Meng knew there were vultures everywhere eyeing his throne, waiting for his downfall.

Every move he made now would decide his fate and that of Oasis Kingdom. He had the power now, and the responsibility. He could not fail.

A girl once told him he was brave. Of course, that was before she found out the truth about his intentions. But for a moment then, she had believed it, and so had he—almost. He had believed that he could save Oasis Kingdom.

And—if he were truthful with himself—she had also helped him envision a future beyond these palace walls, if only for a moment. She made him believe that he could transcend his destiny to become more than someone who had his whole life planned out for him since birth. She had told him stories from the desert, of a world so different from his that it was almost hard to imagine it lay just beyond Oasis Kingdom, separated by a barrier that guarded this land against outside magic.

It didn't feel that long ago, the nights they had sat side by side in the library, warming their icy hands with cups of steaming tea. It had felt like a sweet forbidden reprieve, being holed up in the library, away from the endless demands and conspiracies of the imperial court. Many a time, when he was with her, he would almost forget that he was the Fourth Prince, set to take over the throne.

But he had made his choice. He had chosen duty over her—and even used her—and now he would lay in the bed he had made for himself. He and Desert Rose were from different worlds after all; their paths were destined to be different too.

A gentle breeze ruffled the scrolls on his desk and blew off a couple of them. When he looked up, Windshadow was standing before him in her House of Night uniform, black training tunic belted at the waist, her hair in a haphazard bun. She was a force one couldn't ignore—even without her powers. In her eyes was the same resolute glint he had seen the first time he had met her in a prison cell, where she had spent a week after being caught in a riot. Even now, she hadn't lost sight of her goal.

'How many times have I told you to knock?' Meng griped, glancing at the fallen scrolls.

She reached over to give his mahogany desk two raps. 'There.'

Meng swallowed his irritation at her impudence. It was he who had told her to forgo all propriety with him when he had first enlisted her help.

Tonight, she was a whirling dervish. He could sense her impatience from across the desk, almost as if she couldn't wait to take off into the wind and kill some officials standing in their way. He gave the scrolls another pointed look.

'It's been almost a month, Your Majesty,' she said as she grudgingly picked up the scrolls and set them back onto the pile.

'Yes, Windshadow,' he sighed, already understanding her purpose here tonight. 'We can get to that as soon as I'm through with'—he glanced at the stack of official documents still waiting for him to peruse and approve—'that.'

'The deal was to unleash the magic in this land once I helped you become emperor.' She folded her arms again. 'Desert Rose and I have retrieved the scroll from the White Crypt, and I have done my part.'

Her part had entailed murdering his half-brother, the Crown Prince, so that the emperor's position would be shaken, along with the people's faith in his rule. Her methods were nothing if not extreme, Meng had come to learn, but his mother had approved of the way she had disposed of the Crown Prince.

An emperor must rule with his brain, not his heart, she had told him just days after his coronation ceremony. *What good is a leader who is easily swayed by his own heart?*

He had to focus. The fate of the kingdom and the lives of his people lay in his hands now, and there was much to do.

He returned his attention to Windshadow.

'I've been busy this month, Windshadow. I don't have time to crack my head over riddles in an ancient scroll. Besides, I don't see you offering any answers.'

When Desert Rose and Windshadow had returned last winter with the magically sealed scroll that contained a folk tale, Meng had thought it was a cruel joke played by the ancient sorcerers who had buried it at the bottom of a well in the White Crypt, guaranteeing all but none would be able to unseal the magic in the kingdom. But Duru-shel Minta—which translated to 'the War of the Realms' from the ancient Hesui tongue—was his only clue to restoring the magic that Oasis Kingdom had denied and denounced for centuries. The scroll was his only hope to defeat Han—who, as far as he knew, did not yet know about the existence of the scroll—and stay on the throne.

Meng had memorised Duru-shel Minta by now:

There was a time when heaven met earth
through the sacred Celestial Pool.
Gods and monsters worked together,
each with a task to do.
They guarded their realms and upheld the peace,
kept the magic flowing through.
But when two immortals broke the rules,
gods and demons took to war.
The Pool dried up and magic fell
into the inept hands of men.
And so lies the world, sickened by greed
until the Pool flows free again.
Only the essence of the gods can free
that which has been contained.

But it wasn't just his brother against whom the magic would come in handy. Restoring magic in Oasis Kingdom would also be the first step to preparing it for the long-brewing war with Lettoria and, potentially, the Southern Colonies. Without magic, they were as good as sitting ducks. His father's strategy of pinning all his hopes on a magical, fabled spring had proven impractical. To deal with an enemy that already had the upper hand in magic-infused military prowess, they needed to fight fire with fire.

Windshadow interrupted his thoughts.

'Well, if you don't figure out that riddle soon, you might not get the chance to execute the rest of the plan.'

He frowned. 'What's that supposed to mean?'

'I mean that your brother is on his way home.'

'I know that.'

'Then you must also know that your seat may not stay warm for long.' She took a step closer and leaned forward on the desk. 'I can't sit around waiting for him to usurp your throne.'

Meng knew that his mother had plans for Han, and no doubt expected him to go along with them. But surely she wouldn't jeopardize his position in favour of Han, after everything he had done for her?

'I have things under control,' he said, trying to sound convincing enough for the both of them. 'Just give me some time—'

'The Empress Dowager arrives,' a voice announced from outside the chamber. Meng started. When he turned back to Windshadow, she had already vanished, leaving behind only a gust of wind that teased the scrolls again.

The doors of the chamber parted for the Empress Dowager, accompanied by Blossom, her handmaiden. Even at this hour, she looked impeccably put together, her jade-green robe crisp and pristine, and not a strand of hair out of her bejewelled clasp. She gave an imperious wave, signalling for Blossom to take her leave. The latter bowed and retreated from the chamber.

Meng rose to his feet. 'Greetings, Mother. What brings you here at this hour?'

The Empress Dowager surveyed the chamber, her gaze lingering on the windows and dimmer corners. 'Were you speaking to someone? I thought I heard a second voice.'

'I think aloud sometimes, Mother.'

She appeared unconvinced but moved on from the topic. Her face eased into a smile when she saw the pile of scrolls on his desk. 'You've been working hard, Your Majesty.'

She did that sometimes, called him 'Your Majesty' like it was a compliment for how far he had climbed. But to him it sounded like a veiled threat, reminding him of all that he stood to lose if he didn't watch his back.

He gave her a reassuring smile all the same. 'Not at all, Mother. It's just some paperwork.' He gestured at a carved oak chair by the bookshelf. 'Please take a seat.'

'You will soon fit into this role, Meng,' his mother said as she settled into the chair. 'It has been yours since birth. Advisor Mian read it clearly in the stars.'

He had heard this refrain countless times. As much as his father and ancestors decried magic, they had believed that their destinies were written in the stars, and to defy one's fate was to defy the will of heaven. Meng's birth star, the one he shared with his half-brother Wei, had allegedly shone high and bright in the sky the night they were born. But sometimes, in his dark, private moments, Meng wished the High Advisor had read Wei's fate as his. Sometimes, he wished he could throw all inhibitions to the wind and leave behind his life in the palace to find his place in the vast, wild world.

But he couldn't turn his back on this kingdom. Despite its flaws, it was his home, and he now had the power to change it for the better. He had to.

'I will, Mother,' he replied with more conviction than he had felt in the past few weeks. 'In fact, I have several proposals for which I would like your opinion. Do you remember the scroll that Desert Rose'—he faltered briefly on her name before pressing on, ignoring his mother's disapproving stare—'retrieved from the White Crypt for us last winter?'

His mother made no response.

'She deciphered it for us, too. I would like to study it further and understand what exactly it holds the key to—'

'Meng,' the Empress Dowager snapped. 'What exactly is studying an ancient scroll buried at the bottom of a well going to achieve?'

'It might be the biggest help to us, Mother. It might unlock the magic that's been lying dormant in this kingdom for centuries. Think of how much richer and stronger we could be as a kingdom if we stopped suppressing...'

Meng trailed off as her lips thinned with each passing syllable.

'Your father was the same,' she said. 'Obsessed with that wretched spring and wasting resources on that fool's errand to find it. Are you going to follow in his footsteps? Lose your mind over some fabled promise of magic saving us all? Don't be naïve, Meng.'

'But Moth—'

'*Enough*. I don't want to hear of this again. We have no time to waste on deciphering an old scroll. We need to focus on steadying our control over the kingdom before expanding it. Last year's famine and drought have set us back significantly, and our enemies have been gaining the upper hand.'

'That's what I'm saying, Mother. We are putting ourselves at a disadvantage by denying the magic that still exists in this kingdom. Take Lettoria, for instance. They are far ahead of us with the magical technology they've been developing—'

'Your radical ideas will not sit well with the council. You need to abide by the rules of the court for now and avoid risking an upheaval since you did not inherit the throne properly.'

Her words felt like a slap in the face. *Properly*. The word echoed in his mind. 'You mean by not arranging for the murder of my father?'

The silence that followed was lethal as a blade. Meng could almost hear the drumming of his heart as he watched a thousand emotions flicker past his mother's face.

'No one ascends the throne without making some hard decisions along the way,' his mother said at last, her expression settling back into its calculated calm. 'Everything we did was to get you to where you are now. Are you resenting me for it?'

He had no right to resent her—not when he had gone along with her plans instead of putting his foot down and choosing a different path. He was just as complicit in this elaborate bid for power.

His mother nodded primly, as though she had expected him to realize as much. 'Anyway, once Han takes over the Imperial Army from General Yue, you will have some reprieve.'

Meng found himself leaping to his feet. 'You want to make Han the general of the Imperial Army?' Upon his mother's sharp stare, he settled back into his seat and subdued his tone. 'You believe *Han* is capable of leading the Imperial Army?'

'Military consultant,' she corrected coolly. 'But yes, General Yue will have to run his decisions by him.' She raised her brows at Meng. 'And Han is no less qualified than you in ruling this kingdom. By birth right, he should be the emperor, but of course, your birth star says otherwise. Your brother has lived out in the harshest conditions and survived. I believe he is more than capable of leading our troops to victory.'

Words abandoned Meng. He who controlled the military laid ultimate claim to the seat of power. Surely his mother knew that ...

unless that was her intention? To make Han the true ruler of this kingdom and him the puppet emperor? From her outright rejection of his strategy against the Lettorians to this blatantly biased appointment for Han, it was clear that she had as much faith in his governing ability as she did in his father's.

'Mother,' he said quietly. 'Do you trust me?'

She smiled, but he sensed no warmth in her. He never did, for as long as he could remember. 'Of course I do.'

He wasn't sure what hurt more—that he knew she was lying, that it would never be the truth, or that a part of him still wished she would believe in him someday.

FIVE

Desert Rose

Dusk had settled upon the desert by the time they reached their last pit stop before the Dugur camp. It had taken them five straight hours of travelling after a quick stop for lunch. The first wisp of a night breeze had woven itself around Desert Rose, gentle enough to lull her to sleep. Deep in her dreams were the steady silhouettes of her camp, the faces of her tribe members. Already the air smelled different, threaded with a whiff of mulled wine and—

Someone caught her just before she slid off her desert horse. She jerked awake to find Wei riding next to her. He smirked. 'Bit too confident about your riding skills there.'

Desert Rose drew herself upright, in as dignified a manner as she could. 'Took you long enough to catch up.'

'In case you forgot, I was busy diverting imperial scouts away from you lot.' Beneath the levity in his voice was a tightness that sparked unease in her. If the shadow over his eyes was any indication, he had been busy with something more.

She peered at him. 'What happened?'

He shook his head and glanced at his mother, who was asleep riding behind Desert Rose. 'How is she doing?'

Queen Luzhen—although she had told Desert Rose to address her by her name—had been in poor form ever since they broke her out of prison, but long-haul travelling had worsened her condition further. She could feel Luzhen's shallow breaths against her neck the whole journey.

'Not getting any better,' she replied as they transferred Luzhen to Wei's back. 'The sooner we reach my camp, the quicker she can get treated. We're not far from it now. If we pull through for a bit more, we should be able to reach before night falls without the pit stop.'

Wei nodded. 'I'll inform the others.'

She watched him catch up with Zeyan ahead to convey the message.

The sands shifted with every li they covered, roiling and gathering like a creature awakening. It felt different, almost foreign, like a new, unfamiliar mount she was riding that could buck any moment. The desert had never felt ornery to her until now.

Something else nagged at her, the sense that they were being followed. Could it be her magic drawing out the creatures buried under these sands or were the scouts close by?

Still, they were so close to home now, whatever that might look like. She cast aside her misgivings and raced into the encroaching twilight, letting the desert draw them into its restless heart.

They arrived at the Dugur tribe camp just as the last light disappeared behind the horizon. Desert Rose tried to tame the drumming in her chest as her last memory of being here resurfaced—being woken up in the middle of the night by the clan leaders lurking outside her tent, her father fighting them off as they tried to capture him, her father ordering her to run, her friend Bataar raising a blowpipe to his lips and shooting her in the leg.

The last time she had been here was the night her life as she knew it changed. The night her friend had turned on her and she was forced to abandon her tribe (or had they abandoned her first?). She had tried shutting out those thoughts while she was in Oasis Capital, but now that she was back, so were the doubts and fears. Who in her tribe could she trust anymore?

But whatever she had expected did not prepare her for the sight that lay before them.

The camp was desolate, half-empty with abandoned tents. Instead of the gathering of lamplit tents around the communal square where the clans would gather for dinner, there was only a sinister darkness that allowed the chill of the evening wind to slip through. And instead of the usual crackle of fire, voices, and chatter, there was only silence. The silhouettes of hollowed-out tents drifted and swayed like spectres in the night.

Desert Rose exchanged a look with Qara next to her, then leapt off her steed. She peered into the gloom, cold fear sliding down to her feet. She had spent the past few months wondering what she would return to if she managed to leave Oasis Capital, but no amount of rumination had prepared her for this sense of loss, so deep and unsettling it felt as though she hadn't just been abandoned, but a piece of her soul had been robbed.

Where the ring of tents had previously stood around Heaven's Plate, the stone dais where her tribe shamans held ceremonious rituals and rites, the area was now bare.

For as long as she had been in the Dugur tribe, she had never seen the camp this forlorn.

Next to her, Qara was just as dumbfounded, staring around the camp like a lost child. 'They're gone. They're really gone. Bataar hinted that they might leave, but I didn't …'

Desert Rose whipped around. 'You knew about this?'

'Bataar only hinted at it,' Qara said. 'He said there were firmer lands in the northwest, lands with more protection, whatever that means, but I didn't think they would actually uproot the whole tribe.'

Desert Rose stared at her friend. 'How much more did Bataar tell you that I don't know about?'

On the night she and her father were persecuted by the clan leaders and she was forced to flee from the tribe, Qara had been there to help her, partly because she had an idea something like that might happen. If it hadn't been for Qara, Desert Rose might never have made it to Wei's camp and hitched a ride to Oasis Capital.

Then again, if Qara had shared her speculations and whatever she had overheard from Bataar, maybe all that could have been avoided. Maybe she and her father would have been better prepared for the coup.

'That's all I know, I swear to the gods,' Qara hastened to assure her. 'I never expected any of this to happen. I never thought Bataar would...'

She's feeling just as betrayed as you, Desert Rose told herself. Qara had made the choice to flee from Bataar to the Capital to reunite with her. Whatever information her friend had withheld from her, the fact remained that she was standing by her side now, experiencing the same loss of her home, her people.

Desert Rose headed towards the tent she had shared with her father. Every step she took felt weighted, as though the sand was pulling her into its depths. Theirs was one of the few tents left standing; almost everyone else's had been folded up, leaving behind dry, bare circles. Behind her, she could hear Wei tell his crew to stay put before he caught up with her.

She took a bracing breath, then pushed aside the flap to enter.

The next step she took sparked a sizzling, crackling sound from somewhere inside the tent. A whiff of something foul permeated the air.

'Get back!' Wei yelled, pulling her towards him.

She stumbled into his arms, and he leaped as far away from the tent as he could. A deafening boom reverberated around them as they landed on the ground, Wei's body shielding hers tightly. She squeezed her eyes shut and waited for the dust to settle.

Then came the overpowering stench, a pungent mix of burning earth and steel. She had experienced it in the borderlands, where she had once ventured with the clan boys despite their parents' warnings to avoid that region. The rumour was that the Lettorians had planted exotic explosives there to deter their enemies from launching an attack from the desert.

When they finally raised their heads and peered up, all they could see were wisps of black smoke trailing towards the twilit sky. Desert Rose's eyes watered from the smoke as she and Wei helped each other up.

By the time Qara and Zeyan hurried over to them, she was already charging into her ravaged tent before anyone could stop her.

The damage wasn't widespread, but it was thorough. The felt tent, though fire resistant, was ripped to shreds by the blast, and everything else inside was in pieces—the low wooden table where her father often sat sharpening his tools and drinking buttered tea, the wooden rack with her beloved collection of carved daggers, and even the pewter kettle that her father used to make medicinal tea when she fell sick.

Qara, Wei, and Zeyan caught up with her as she surveyed her ruined home, now aglow with remnant embers. Surely something could be salvaged. Surely not everything was lost. Her eyes roved around the tent, searching for something—anything—still intact.

'How would the scouts know to lay traps here?' Qara asked, taking in the sight. 'They couldn't have arrived sooner than us.'

Desert Rose stooped to peer at the debris on the ground, the fine black powder strewn amongst it. Her father had taught her about this explosive.

'Devil's Fire,' she reported, straightening. 'That's what triggered the explosion. It ignites upon contact with anything, and they laid it at the entrance.'

'Devil's Fire is a weapon specially made in Lettoria,' Wei remarked next to her.

Desert Rose nodded. 'It's not the scouts who laid the traps.' She turned to Qara. 'It's our people.'

Qara's eyes widened. 'You mean … Bataar and the clan leaders?'

Something unspoken passed between them, the understanding that their old friend and tribemate was truly no longer on their side. That he would ambush them this way, knowing the first thing they would do was rush to their tents.

Desert Rose squinted in the dark and continued surveying the debris, trying to sift out any clue that would point her in the right direction now that they had come to this dead end.

'The tribe must have gone northwest,' Wei was saying as she went to her splintered bedside drawer. 'The clan leaders were never in true alliance with Oasis Kingdom. They're working with the Lettorians.'

Bataar had told her the clan leaders had an alternative plan, that things were not as they appeared. But nothing he said could change the fact that they had betrayed her father—and her. Even if they had an ulterior agenda, they had still forced the chieftain out of the tribe.

Either way, whichever side they chose, one thing was for certain: she would never join them.

Desert Rose unhitched the broken drawer, half expecting to find its contents destroyed too, but the bird-shaped enamel box tucked away at the back had suffered merely a few scratches and dents. She clutched it tightly as a wave of emotions surged forward. Apart from the double knives her father had given her, this enamel box was one of her few prized possessions. It was the first gift her father had given her after adopting her. Sometimes, he would leave her a short message written in Capital script on a scrap of paper to teach her how to read.

She opened the box and gasped, her fingers already fumbling to pull out the folded scrap of paper tucked inside. A chill skittered down her back when she saw her father's familiar handwriting.

'Not everyone's gone northwest,' she murmured, staring at the bold characters.

Qara and Wei turned to her.

Desert Rose held up the piece of paper and showed it to them. 'I think I know where my father is.'

SIX

Wei

There was a stone that sat in Wei's chest, and each day it grew larger.

It began with the news of his brother Yong ascending as crown prince, just a year after Wei left Oasis Kingdom. The stone in his chest grew with each piece of intel he received from Matron about the goings-on in the palace: his mother being framed for attempted regicide and her subsequent imprisonment, then the murder of his brother, and now Han returning to the Capital.

Now, even though he was reunited with his mother and they had left Oasis Kingdom behind, Wei felt that deadweight sitting on him like an executioner's block.

He was watching her waste away day by day under the punishing elements, her already frail body undergoing a second round of turmoil after what she had been through in prison. Maybe it was a mistake to take her this deep into the desert towards an uncertain future and a certain peril. Maybe she would have fared better in Oasis Kingdom than out here with him. After all, her home had been Oasis Kingdom for decades. She had lived as a dignified queen. But as long as Wangyi was in power, there would be no way for his mother to reinstate her position and live in peace.

Unless Wei were to become emperor.

This was not the first or only time he had toyed with that preposterous idea, but perhaps the only way he could protect his remaining family and end this life of running and hiding was to get on that throne.

Wei had turned his back on Oasis Kingdom a long time ago. He owed nothing to a kingdom that didn't want him. But what if he could tear down what destroyed his family and rebuild something better in its place?

Wei glanced at the girl riding next to him now. A few months ago, he couldn't imagine himself laying his hopes on her, much less following her into the depths of the desert. But she was no stranger now—she was an ally, a friend who had saved his life multiple times now, and she had promised to help save his mother.

Desert Rose rode with renewed determination, her gaze keen and bright now that she had a new destination. All that was written on that piece of paper in rough Oasis script was *Ghost City*, which couldn't possibly be an actual place. Yet, she seemed to believe in her father's message wholeheartedly, ignoring the likelihood of them walking into a trap.

The darkness grew deeper the longer they rode, until they were practically swimming in it. Out here in the profound silence, every rasp and creak—and even the distant howl carried over by the wind—sounded like a cacophony. Shadows flitted by like ghosts in the night, but there were no other travellers in sight. Their torches were now both a crutch and a beacon for night-time creatures, and Wei had spent enough time in the desert to know that he would rather not encounter the monsters it bred.

Before he could ask Desert Rose how much longer the journey would take, she pulled to a stop.

'We're here,' she said.

Here was the middle of nowhere, as far as Wei could tell. He squinted at his surroundings, trying to make out the silhouette of tents or camels, anything. But there was only the unending stretch of bruised sky and empty land sprawled out all around them.

Desert Rose and Qara hopped off their camels and started tapping the ground with their feet. The sands rustled as an unearthly howl trailed off in the distance. Wei shared a look with Zeyan and Beihe, wondering how long he should wait before questioning her plan.

'Rose, what—'

'Shh!' She continued roaming around the area with her torch held close to the ground as she tapped it intently.

His mother stirred behind him. 'Wei? Where are we?'

He turned around and patted her hand. 'Wait here, Mother. I'll give the girls a hand.'

'Here!' Qara hissed a few feet away. They hurried over to her, relying entirely on their torches to wade through the darkness. Qara dipped her leg into the sand. It rode all the way up to her calf. 'I think this might be the entrance.'

Desert Rose nodded at Wei, ignoring the confusion in his eyes. 'Start digging.'

But before he could start, a rampant wind made the sand skitter and swirl into a fury. In the distance came a piercing howl. When the dust settled, a pair of bone-white figures appeared before them, not quite spectres but not corporeal either, drifting a few inches above the ground with their elongated limbs dangling like cut nooses. They loomed closer, their silhouettes cutting through the dark.

'Are those ... desert ghouls?' Zeyan said, rubbing his eyes.

In all his time spent in the desert, Wei had come across an assortment of creatures, supernatural and otherwise. *This is but one of them*, he thought, tightening his grip on his sword hilt. According to lore, ghouls typically showed up to feed on remnant souls in dead bodies. There was no reason they should appear here now, unless ...

'Ghost City,' he murmured, turning to Desert Rose. 'This is a graveyard, isn't it? Your father sent you to a graveyard?'

Doubt flickered across her face. 'I'm sure he has his reasons.'

The ghouls swooped towards them, their raucous howls piercing through the thick desert night. Wei unsheathed his sword. Desert Rose threw out her hands before her. His blade swung through thin air and came into contact with nothing.

Unfazed by Wei's attack, the ghouls lunged towards Desert Rose, their long, emaciated hands tipped with blackened nails as sharp as knives. They swiped at her with surprising viciousness and speed, one of them slashing her right cheek just before she dodged.

Wei grabbed Desert Rose's hand and pulled her behind him, out of the ghoul's reach. 'Keep digging,' he called to Zeyan and Qara. 'We'll distract them.'

He and Desert Rose took off in the opposite direction, running helter-skelter across the sand, away from the warm glow of torches. In the unrelenting darkness, there was no telling where they might lose their footing and tumble down a sand cliff. All that mattered was that they bought Zeyan and Qara enough time to find the entrance to Ghost City.

The pair of ghouls spiralled towards them, close on their heels. Another pair rose from the ground, joining them.

'We have to split up,' Desert Rose said, attempting to tug her hand out of his. 'They're drawn to my blood.'

But Wei didn't let go. 'All the more we should stick together.'

They doubled back before they lost sight of the last glimmer of torch light, narrowly evading the nearest ghoul's grasp. Desert Rose threw out her arms, an action Wei now recognized as her trying to summon her powers, but now that they were well into the desert, drawing water to her would be a larger feat. A weak trickle of water streamed towards the ghouls, barely impeding them in their pursuit.

Then came a noise: an urgent hiss that sounded human, though it was hard to tell for sure out here.

'Over here!'

The voice came from the ground. More precisely, it came from a hole in the ground a few feet away from where Qara and Zeyan were digging. Wei and Desert Rose shared a look, then sprinted towards it.

Under the frail light of the torches, Wei could just make out the silhouette of the newcomer as she emerged from what appeared to be an underground stairwell. She was a stout old lady in a rough-hewn fur coat that concealed an assortment of coloured knotted threads and tiny bells. Close by her side was a woman not much older than Wei's mother, also dressed in distinctly Dugurian clothing.

'Anar Zel!' Desert Rose and Qara cried in unison. 'Yanda!'

'Get in here,' the woman named Yanda said, beckoning them all towards the stairwell. 'Hurry! Anar Zel will take care of those nasty things.'

Desert Rose attempted to go to Anar Zel's aid, but the older woman snapped, 'Stay in there.'

Wei helped Desert Rose and Qara down the dark mouth of the stairwell before heading back for his mother, though Beihe was already helping her over.

Once they were all packed underground, Anar Zel swept her arm in a dramatic arc, sending a wave of sand sliding over the entrance of the stairs. They huddled close on the steps beneath her. Outside, the ghouls' shrieks intertwined with the frenetic tinkling of Anar Zel's mini bells as she fought them off.

Wei had encountered enough shamans and priests during his time training in the mountains, and in the desert searching for the spring, to know that this lady had to be the tribe matriarch, the one who typically protected and governed the tribe socially and spiritually so the chieftain could focus on territorial and political dealings.

With bated breaths, they listened to the fight outside. The air in the stairwell was surprisingly comfortable—not too dry or thin or damp—which was likely thanks to Anar Zel's efforts in regulating it. For the first time since they left the Capital, his mother's breathing sounded less shallow as she settled onto the steps and leaned against the wall. The knot in Wei's chest loosened a little.

Desert Rose was staring intently up at the opening, as though praying for Anar Zel to come through it any moment. In her eyes was the otherworldly gleam that appeared whenever she used her powers. Blood trickled down her cheek where the ghoul had clawed her. Wei reached over to wipe it away gently with his fingers. She jumped at his touch and turned to him. They held each other's gazes in the gloom until Anar Zel descended the steps with almost stately ease.

Outside, all was calm again. There was neither the howl of ghouls nor the rustle of sand.

The old lady turned to Desert Rose. 'Well,' she said with a hint of irritation. 'What took you so long?'

SEVEN

Desert Rose

Desert Rose had grown up hearing about the Darklands. Her father used to tell her about that desolate land and its undead inhabitants. Beneath the restless sands was a catacomb ruled by the mythical Ghost King, who reaped and governed the souls of corrupt men who died in the desert.

The thought made her uneasy as she followed Yanda and Anar Zel down into a winding labyrinth steeped in darkness. Every sound gradually receded into a stifling silence broken only by the shuffling of their footsteps. The passageways were wide enough to fit two people at once, but Desert Rose felt like the walls were closing in on them the deeper they wound.

Nonetheless, she placed all her trust in her fellow tribeswomen and stayed close to them. Papa had directed her here; maybe he *was* here.

'He's not here with us, child,' Anar Zel called over her shoulders, as though she had heard Desert Rose's thoughts.

The sinking feeling in her chest was all too familiar. 'But he led you all here?'

'Scarbrow didn't go quietly with Blackstone and the other fools, of course,' she said. 'He knew long ago that the coup would happen

43

and was well prepared for it. He had warned us about Blackstone too, although anyone could see through that traitor and his ambitions.'

Desert Rose tripped over a rock in her eagerness. Wei's hand shot out to steady her. 'Does that mean Papa escaped? Do you know where he went?'

'He told no one about his plans, although he did say he was going to look for the cure.'

The cure. It was the same thing Bataar had told her. So did Golsha, the Dugur-tribesman-turned-Capital-merchant. Had her father already known what she was and what she could do? Golsha's words rang in her head again. *An abomination,* he had called her. Did her father also think her power was abominable enough to require a cure?

Desert Rose was suddenly aware of Wei's silent gaze on her, reminding her of the time they were stuck on Yeli Mountain after escaping a vicious fire. She remembered his exact words to her after she told him what Golsha had called her.

For what it's worth, I don't think you're an abomination.

The memory of his words quelled the disquiet in her heart just a little.

'Scarbrow told us no one would be able to track us down, but he said you would come eventually,' Yanda said, interrupting their moment. 'We were worried you wouldn't be able to find us when you returned.'

That they had been waiting for her and Qara to return, that her father had trusted her to make the journey back home, made Desert Rose's heart swell again. She had not let him down. She was home among her people again. Well, half of them, anyway.

A light appeared at the end of the tunnel, growing brighter as they approached it. They stepped out into a cavernous space that appeared to be a ceremonial square, with four carved pillars at each corner and a stone dais in the centre. The walls and ceiling were covered in religious paintings, illuminated by torches parked in uniform stone brackets.

The square was large enough for a camp to be set up. About fifty of them—mostly women and children—from various clans within the

Dugur tribe milled about, the mothers sitting around a small fire in the centre of the square, chatting and drinking from clay cups, as the little ones chased each other around the tents. The shamans sat in a circle around the dais, meditating.

It was a sight so familiar—a glimpse of the normalcy Desert Rose had missed—that it made tears well up in her eyes. Her tribe was not destroyed, not completely. There were still those who did not place their faith in Blackstone, those who remained loyal to her father.

Qara sucked in a breath, staring around in wonderment. 'This place...'

'The most dangerous place can also be the safest,' Yanda replied with a conspiratorial smile.

'And you've all been staying here this whole time?' Desert Rose asked. 'Among the dead?'

'The dead don't find trouble with us if we don't cause it,' Anar Zel replied, although Desert Rose didn't miss the glance she sent Wei and his crew. The tribe matriarch hadn't questioned their identities the whole way here, but she had led them into her new makeshift home on account of them being Desert Rose's friends.

Before she could make the introductions, a tribe member cried, 'Rose! Qara!'

Almost at once, everyone scrambled to their feet and rushed towards them. And then they were engulfing her and Qara in tears and warm embraces. Desert Rose hugged them back just as fiercely, no longer holding back her own tears.

Amid the reunion, she saw Anar Zel reach out to take Luzhen's hand, having sensed the frailty of her energy. 'You have suffered on this journey,' she said, to which Luzhen replied with a wan smile. 'Come. I may have something to help.' She led Luzhen to the other corner of the square and made her settle onto a large rug while she busied herself with an assortment of herbs.

'Everyone,' Desert Rose said, raising her voice over that of her tribemates. She gestured at Wei and his crew lingering behind her and beckoned them over. 'These are my friends from the Capital. Meet Wei, Zeyan, and Beihe.'

'Oasis Capital?' someone asked. Wei eyed the group, shoulders tensed.

'Oasis Capital,' Desert Rose affirmed, shifting closer to Wei. 'My friends,' she repeated for good measure.

'Well, let's get our guests something to drink then,' Yanda said, shuffling everyone back into the square. Once they were settled in, she poured them all a cup of mare's milk each. 'This is in short supply these days. We have to take turns sneaking out to a market to barter for supplies, so savour every drop.'

Wei, Zeyan, and Beihe exchanged hesitant glances. Only upon Desert Rose's urging did they gulp down the milk with the gratitude of men lost in the desert.

'What happened, Rose? Tell us everything,' Yanda said. The other tribespeople pressed around them, all ears.

Desert Rose drew a deep breath and shared a look with Qara. Together, they described everything that happened from the night of the White Moon Festival, when Blackstone had led the clan leaders to ambush her and her father after the bonfire celebrations. Desert Rose told them about her journey to the Capital, how she met Wei and his crew along the way, how she ran into Bataar and the other clan members in the Capital, and their involvement in the Spring Ceremony upheaval that led to the fall of the Fifteenth Oasis Emperor (though she eliminated the parts where she discovered her power and killed the emperor). Qara narrated how she had been taken by the shouren after escaping from Bataar, reuniting with Desert Rose to finally flee from Oasis Kingdom, and finally, their month-long journey through the desert that brought them to this moment.

Everyone was silent when the two of them finished speaking, save for the children still blithely engaged in their game of catch.

Finally, Yanda spoke.

'Blackstone convinced everyone else that the tribe was in danger if we continued to stay here, that our only chance of survival is to move to where the north-western countries can protect us. He said Scarbrow has abandoned the tribe.'

Rage coursed through her, white-hot. 'Papa would never—'

'We know, Rose,' Klutan said quietly. 'We trust Scarbrow with our lives. But he told us to stay put until he returns or you find us.'

'Papa … was expecting me to lead the tribe?'

'Anar Zel was betting on you to find us first,' said Aish. 'She said she believes in the prophecy.'

'The prophecy?' Wei echoed.

'Of the Elementals,' Desert Rose supplied. 'It's a story we were told as children.'

'What does the prophecy say?'

'That one day, out of five Elementals, the surviving one will lead the Damohai, Children of the Desert, to rebuild their empire and restore the balance between Heaven and Earth.'

But what did the prophecy of the Elementals have to do with her?

'Sounds like a huge responsibility,' Wei said.

It was hard to think of it as anything more than a myth, a bedtime fable she heard growing up, and even harder to believe that anyone was coming to save the desert or its people. Desert Rose had always reserved her doubts about the Elementals. Sometimes, it felt like the gods had given up on them, left them stranded in a world that moved and changed faster than the shifting sands, left them caught among warring nations that sought to exploit the desert and unearth its treasures.

Yanda nodded. 'Anar Zel believes that the last surviving Elemental will be the one to save us, not Blackstone and the clan leaders, not even Scarbrow … if he's still alive.' She glanced at Desert Rose, who chose not to acknowledge that last part.

Later, after the lamps in the chamber were dimmed and everyone retired to their corners, Anar Zel pulled Desert Rose aside.

'You must find the spring,' the matriarch said with surprising urgency.

Desert Rose peered into her kohl-lined eyes. 'I—what?'

'The Immortal Spring. You must find it,' Anar Zel insisted. 'Your life depends on it.'

'I don't understand. Papa never wanted anyone to go looking for the spring. He butted heads with Blackstone over this. Why do I have to find it now?'

'I saw what you did out there when you fought those ghouls. When did your power reveal itself?'

'You ... you knew?'

'Of course I knew. You think Scarbrow could bring a lost child home without having me check your provenance?'

She knew all along. So did her father. Even Golsha—he had guessed there was something different about her. And they had all kept it from her, suppressed her powers with Anar Zel's special concoctions. It all made sense now, how overprotective her father had always been, how he never let her come close to any supernatural creature—even though there were plenty in the desert—much less fight them, how he had even told her not to reveal how quickly she could heal.

'We did so to protect you,' Anar Zel said, as though she had heard her thoughts again. 'We weren't sure what you could do, and we couldn't very well toss you back out into the desert. It would be blasphemous to abandon a child of the gods.'

Desert Rose stared at her, dumbfounded. Anar Zel had always been the staunchest believer in the gods, Heaven's will, and destiny. But this was ludicrous. 'You don't actually think I'm an Elemental, do you?'

'I believe all the evidence I see.'

'But that's just a myth,' Desert Rose argued.

'All myths stem from truth, child,' said Anar Zel.

'I ... I can't be ...' She glanced around wildly, hoping that a sensible counter argument would land before her, but instead, she caught Wei's eye and realized he was listening to the conversation too. 'I'm just Rose. Just Rose,' she repeated, but she no longer knew if she was merely trying to convince herself.

'Whether or not you choose to accept your identity and destiny, you have to find the spring. For the sake of the tribe ... and your life. This is your destiny.'

Destiny. She had once scoffed at the idea. *I don't believe in destiny,* she had told Prince Meng. *I believe we are the makers of our own lives and are only as free as we allow ourselves to be.* Yet, she now had a new identity, a new fate, thrust upon her.

And what about Windshadow? If being able to manipulate water made her an Elemental, the wind-wielding desert girl had to be one too. Had Windshadow already known what she was, what they were? *You and I—we're gifted.* Those were her words.

'There was another girl,' she said. 'I met her in the palace. She was from another tribe …'

Anar Zel nodded grimly. 'There's been talk that the Lijsal tribe has one too. Your paths will cross again, when it's time.' Her gaze turned pensive. 'The one who unblocks the spring is deemed the surviving Elemental. They will win the favour of the gods, right the wrongs of their ancestors, and bury the past, restoring peace between heaven and earth and in turn ascend to the celestial kingdom.'

'So the reward for staying alive is going to the heavens?'

The older lady raised her brows. 'Would you rather be killed by the others?'

Either way, it seemed like the wrong end of a deal.

'I don't want this wretched destiny,' she said. 'The gods can stick it up their celestial—'

Anar Zel hissed.

'Anar Zel—'

The old lady held up a hand. 'We will talk tomorrow. I need to check on Luzhen, and you need rest.'

But how could she sleep after a revelation like that? Even as she settled into the makeshift bed she shared with Qara and Yanda, her thoughts remained in a tumult until she finally got up and went over to the central square, where a small fire was still kindling.

Wei was there, lying on a rug next to the fire, watching the embers smoulder and glow. He started to sit up when he saw her approach, but she gestured for him to stay put because he looked as worn out as she felt. Without a word, she lay down next to him.

It had almost become a routine for them in the past few weeks when they were on shift duty to look out for scouts who might ambush them in the night. Wei would sometimes stay a little longer, or Desert Rose would join him a little earlier, and they would sit next to each other in a strangely comfortable silence. Sometimes they would chat, but they often didn't have to; sometimes they would trade stories of their childhood but otherwise, they would lean against each other, simply grateful for the companionship.

This time was no different as they lay side by side on the rug, facing each other in silence. She watched the gentle rise and fall of his calm, breathing form, which made the storm inside her subside.

It seemed surreal that they had ended up here, in an underground tomb, after a whole month of being on the road. The floor beneath her might be hard and uncomfortable, and they might be lying among the dead and the ruins of a fallen kingdom, but she no longer felt unanchored, as though she was wading through silken sand on the highest dune.

Wei traced the gash running down her cheek with his gaze—now merely a tender scar. A chilly draught curled around them, but his fingertip burnt where it touched her. She wasn't sure if it was the wind that made her shiver.

'It's not as bad as it looks,' she said at last, although she couldn't be certain.

The first time they met, they had fought off a sand hound together and the creature had clamped its venomous teeth onto her arm. Wei had painstakingly purged the venom from her wound, but she had healed in less than a day—likewise, for the other injuries she had sustained along the way.

'I thought you heal exceptionally fast,' he said. 'Why is this taking longer than usual?'

She shrugged. 'Doesn't sting as much anymore, at least.'

They fell quiet.

'I know you heard us just now,' she said.

'I wasn't eavesdropping.'

She raised her brows. 'A bald-faced lie.'

'I happened to overhear the conversation, then got too interested to leave.'

'Well,' she prompted, aware that he was stalling for time. 'What do you think?'

His expression was unreadable. 'I think we can't root out any possibility.'

'You think I'm a descendent of a supernatural race of desert warriors?' Her tone was light, almost teasing, but he didn't seem to find it as laughable as she did.

'When you've lived out in the desert, you start to believe anything is possible,' he said.

He wasn't wrong. Anything was possible, especially in the chaotic wilderness of the desert. So, why not the fact that she might be an Elemental, one of the five chosen saviours of her people and the guardian of a celestial relic?

She snorted. 'No. My story will be written by me, not the gods. I'll decide what I will fight and die for.' If she believed in the idea of destiny, then she had already surrendered to the whims of Fate.

'For a Dugurian, you sure don't seem very respectful of the gods,' Wei said with a wry smile.

Perhaps a part of her sought to defy them. Perhaps she already knew she was hurtling towards something much bigger than herself and there was no stopping it. Or that she was actually more afraid than she was willing to admit.

She looked at Wei lying next to her now, his familiar gaze taming the whirlwind inside her mind. He said nothing more, although he seemed like he understood what was going through her mind.

He reached out again, this time laying his palm against her cheek gently.

'At least you're home now, in a way,' he said softly. 'Whatever happens next, you know you're not alone.'

She nodded, letting those words wash over her as her eyelids grew heavy. For the first time in almost a month, she fell into a deep, long sleep.

Longing is love without a home.

—Dugurian proverb

EIGHT

Meng

The First Prince returned with much fanfare—the Empress Dowager made sure of that.

The day began with servants and maids setting up the decorations for Han's homecoming. By the time Meng had roused, the Red Circle, where the imperial family resided, was already adorned with deep vermillion and black silk—colours reserved for generals awarded with the highest honour in protecting the kingdom.

Meng wandered around the grounds, watching the servants scurry about under Matron's watchful eye. In a few hours, they were all to gather at the Five Wall Court. That was where he had last addressed the Imperial Army upon ascending the throne, and where he would now officially welcome his brother home. Han had always loved ceremonies—the stateliness and grandeur would make him stand a little straighter and walk a little taller—while Meng, like his half-brothers Yong and Wei, couldn't wait for them to be over.

This felt like the beginning. But of what, Meng wasn't quite certain. There was a change in the air, a cold wind that settled inside him at the thought of having Han back in the palace. While his eldest brother had never been outright cruel to him like he had been to Wei, Meng had never been in his favour either.

Don't think like that, Meng chided himself internally. He was the emperor. He held all the power now. He could remove any threat that he had to, even if that threat was family. The only thing holding him back from hereon would be his conscience, though lately it was the thing that crept into his dreams and kept him up at night. Yong's purpled lips, the sword lodged in his father's throat, Desert Rose's look of disbelief and disappointment in him.

Some days, Meng wasn't sure if getting on the throne was worth anything at all.

* * *

Seated next to his mother in the courtyard overlooking the Five Wall Court, Meng stared out at the crowd gathered below. He scanned the faces of the court officials lined up in neat rows at the front, the magistrates and nobles behind them, and finally the generals and soldiers. Each held more misgiving than the last, similar to the response Meng received when he was declared the new emperor.

This time, more than doubt, he saw fear in some of them. But some looked eager for what lay ahead.

High Advisor Mian stepped up to the podium. 'Today,' he intoned, 'the imperial family welcomes home a son who has braved the perils of the north. Today, we are replete with joy and relief over the return of the First Prince Zhaohan. Today, our lost prince is finally home again.'

Lost prince. As though Han had been no more than an innocent child who had strayed too far from home. Not an ambitious son who had plotted against his father and was thwarted in his bid for the throne. Not a disgraced outcast exiled to the northern border of the kingdom. While he had formerly been denounced by their father, he was now celebrated as a survivor, a hero, by their mother.

Next to him, the Empress Dowager beamed as brightly as the sun that scattered its rays across the courtyard.

And she says she never plays favourites, Meng thought as he rose from his seat and offered her his hand. They made their way to the front of the courtyard as Mian stepped back with his head bowed. Meng glanced at his mother, who urged him on with a nod.

'The First Prince, Zhaohan,' he announced flatly.

Han strode out from the alcove behind them, dressed in a black silk robe embellished with gleaming crimson trimming. Everything about him commanded attention and awe—his towering, sturdy build hardened by life in the wilderness, his decisive gait, and piercing gaze. He was a man who still believed in his worth, despite his dishonourable past. Even Meng could not help but stare.

He watched as his brother—someone so familiar yet entirely foreign—approached him. He observed the same old defiance and proudness in his face but also a newfound savagery that had settled in the corners of his eyes, the curve of his lips. Meng had always thought his older brother bore a striking resemblance to their mother, and it was only now as he looked Han in the eye that he understood why. They shared the same hunger, the same ambition and ruthlessness to achieve their goals.

'Your Majesty,' Han greeted, but there was something unsettling about his tone, as though he was secretly laughing at the fact that Meng was an emperor. A few weeks ago, Meng too had had his own doubts, but to see the scorn in his brother's eyes, to hear it in his voice now, made an ugly, angry creature rear its head inside him. *You were unworthy of the throne*, a small voice in his head said. *I managed to claim it.*

Meng quelled the voice, half-ashamed, and gave his brother the most perfunctory smile. 'It's good to have you home, Brother.'

Han's smirk deepened—there was no mistaking it now. His brother was mocking him, as though he was certain it was only a matter of time before Meng fell off his throne.

What he had been doing in the past month seemed like child's play now that the real threat stood before him with his teeth bared in a predatory smile. Family, survival, and the desire to rebuild his kingdom were the reasons Meng had so scrupulously planned to assume the throne.

But his brother had different motivations, and he had far fewer qualms about doing what it took to get what he wanted.

'It's good to be home, brother,' said Han, laying a hand on Meng's shoulder. His grip was far too tight.

* * *

'He means to take over the throne. You know that, don't you?'

Meng knew it was her before she spoke. No one else appeared in his room without warning like that, especially in the middle of the night. He shot Windshadow a look. She had that way of getting under his skin with just a lilt in her voice. 'I'm not a fool.'

It had been two weeks since his brother was back, and he knew it was not by any measure of fortune that he was still alive and on the throne.

'So how should I get rid of Han?' Windshadow asked. 'Same way as with the crown prince?'

His irritation flared stronger at the callous way she mentioned Yong's murder. While he had spent many sleepless nights over his half-brother's death—the one he had orchestrated under his mother's order—Windshadow had seen it as nothing but another task to execute to get them closer to their goals. Sometimes, he wished he had her lack of conscience. Sometimes.

'We are not killing Han,' he said.

Windshadow leaned across the table and looked him in the eye. 'It's kill or be killed. Surely you know that. You grew up in the palace.'

'I will not kill Han. Not until I know what he intends to do, at least.'

She cocked her head, frowning. 'You didn't show mercy with the crown prince. Why not do the same with Han?'

'Enough,' he snapped. This was the first time he had ever lost his cool with her.

She seemed unfazed, only annoyed. 'Your bleeding heart is not going to serve you as the emperor. I hope you make a decision soon, Your Majesty.' Without waiting for his answer, she vanished into a gust of wind and slipped out through the ajar window.

A servant's cry rang out from outside. 'The First Prince arrives!'

The doors to Meng's chamber swung open before he could think to protest. Han strode in with the confidence of a man who believed he belonged here, surveying every corner of the chamber before finally greeting Meng with a hint of sarcasm.

Meng reclined in his seat pointedly, just to demonstrate that he was the master of the room. Petty, he knew. But there was something about Han that compelled him to calculate every word, gesture, and expression.

'What brings you here at this hour, Brother?' he inquired.

'Just a friendly visit. I thought I'd catch up with my little brother after so long,' Han said. 'You don't mind indulging me, do you?'

Meng arranged a smile on his face. 'Of course not. Although in the future'—he sharpened his tone—'I would appreciate it if you announced your visits in good time.'

And there was the smirk again. 'Not bad, Brother. You sound almost like an emperor. Might fool me if I didn't know better.'

'Why exactly are you here, Han? I'm fairly certain you're not here merely to express your doubts about my leadership.'

His smile deepened. 'No, that would be too trite. I'm here to remind you that an emperor is only as powerful as his people allow him to be. There's no mandate of Heaven, nor are you the Son of Heaven—especially not when we both know what you did to get here.'

Meng stiffened, though he tried to keep his face impassive. His brother had only been back for a couple of weeks, he couldn't possibly know everything that had happened recently.

'Mother tells me everything, in case you didn't know. How you arranged for our father to be poisoned, conspired with a girl from the desert to steal the throne, then claimed it was your destiny to be emperor.'

Despite himself, Meng abandoned all pretence at last. 'I'm fairly certain you would have done the same, if not worse.'

'I'm not judging your ambitions, little brother, only your execution.' A smile toyed around the corners of his lips.

'What is it you want from me?' Meng snapped.

Han straightened, satisfied that he had gotten a reaction out of him. 'We live in chaotic times, Brother. And the throne is reserved only for the victors, the ones hungry enough to not just steal it, but stay on it.'

Another far-off cry cut through the night before Meng could respond. This time, it was not the announcement of an unwelcome guest. Meng turned sharply in the direction of the sound. He could hear the offending servant boy being shushed by someone, but the boy's voice just outside his chamber was clear as a bell.

'The prison is on fire! The shouren have escaped!'

NINE

Windshadow

Windshadow careened through the hallways, not bothering with discretion, even as she stirred up a gust strong enough to drag down the silk cloth adorning the roofs of the buildings in the Red Circle. These days, her anger and frustration took the form of a gale inside her, ferocious enough to eat her alive.

She was familiar with rage; it was what fuelled her and guided her every step. She knew rage like an old friend, ever since she was an orphan child, constantly picked on for wanting to spend time observing the golden eagles take flight and playing pretend games instead of joining the others in rituals and ceremonies. She knew what it was like when the urge to tear up everything in her path was the only thing blazing the way ahead.

But the frustration was new. And it stemmed from Prince Meng's overly cautious nature and the excessive prudence with which he made every decision. He was good at strategy but often terrible at execution. If it weren't for her urging him to do what needed to be done, the crown prince might still be alive, and so would Golsha, and Prince Meng wouldn't have become emperor at all.

He hadn't been this hesitant before he acquired the throne. Before, he was focused, intent on his singular track towards becoming the emperor. Even if he hated many of the things he had to do, he made sure they got done. But that changed after that evening in the Astronomy Tower, when Windshadow framed Desert Rose for murdering the emperor. It had probably seemed like she and Prince Meng had conspired to make Desert Rose the scapegoat when it was really just a matter of bad—or good, depending on how you looked at it—timing. Since then, Prince Meng had let his guilt eat its way through him and it was affecting his acumen.

Windshadow returned to the House of Night just as Shimu gathered all of them in the common room. She snuck in through the window and slipped back into human form in time to join the rest of the Cranes.

'There's been a fire at the imperial prison. We suspect foul play, or worse, a prison break,' said the housemistress, her gaze steely and sharp despite the hour. 'Black Cranes will guard the Red Circle. Blue Cranes will investigate the fire and take down any suspects you see.'

A fire, Windshadow mused. *This could be interesting.*

Windshadow and the other Blue Cranes, Liqin and Xiyue, made their way to the imperial prison, where Prince Wei had broken out his mother, Queen Luzhen, not long ago and fled the Capital. Security had been heightened since then, but clearly not enough if this freak fire managed to break out in the dankest recesses of the dungeon.

Everyone's guess was the shouren. Ever since the beast-people stormed the palace during the Spring Ceremony and attempted a coup on the last emperor, they had become the biggest enemy of the people. Never mind that they had, before this, never caused any harm or trouble, or even shown themselves in broad daylight for fear of persecution.

But the fate of the shouren were of no concern to her. She had enough to worry about to care about the magical folk in this magic-loathing kingdom.

With Liqin off to scout the area, Xiyue and Windshadow slipped in through the back entrance of the prison, closest to where the fire broke out, and made their way down the narrow flight of stairs to the cells.

The inmates were restless. Windshadow could feel their fear ripple through the winding passageways. But while thick black smoke and an acrid stench hovered in the air, there were no more flames, not even embers. It was as though the fire had died as quickly as it broke out.

'Has the fire been put out?' Xiyue whispered, glancing around in confusion. 'But we came as soon as we heard the news.'

The cells in this section—at least twelve of them—were empty, and what sparse quarters that existed before were now razed to nothing. But it wasn't just the walls and ground that were charred. The bars of the corner cell were melted and wrought, but also perfectly twisted, as though the flames had yanked them apart and allowed the prisoners to escape.

Windshadow ran a finger down a distorted bar and peered at the damage. What kind of fire could melt iron so quickly and methodically?

'Shimu was right,' Xiyue murmured. 'This is connected to the shouren. But who would break them out?'

Ignoring her, Windshadow continued to scrutinize every corner of the cell. There weren't many clues she could glean from a near empty cell where everything from the clay bowls to the straw mats had been burnt to crisp, but there had to be something.

'If this is an inside job, that means they have powerful backing,' Xiyue continued surmising.

'Keep your thoughts in your head. Do you want the whole prison to hear you?' Windshadow said.

Then she saw it, something that didn't quite fit into the picture.

Strewn amongst the soot and ashes was a loose dusting of fine reddish sand, the very kind that she had left behind at the crown prince's chamber last winter after slipping inside to poison his food. The kind that had allowed Prince Wei to uncover her role in the murder.

Coincidence? Windshadow didn't believe in that.

The fire. The desert sand. The shouren escaping—or being freed.

Someone else had been here. Someone else who shared the same ability as her.

* * *

Later that morning, Shimu addressed her and the other assassins-in-training in the armoury with her usual demeanour—hands pressed behind her spear-straight back and chin tilted high. Both the Black Cranes and Blue Cranes mimicked her posture, ready to receive their assignment for the day.

Since there had been no clear winner of the trials after the mayhem at the Spring Ceremony, the Blue Cranes had to resume regular training for Shimu to assess their skills and later place them in different units. Until things settled down, they would continue to train at the House of Night and be deployed to wherever they were needed. But after last night's freak fire, their training schedule was interrupted by the need for heightened protection of the imperial family and covert investigations.

Windshadow couldn't care less about her placement anyway. What did it matter if she became an Imperial High Guard or Nightwalker? She wasn't here for a title; she had bigger goals than that. Her destiny lay beyond the confines of Oasis Kingdom, and soon she would fulfil it. For now, though, she would have to continue playing her part.

'Fengying, Xiyue,' Shimu said after Liqin reported what she had observed from scouting the prison grounds last night. 'What about you two?'

'It's strange, Shimu,' Xiyue said, her large round eyes widening further in wonder. 'The fire had already died by the time we arrived, and we didn't even see anyone trying to put it out.'

Shimu narrowed her gaze but withheld her opinion. She turned to Windshadow. 'What else did you find out?'

'Just like what Xiyue said,' said Windshadow, looking Shimu in the eye. Until she figured out who or what was behind the fire and prison break, she would not surrender any information she had discovered. 'The fire was gone by the time we got there, and the devastation was complete. Even the prison bars had melted. None of the prisoners saw anything, at least based on what I overheard.'

Shimu frowned. 'We must prepare for a possible attack soon, most likely from the shouren again. Xiyue, you will continue to watch the prison in case of another attack. Liqin, you will guard the sentry post for potential attacks on the palace. And Fengying, I want you to do a full surveillance of the palace for any new faces, anyone who might be hiding in the shadows and uncover their background. All three of you will report in detail to me daily.'

Windshadow received the order along with the other girls, her mind already racing to work out the answer to this mystery. Someone had let out the shouren, she was certain of it. No fire was this methodical and careful; it would have spread to the other cells and the other prisoners would have heard the commotion.

Why then would the perpetrator let out the shouren? Were they in alliance with them? The beast-people were an elusive bunch. Many people believed that they no longer existed, having been exterminated during the Great Purge upon the birth of Oasis Kingdom. But the shouren always lurked within this land, possibly biding their time to take back their rightful place in the kingdom.

Whoever let them out must have some use for them, unless it was another shouren who did it—which seemed unlikely because they hardly ever operated alone, drawing strength through their numbers.

Later, as she duelled with Liqin, her thoughts kept her preoccupied—although she was still a better fighter than the Capital girl with her mind elsewhere.

Yet, she had the unshakeable sense that she was being watched. It began as a prickle on the back of her neck, a shift in the wind, then a heavy presence near her like an invisible weight resting on her shoulder. Every instinct went on full alert.

The First Prince stepped out from under the eaves a moment later, the timing too exact for him to have just been passing by. How long had he been lurking there?

Shimu gathered the girls as Prince Han approached, looking every bit like a respectable prince in his resplendent black and gold-trimmed robes. But something in his eyes reminded her that he belonged out in the wilderness. It was different from Prince Wei's brow-beaten look that retained a thirst for adventure; the First Prince was more like a starving wolf ready to devour anything in its path. It raised her hackles and made every inch of her body stand on guard.

'Greetings, Your Highness,' Shimu said. The girls echoed after her. 'What brings you to the House of Night? We don't often receive visitors here.'

'Consider it a call of duty to better understand the defences within the imperial court. I understand the trials did not go as planned last season, so I would like to directly pick a personal guard from here.'

Liqin and Xiyue exchange uncomfortable glances. Even Shimu looked slightly flustered. But Windshadow kept her expression as placid as she could, giving nothing away.

'I was not aware of this ... arrangement, Your Highness,' said Shimu.

'Well, you are now,' Prince Han drawled as he circled the three girls, lingering the longest around Windshadow. 'A desert girl,' he murmured, eyeing her from head to toe.

As unnerving as Prince Han's attention was, Windshadow was determined not to crack under his scrutiny. She levelled her gaze at him and observed him back. The shrewd slant of his brows, the thoughtful smirk, the hunger in his eyes that reminded her of the skin-hawks in the desert—vicious predators that would rip the skin clean off their prey before devouring them whole.

'Your sparring skills are remarkable,' he said. 'One of a kind, I might even say.'

'Thank you, Your Highness,' Windshadow said, her words clipped.

As he leaned closer to her, his voice dipped. 'I wonder what use my brother might have for you to keep you so close.'

Steady, Windshadow, she thought. *He's just baiting you.* He had only just returned to the palace. How could he know about her alliance with Meng?

Shimu and the other Blue Cranes peered at them curiously, but no one dared to utter a word.

'You will soon learn that I have my ways of forcing the truth out of you, Desert Girl,' Han muttered, still leaning too close for comfort.

'My name, Your Highness,' she said, 'is Windshadow.'

Han smirked, straightening. 'I would like her to be my personal guard,' he said to Shimu, eyes still fixed on Windshadow.

Shimu cleared her throat. 'I'm afraid—'

'That was not a request.'

'With all due respect, Your Highness,' Shimu persisted. 'Only the emperor has the power to assign the girls from the House of Night their roles.'

'If you insist on such trifling procedures,' he replied, shooting Shimu an almost mocking glance, 'rest assured I will acquire the emperor's permission.' He turned back to Windshadow. 'Would that be a problem for you, Desert Girl?'

'No, Your Highness,' she said, mimicking his tone. She had encountered one too many condescending Capital men to bristle at this one now. 'It would be an honour to serve,' she added, staring him dead in the eye until he departed.

Maybe if she was lucky, she'd get to kill Prince Han in his sleep as soon as tonight.

* * *

The First Prince was a light sleeper, but Windshadow expected nothing less. For someone who had lived out in the brutal North, hypervigilance was a skill essential for survival.

He trusted no one. She could tell from the way he doubled bolted his doors, checked his knife under his pillow, and positioned his hand close to it before he slept. Almost as though he expected a night-time assassination like what she was about to serve him.

Windshadow remained tucked away in the draughtiest corner of his bed-chamber until his breathing slowed. Everything had happened too quickly in the day for her to devise a plan with Prince Meng, so she would have to act on her own now. Prince Han had towed her to his quarters and told her to unpack her sparse belongings in the servant's quarter next to his.

He wanted her on a short leash, she knew. Perhaps he already had an inkling of what she could do. If that was the case, then this was all a test. Here he was, presenting her with the perfect opportunity to slit his throat in his sleep. All she had to do was take it—and walk right into his trap.

Yet, this was an opportunity too good to be missed. He was mortal, no matter how hardened he was by his time in the wilderness. And anything that could bleed could be killed.

She slipped out from behind the drapes towards his bedpost and materialized in full form, her dagger cold and steely in her hand. Next to her, a lone candle—the only source of light in the room—flickered in the breeze, throwing her shadow long and sharp across the floor. She extinguished it without a sound.

Even in his sleep, Han appeared fully aware of his surroundings, his expression carefully placed and his brows fixed in two shrewd arches. Windshadow hesitated, just for a moment. The hilt of her dagger bit into her palm.

She raised her weapon.

A low roar rushed by her ears as a gust of fire struck her hand. She gasped at the burn, releasing her grip on the dagger just as Prince Han rolled out of the way. The dagger lay useless on his pillow, snagging on the sheets.

Windshadow stared at her hand, incredulous, watching as it turned an angry shade of red.

She leapt away and spun around to see a figure step out of the darkness. He was a lanky boy not much older than her, but his magic felt much stronger, as though he had spent more time cultivating his power. He had the smooth bronzed skin of someone who grew up in the open desert, and in his eyes the malice of someone who had stomached enough rage in his life.

He measured her with the look of a skin-hawk eyeing its prey, toying with a flame in his open palm.

Windshadow watched as blisters began to bubble under her skin. Just as the pain began to set in, her skin healed.

Behind her, Prince Han remarked, 'How nice of you to visit, Desert Girl.'

She shouldn't be surprised. She had known about the Elementals ever since she was a child; she had known about her powers even before she learnt to wield a sword. She had even met the Water Elemental and called her azzi, her desert sister. It shouldn't come as a surprise that a Fire Elemental would exist.

What surprised her instead was that he was standing right before her, in the flesh. Windshadow thought she knew rage, but this boy's rage simmered and bubbled, rippled and roared, almost as if it had a life of its own. Almost as if it had made a home inside him and become him.

'I am not your enemy,' she said coolly, inching to the side so that she could put some distance between them.

'A bold claim from someone who just attempted to slit my throat,' Prince Han drawled as he pulled on a silk robe. 'For an assassin, your intentions are very predictable. Or should I say impulsive? I was expecting you to lay low for at least a day or two before attempting to murder me in my sleep.' His eyes glinted in the gloom. 'You must be desperate.'

She gritted her teeth, her gaze shuttling between him and the fire-wielder.

'Oh, don't mind Lazar,' Han said. 'He won't burn you to a crisp as long as I decide to spare your life. Very handy to have one of your kind at my beck and call, I must say.'

Windshadow ignored him and addressed Lazar. 'What's in it for you?'

'I don't believe it's any of your concern, azzi,' he sneered.

Gods, Windshadow thought, *they're equally unpleasant.* No wonder they could conspire together. But she didn't believe for a second that the desert boy would stay by Prince Han when the moment came for him to save his hide. No one from the Khuzar Desert would put their lives in the hands of someone from Oasis Capital. As the saying went, in the Capital, hands are full but hearts are empty.

They were watching her, as though expecting her to fight back and reveal what she could do. But she was not going to show her hand just yet, not until she found out this boy's origins, his motives, and the extent of his capability.

She drew herself into a gale and swept out through the window, putting out the lamp behind her.

Han's laughter trailed after her as she blustered out of his chamber, her rage driving her deep into the night. She hated fleeing like a coward, but the time was not ripe yet and she had to pick her battles for now.

She raced towards Meng's chamber, throwing all caution to the wind. There was another Elemental living under his roof, one who was on the side of the enemy, and they were running out of time.

Elemental Magic

Little is known about elemental magic.

Much of what we understand now was gleaned from folktales passed down through generations in verbal storytelling and written script. Over time, original accounts of a period in history when gods roamed the earth and walked among humans—when magic was pure and revered, wielded by beings closest to the gods— became distorted.

The stories about the Immortal Spring and the Damohai spread through the ancient sandstone city of Nakh-Dul, the mountain tribes of Arkana, the nomadic tribes in the Khuzar Desert, and even the southern river cities along the Nam Huong river.

But not all versions of these stories agree with one another. Especially when it comes to the Elementals and their magic.

Descended from the Damohai, the five Elementals are regarded as myth—as abominations or saviours to a lost people. The views regarding their magic are thus conflicted. Some say it is stolen from the gods. Others see it as a gift, a manifestation of the gods' benevolence towards mortals. And many believe it is a sign that the age-old enmity between the Celestial and Earth Kings is coming to an end. Those who believe in the latter regard the Elementals as the harbingers of a new age, reincarnation of deities—or what folks from the West would call 'saints'—come to bless humankind with eternal peace and prosperity.

Mortal rulers have long regarded the tales about the Damohai and the Elementals with some degree of wariness. Some seek them out to exploit their magic, and others aim to exterminate them, fearing a rebellion if the people began to lose faith in mortal kings.

After all, according to the prophecy, the surviving Elemental must prove not only his mettle and might, but also his character to earn the esteem of the gods. And only a worthy Elemental can become the true guardian of the spring. Only having put an end to these troubled times, where corrupted magic lies in corrupt hands, can he take his place among the gods.

But Elemental magic and its limits remain largely a mystery. Is it strong enough to restore the balance between the realms, or kill its bearer before he arrives at the spring? Or will the ambitions of men interfere with his destiny? Whatever the fate of the surviving Elemental, so becomes the fate of the world.

Meanwhile, kingdoms lie in wait for the appearance of these prophesied characters, for the day they bring about a new order between Heaven and Earth.

—Excerpt from *'Land of Sand and Song: Tales from the Khuzar Desert'* by Lu Ji Fang

TEN

Desert Rose

It started as a trickle, steady but insistent, like a pulse beating under Ghost City. Desert Rose wasn't sure if she was dreaming when she heard the faint sound of streaming water.

The noise grew in urgency. Her eyelids flew open.

She stared out into the pitch-black cavern where the lamps had been snuffed out, save for one in the kitchen area. Something under her skin was thrumming and her body felt warm, as though something had awakened in her; as though something was responding to the water she heard.

For a moment, she lay in the darkness next to Wei, watching the gentle rise and fall of his sleeping form. During the night, his hand had found its way to hers and lay warm and solid on top of hers. She held onto that fleeting moment of comfort, where her heart felt grounded and at peace, willing her body to fall back into calmness.

But the sound never abated, breaking into her thoughts even as she tried to go back to sleep. The buzzing in her blood made her heart race and her head swim. How could there be water here—in the parched, arid depths of a catacomb buried in the heart of the desert? Where could it possibly come from?

With some reluctance, she pulled her hand out of Wei's and got up. She stood still for a moment with her eyes closed, feeling the skeins of energy tug at her. She let her feet guide her across the complex, careful not to trip over Zeyan and Beihe lying asleep not far away.

The sound came from behind one of the pillars, near a wall carved with murals. More accurately, it came from a boulder resting against the wall—if the way it crescendoed was any indication. She peered at the boulder closely, not quite sure what she was looking for. She ran her foot over the ground at the foot of the boulder and found a gap.

There was a hole underneath the boulder. Was there another tunnel beneath? There was only one way to find out.

'What are you doing?'

Desert Rose jumped and spun around to find Wei looming over her, silhouetted by a small torch perched on a wall bracket behind him. In her preoccupation with the boulder, she hadn't noticed him appear behind her.

She scrambled to find the words, an explanation that did not sound completely ludicrous but failed. 'There's water flowing under this rock. Help me move it.'

His brows slid up, but he didn't question her credibility. 'And how do you propose we do that?'

'You push, I'll move it with water.'

'But what are you hoping to find? So what if there's water under this rock?'

She couldn't explain it even to herself, much less convince Wei that this was a worthwhile endeavour. But the way her body was responding to the water was undeniable, and she had learnt not to ignore or suppress that part of her. She had unleashed it, and there was no going back.

And with what Anar Zel just told her about the Elementals, it seemed imperative that she understood her new abilities, what they responded to, and what exactly she could do.

'Just trust me on this,' she said.

Wei didn't ask any further questions, only propped both hands against the rock. 'Ready whenever you are.'

She closed her eyes in concentration, letting her power course through her. It was becoming a familiar sensation. Her mind latched on to the water all around her and reeled it in until she could feel the threads thicken into a rope, a sash, a thick blanket she could almost hold in her hands.

The ground rumbled, hard enough to shake the ground. She opened her eyes and glanced at the square, but no one stirred in their sleep. She tried again, gathering more water she could get hold of. The rock trembled and dislodged from its position. Wei dug his feet into the ground and pushed it with all his might as she continued to wield her power.

At last, the rock rolled free, revealing the hole in the ground. It was no larger than the size of a pushcart wheel, just enough to fit one person at a time.

Desert Rose could feel the water rushing beneath as surely as the blood running through her veins. There was life underneath these cracked, barren grounds, and she was somehow drawn to it, tied to it.

She dipped her foot in and found a step. Then another. And another. Soon, she found herself descending a flight of stairs leading her further down the catacomb.

Wei's laid a hand on her shoulder from behind. 'Rose, are you sure …?'

She nodded, taking another step down. The water was calling out to her now, pulling her towards it as it rose in an urgent crescendo, although the ground remained dry with every step she took. Darkness swallowed her whole. She groped for support—a wall, anything. But the emptiness that lay before her was vast, almost infinite.

A gentle whoosh behind her brought along a warm glow that lit up the stairwell. Wei was close behind her, torch in hand.

'Better to have two fools embarking on a suicide quest together,' he muttered when Desert Rose grinned at him.

A rattle and hiss, followed by an unearthly shriek, made them both jump. Their smiles slipped off their faces as they reached for each other's hands.

'It's not too late to turn back,' said Wei.

'You can if you wish,' she replied. She had come this far; she couldn't go back now. The answer to who she was and what she could do felt right within reach.

The water slowed to a steady stream when they reached the end of the stairs, as though cowed by the interruption. She strained to hear it, but a spectre cut through the gloom and dove straight towards them. Wei yanked her out of the way and they whirled around to find a figure emanating a pearly glow drifting before them.

Calm down, Rose, she thought as a chill ran through her. *This is Ghost City after all. Nothing to jump out of your skin about.*

But it wasn't just one spectre. The chamber was suddenly illuminated by multiple glowing figures closing in around them like a pack of wolves, their sunken, gaping faces looking almost feral.

'Brilliant plan,' Wei muttered to her as they pressed their backs close against each other.

'I don't hear you proposing a better alternative,' she retorted.

She threw out her hands as one of the spirits lunged for Wei, directing a jet of water at the spirit. It struck the spirit square in the chest as though it were corporeal and flung it backwards against the others.

Still, they were relentless. They swarmed in, one of them swooping towards Wei and knocking him off his feet with unexpected force. Wei let out a cry as the spirit settled inside him, then a grunt as he landed on his back.

The water began to peter out. Desert Rose's hands started shaking as she kept up the stream of water. *Get up, Wei.* In this barren underground chamber, so deep she could hear nothing but her own laboured breathing, drawing even the slightest drop of moisture was a feat.

But Wei did not get up. The spirit remained inside him, emanating a glow that brought a green tint to Wei's pallid face. Sweat beaded on his skin as he struggled to return to his feet, but the spirit held him down as the others rounded in on him.

'Cease,' a voice bellowed over the din and echoed through the chamber.

Desert Rose jumped. The spirit fled Wei's body and joined the others as they shuffled into two lines facing each other. While she helped Wei to his feet, a hush fell over the chamber.

A statelier-looking spectre cut through the throng towards them, wizened and opaque, but there was no mistaking his wrath. His image rippled, as though his anger was rolling off him in waves, making the crown that sat atop his head tip perilously. He was dressed in a ceremonious Old Kingdom-style robe that trailed behind him whenever he moved; when he spoke, his voice rumbled deep and gravelly as a shuddering mountain.

'He who intrudes upon my land shall surrender his soul.' He spoke in the ancient tongue that only a few of the tribe elders spoke, but both she and Wei understood him perfectly.

'She, actually,' Desert Rose said. Wei shot her a look. 'We?' He rolled his eyes.

'Foolhardy intruders. You will bow before the Ghost King.'

Desert Rose froze. 'The Ghost King?'

Wei glanced at her askance and muttered, 'Does this mean we're actually in …'

Her voice came out hushed. 'The Darklands.'

She had got lost here once when she was fourteen. The Darklands aboveground was terrifying enough, a desolate pitch-black landscape that seemed to stretch on forever, but nobody—not even the tribe elders who told campfire stories about this place—had spoken much about what lay below this fabled wasteland. All she knew was this was where the souls of men who died in the desert roamed for all eternity.

She had also heard about the Ghost King misleading errant travellers until they lost their way and lost their minds, before harvesting their souls for his phantom army. She had always thought those were cautionary tales the clansmen told to dissuade those with curious minds and hearts for adventure.

But now, standing face to face with the lord of all those aggrieved souls in his underground lair, she wasn't sure anymore.

She bowed the way she would to her tribe elders, with one hand over her heart and another around her torso. Wei mimicked her.

'We mean no ill will,' she said. 'I just…' How could she explain the unexplainable pull she had felt that led her here? Would the Ghost King even care if he was ready to reap their souls?

'The last time an Elemental trespassed upon the Darklands, he said the same thing,' said the Ghost King.

'An Elemental?' It was the certainty in his voice that unsettled her. That he uttered it as fact, not conjecture, made everything irrevocable, inescapable.

She was an Elemental, and it was clear which one of the five she was. If so, then that would make Windshadow one as well. Did that mean the rest of the prophecy was true, too? That she was destined to kill the others or be killed to make it to the Immortal Spring? Where then were the others?

'Rose?' another voice rang from the back. There was no mistaking that familiar timbre. She had fallen asleep to the sound of it as it told her folk tales from the desert, hummed the melodies that felt like warm hugs on frigid nights. It was the last voice she heard before she fled her home that winter's night, before everything fell apart.

'Papa!' Desert Rose cried, her heart already swelling at the sight of his familiar silhouette. But as he made his way to the front of the line, the glow around him became more apparent.

He was no more than a soul, just like the rest of them.

'Papa...'

The Ghost King held out an arm to stop her from going any closer to her father. 'His soul belongs here.'

Tears clouded her eyes as she continued staring at her father. 'Does that mean ... you're dead?'

'Not quite,' her father said gently.

'I don't understand.'

'Anar Zel and the others needed refuge. I had to ensure they had somewhere to go until the tribe business gets sorted out.'

Realization dawned upon her. 'So you traded your soul for the safety of the tribe members? They're living comfortably up there because you made a deal with the Ghost King?'

He nodded. 'Temporarily.'

'For how long exactly? What about Blackstone and the other clan leaders? They've gone northwest to—'

'I know about their foolish alliance with the Lettorians.'

'Then why would you stay here? It's not like you.'

'Because I knew you would come. This war is bigger than us, Rose. Bigger than the tribe and the warring nations. It's in the prophecy.'

The prophecy. There was only one, the one that she had heard ever since she was a child. Five Elementals. One survivor. The guardian of the Immortal Spring and keeper of the peace between the realms.

Some of her tribe elders heralded it as the beginning of a new age, a golden age where they would all be saved, but others—like her—only saw it as a myth passed down to keep her people clinging to hope.

'Your father was counting on you to find him and fulfil your destiny,' said the Ghost King. 'You are the one who can free us all.'

'There has been news of an Elemental in Lettoria. It's how they managed to advance so quickly in military strength,' said her father.

Desert Rose shared a look with Wei. Things were starting to fall into place. 'So I have to go to Lettoria and kill an Elemental to weaken Lettoria, defeat Blackstone and the clan leaders, and get one step closer to the spring?'

'And your destiny.' Her father's gaze was infinitely sad.

'You—you knew what I was all along?'

'I've tried to protect you from it all this time. Your abilities would have attracted all the wrong sort of attention.'

All those times he had made her drink *mukh* water concocted by the tribe healers, told her to hide her abnormal healing ability, and forbidden her from hunting with the clan boys, she had assumed he was just being overprotective of the orphan girl he had picked up in the desert.

'But even then, a few tribe members knew,' her father added.

She recalled how Golsha—the ex-tribe member who had left the desert to forge a new life in Oasis Capital as a merchant—had called her an abomination. How Anar Zel had tried so hard to school her in the natural arts so she would have better inner control. How the tribe healers had handed her mukh water and pretended not to notice how quickly she healed from every injury she sustained.

'That was how I managed to find my way back home the last time I got lost for two weeks,' she said. 'How I managed to survive the desert as a child before you found me.' Something else Golsha said came to mind. 'Golsha said you were looking for a cure for me.'

Again, the sad look settled in his eyes. 'It's for the event where your powers are too strong for you to control. But your destiny is larger than any cure I can possibly find. There is no changing who you are.' He took a tentative step forward until the Ghost King shot him a look.

'You said Rose can free you all,' Wei piped up, addressing the Ghost King without flinching. 'Who exactly does *all* include?'

'The surviving Elemental will restore the balance between the realms and free our souls from this limbo.' He turned to Desert Rose. 'Your father's soul will remain here until the spring's rightful guardian claims her place.'

She glanced at her father and read the unspoken truth in his eyes. The fate of the Dugur tribe now rested on her. It was up to her to save not just him and the tribe, but also the world as she knew it.

She used to reject the idea of destiny. Yet now, she had her own fate laid out for her. The thought felt large enough to consume her, but it also awakened something in her, as though she had been waiting for this very moment of reckoning.

'It's here, isn't it? The spring?' she said. She could feel it, pulsing through the ground like a life force. Like it was running through her, too. But it was too faint to grasp, like mist that threaded through her fingers.

'You don't have to concern yourself with its whereabouts,' said the Ghost King. 'The spring will reveal itself to you the closer you get to being the last Elemental standing.'

She had to do it. For her father, above all. Her tribe. Her home, a land once ruled by her ancestors. She had a chance to restore everything to its rightful place and save the people she loved. She would do whatever it took to do so.

She turned to Wei, who seemed to already know what she was thinking. 'How many days is it to Lettoria?'

An explosion outside reverberated through the underground chamber, cutting off Wei's reply. They exchanged a look. With one parting glance at her father, who urged her on with a nod, she charged back up the stairs together with Wei.

They emerged to find the chamber shrouded in smoke, but the damage revealed itself when the dust cleared. One of the pillars had been blasted through and half the ceiling had collapsed. An eerie silence settled—where before there had been the laughter of children and the sound of chatter, there was none now.

Fear seized Desert Rose. *No. No, no, no.*

She and Wei split up and picked their way through the rubble. She cast her gaze around wildly, looking for signs of her tribespeople, but there was only crumbled stone all around. Were they all buried underneath?

'Mother!' Wei called. 'Zeyan! Beihe!'

'Qara! Yanda! Anar Zel!' Desert Rose yelled, trying to quell the mounting terror in her heart.

'Rose!' a familiar voice replied from the middle of the chamber.

Relief washed over her as she scrambled in the direction of the sound of Qara's voice. Wei joined her right away, offering her a hand as they picked their way towards what used to be the dais. Now, a massive stone slab that was part of the collapsed ceiling covered it almost entirely.

Desert Rose only spotted them when she went around to the other side of the slab. They were all huddled within the space between the dais and the stone slab—Zeyan, Beihe, and the tribespeople, from wide-eyed children wrapped in their mother's embrace to exhausted-looking elders. Among them, the shamans who had been praying in a circle earlier had their eyes closed in concentration as they recited a stream of chants. Silvery light unspooled from their fingertips and formed a dome around them that seemed to withstand the weight of the stone slab, protecting everyone under it.

'Rose!' Qara rushed towards her. 'Thank the gods you're okay!'

'What happened?' Desert Rose asked.

'We were ambushed. Everything exploded before we could see who it was. The question is, how did they manage to get in here?'

The stone slab lying atop the dome started to tremble. It was taking the shamans all their energy to prop it up. Desert Rose and Wei attempted to lift it off, but it was too heavy to budge until she gathered a wall of water to hoist it up. Qara ushered everyone out from underneath it. Most of the tribespeople were still in shock, but those who had noticed her magical ability made no mention of it, merely regarding her with slow caution as they picked their way out.

Who could have attacked them? There was no way anyone could have followed them in after Anar Zel sealed the entrance. This meant they had to have entered from somewhere else and lain in wait until everyone was asleep to set off the explosive. This wasn't the act of desert bandits or grave robbers, who were usually more interested in valuables than the messy business of killing people.

'Where's my mother?' Wei asked when the last of them emerged and there was no sign of her.

The last time Desert Rose saw them, Wei's mother and Anar Zel had gone to a far corner, where Anar Zel attempted to restore Luzhen's energy.

'Mother!' Wei called, his cracked voice echoing around the chamber in the silence that followed. Desert Rose, Qara, Zeyan and Beihe joined him at the far corner of the chamber and came to a dead halt next to him.

Luzhen and Anar Zel's mutilated bodies lay sprawled at the foot of the wall, their blood streaked across the murals. Desert Rose felt her body go numb. Next to her, Qara burst into tears. Wei was completely still but his gaze was empty, as though his soul had escaped from him.

They had been too far away from the shaman's reach to be protected, and Anar Zel, as skilled as she was in the natural arts, had likely been so focused on healing Wei's mother that she didn't have the spare energy to fend off the attack.

Desert Rose reached for Wei's hand. It was limp in hers but started to tremble as they approached the bodies. His grip tightened the closer they got until they stood before the horrific sight. Wei sank to his knees, his eyes bloodshot and jaw clenched tight, as he took his mother's hand.

Next to her, Anar Zel, who had always seemed formidable despite her slightly hunched back and grey hair, now looked every bit her age. This was not the way she should have gone. She was the matriarch of the Dugur tribe, who healed and defended them all alongside her father, the chieftain. Her death should have been dignified and peaceful, if not grand. Not like this.

Out of the wreckage, she spotted it. Half obscured by sand and rock fragments, the glint of gold under a remnant flame next to her that Qara put out. She reached for it, already recognizing it. She had seen that vermillion and gold imperial emblem everywhere in the palace last winter.

How had Oasis Kingdom's scouts managed to find them here?

Desert Rose's hand shook as she showed Wei the emblem. Recognition settled on his face at once. A part of her struggled to come to terms with the truth, but there was no denying the evidence she held in her hand now.

Meng did this. He had sent these scouts, and they had been ordered to set off this explosive, to ambush them indiscriminately. Had he changed his mind about catching them alive after all? The Meng she knew might have been trapped and misguided, but he wasn't cruel.

Then again, she had been entirely fooled by him the entire time she had been in the palace. All those nights in the library, the help he offered, the tea, his gentleness and hunger for stories—everything had turned out to be a lie just to advance his aim.

Perhaps she never knew him at all; perhaps he truly was this unscrupulous.

'He did this,' Wei said, echoing her thoughts as he took the emblem from her. Fury gathered in his onyx eyes. 'First Yong, now Mother. He did this.'

Desert Rose was no stranger to vengeance. It had stoked the fire in her ever since the clan leaders overthrew her father and persecuted her. It had lived under her skin, a constant reminder of her goal, her responsibility, the injustice she had suffered. The betrayal.

She saw all that now in Wei, brimming with fresh hatred, grief spilling out of him. She heard in his voice that urgency that had spurred her on when she trained in the House of Night.

He gripped the emblem so hard his knuckles turned white. 'We'll head to Lettoria in the morning.'

There is a time to wait and a time to take action. To miss the boat on either will cost you your victory.

—*The War Handbook*, Lu Cao

ELEVEN

Meng

The air stirred. A slight breeze slipped in through the windows, rustling the curtains.

Meng turned over in his sleep, ignoring the faint rustle at the foot of his bed. It was not until he felt a weight sink into his bed that he roused to find Windshadow perched before him, looking, for the first time since he met her, rattled.

He sat up hastily. 'Windshadow, we've talked about this.'

She ignored him, wasting no words. 'There's another Elemental in the palace, and he's out for blood. He's working for Han.'

Meng took a moment to digest her news. Of course Han would not return alone; he knew better than to come back unguarded to challenge the throne. What surprised Meng was the fact that his brother had found an Elemental too, one who could unnerve Windshadow, the most dauntless person he had met. When she first discovered Desert Rose was a fellow Elemental, there was only excitement.

'And I have reason to believe the Fire Elemental is the one behind the prison fire that freed the shouren,' Windshadow went on, interrupting his thoughts.

What would his brother gain from setting free the shouren prisoners? Was he perhaps trying to win them over? What exactly was his plan? Was their mother in on this?

Meng closed his eyes as a bone-deep weariness settled upon him. He was wrong to think that his destiny ended with taking over the throne; it was much harder to stay on it than to attain it.

'You need to lie low for now,' he told Windshadow at last. 'Until we learn of their intentions.'

She shot him a look. 'No offence, Your Majesty, but I'm not certain how long I can sit still, given that your brother who has a chip on his shoulder has returned, and there's a powerful Elemental roaming around the palace.'

Desert Rose had once told him about the Elementals and the prophecy, in one of their long, quiet conversations in the library. How they were to kill or be killed by one another. It sounded like an old wives' tale, but Meng knew better than to dismiss them as such. The world was far bigger than Oasis Kingdom and its magic-resistant wall, and some destinies were far larger than his.

'What do you propose we do about the other Elemental then?' he said.

'I could assassinate them both,' Windshadow said, her eyes glinting.

Meng sent her a look. Everything seemed to end with that one solution for her. 'I would be the biggest suspect if my brother was killed.'

'I suppose you'd prefer if he killed you first,' she said.

She was right. His brother would show no mercy when it came to the throne. Han had always believed himself to be the rightful successor. There was no doubt that he would do whatever it took to seize power.

And the difference between Meng and his brother was that Meng had far more to lose.

But surely his mother wouldn't allow her sons to go at each other's throats for the throne. Besides, according to High Advisor Mian, Meng was destined to take the throne; it was written in his stars from the moment he was born. She had told him that enough times for him to almost believe it.

'I still think we should find out what they're planning before making our move,' he said at last.

Windshadow raised her brows. 'Well, then I hope you find out soon, because they're certainly not wasting any time.'

Before he could reply, she disappeared in a gust of wind and swept out of the chamber, leaving him at odds with himself for the rest of the night.

At dawn, the messenger arrived.

* * *

The next morning, the hallways leading from the Red Circle to the Hall of Harmony seemed exceptionally deserted. Meng quickened his footsteps, leaving his servant hurrying to keep up. Windshadow was right: Han was certainly not wasting any time.

'Prince Han has called for an urgent Council session and requested for Your Majesty's presence,' the messenger had relayed in his chamber at the crack of dawn.

On any regular occasion, it would be preposterous for the emperor to respond to a prince's call for a council session. But the rules were different now—Han cared nothing for court protocol, and Meng was on his own in fending for his position.

The council was already gathered in their two regular columns leading up to the dais, murmuring furiously amongst themselves. Han stood at the front of the left row, carrying his usual air of casual confidence, disengaged from the chatter among the council members. At the front of the hall sat the Empress Dowager, looking mildly annoyed by the chattering ministers but otherwise composed.

Meng had the sense that something large was looming, and he hated that feeling of being blindsided. The fact that all the council members were gathered here when only the emperor had the power to call for a council session was enough of an indication that something was amiss.

Meng took a deep breath and nodded at his servant to announce his arrival. Han's gaze cut straight to him as he stepped through the doors. Meng sent his brother his most imperious look and took his seat on the gilded dais before everyone.

'What calls for this, Prince Han?' he said, glancing at the ministers. 'I don't recall the council responding to anyone's call for a session apart from the emperor's.'

A few council members exchanged guilty glances but the rest stood still with stony faces. A few stared at Han for their cue. Meng turned to his mother, who watched on indifferently.

'I apologize for the intrusion on an early morning, Your Majesty,' Han said, sounding anything but sorry, 'but this was quite an emergency.' He turned to address the ministers. 'We are gathered here today for an interrogation of sorts.'

The Empress Dowager showed no sign of surprise or bemusement, so Meng could only assume that Han had already let her in on this. His trepidation rose in him like a wild animal as he surveyed everyone before him. Even now when they were both grown, his brother was able to worm under his skin.

'Explain yourself, Prince Han,' he commanded, trying to keep his voice loud and steady.

'Bring out the suspect,' Han called.

A pair of guards stepped out of the shadows, their grip firm on a girl in chains between them.

Something was wrong. Windshadow, a girl made of spite and vengeance, who had on multiple occasions urged him to kill or be killed, was barely fighting back at all. Instead, she slumped forward, barely able to walk on her own, her ashen face downcast.

It wasn't until he spotted the bits of emerald-green leaves strewn around her sweaty neck that Meng realized why.

Ticha. The leaves used to cleanse every visitor at the gates of Oasis Capital were meant to filter out magical folk before they could step foot into the kingdom. Windshadow had always been careful to evade the magic-detecting herb widely used in the kingdom and particularly the palace. How did she get captured this time?

Meng tried to hold up an impassive expression, but he was powerless against his own racing heart.

Han knew. He knew what Windshadow was, what she could do. That was how he managed to nab her, lock her in her human form, and debilitate her. And now he was about to expose her—and, indirectly, him.

'She trains at the House of Night, a fact our emperor is aware of,' said Han.

Every pair of eyes turned to Meng. The ministers began whispering among themselves as their gazes shuffled between him and Windshadow.

Han's voice cut over the din. 'However, I have reason to believe that this witch'—he jabbed a finger at Windshadow—'is responsible for the recent prison fire that freed the shouren.'

Windshadow struggled to raise her head. Even so, the malice and hatred in her eyes burnt bright when she glared at Han.

'What evidence do you have that this girl is behind the prison fire?' Meng demanded.

'Her housemistress revealed that she was not in the dormitory on the night of the fire. We also found some rather interesting residue at the crime scene: sand. More specifically, sand that is only found in Khuzar Desert, which, I believe, is where the suspect hails from. This residue I also found in my chamber, where she visited me last night to put a dagger to my throat.'

The whispers turned to urgent murmurs.

Meng caught Windshadow's eye at last and was met with her usual defiance. She hadn't told him about her failed assassination attempt, only the part about Han's fire-wielding assistant. That was the thing about her—she operated on her own, and on her gut, and too often she would inch too close to danger and put both their positions in jeopardy.

'But perhaps most interestingly,' Han went on, 'this unique type of sand was also found in the emperor's chamber when I visited him on the night of the prison fire, just before the fire broke out. It is therefore a logical conjecture that the girl visited the emperor in his chamber, then went to set the fire and free the prisoners while the emperor and I were engaged.'

The ministers' mutterings reached a fever pitch. A couple of them glanced at Meng reproachfully, while others shot looks of pure hatred at Windshadow.

'Based on such incriminating evidence, I believe that the current interim emperor's integrity is far too questionable for him to govern and safeguard this kingdom,' Han finished, pulling his best solemn look.

'Preposterous,' Meng snapped before he could stop himself. But he knew he was outmatched this time. All his careful planning and observing hadn't prepared him for this assault on his integrity. Even if Han's accusation was far from the truth, the evidence he provided was indubitable.

Already, the ministers were regarding him differently. While before they might have been willing to give him a chance to prove himself, their unanimous look of disapproval now told Meng all he needed to know about their eroding faith in him. As the interim emperor, he was already grappling with his shaky position. But now, anything he said would sound like a poor defence.

Windshadow was watching him. So was his mother. Han. The ministers. Each waiting to see what he would do or say next.

Another voice—female—interrupted them before he could find the words. 'The Fifteenth Oasis Emperor was aware of this before he passed on.'

Matron stepped out from the back entrance of the hall alone, looking stoic and unwavering as always. As she came to her usual position one step to the left behind the throne, where she used to stand next to his father, her gaze remained steady, even when the council members frowned at her presence and Han stalked towards her.

The Empress Dowager narrowed her eyes at her. 'I don't remember you being invited to this private council, Matron.' Underneath her imperious drawl lurked a barbed warning.

'My place is next to the emperor, as long as he will have me there, Your Majesty,' Matron replied coolly.

'How dare you,' the Empress Dowager snapped, her lofty demeanour slipping.

'I mean no disrespect, Your Majesty,' said Matron. 'But I have served as lady-in-waiting to two emperors, and I will serve the Sixteenth Oasis Emperor as he carries out his duties without the distraction of those attempting to cause unrest within the palace.'

The Empress Dowager drew in a breath, ready to call out her insolence again.

'Regardless,' Han broke in. 'My father being aware of this witch's presence does not mitigate her crimes or negate the fact that the interim emperor not only allowed her to continue training at the House of Night, but also kept close contact with her.'

The ministers nodded in agreement. The Empress Dowager remained impassive, keeping her gaze fixed straight ahead, offering no help at all.

Moments passed. Meng felt his stomach sink. This was a test, and he had failed. Failed to keep the throne against a simple accusation, failed to prove his mettle as emperor, failed to live up to his destiny.

His mother had never truly cared about his future or destiny, despite all the time and effort he had spent carefully planning his next step, navigating the fraught politics of the imperial court, and executing his mother's plans even when they went against his conscience and better judgement. Despite all the sleepless nights where he lay wrought by guilt and sorrow and bone-deep exhaustion because his mother had convinced him that he was the only person who could save and protect their family.

In the end, everything he had done out of duty and love for his mother had only served to secure her position in power.

Had she planned this all along? Had she helped make Meng the emperor so that he could reinstate Han? Had he been nothing but a stepping stone for his older brother? Their mother had never made any attempt to disguise the fact that Han was her favourite, after all.

Meng was on his own now, truly, with all evidence stacked against Windshadow and him. It was up to him to fend for the both of them.

'Do we all truly believe that my father and I would have a Ling living with us under the same roof without understanding her intentions and abilities?' The ministers drew in a collective breath at the mention of the race of magical beings and practitioners—it was profane to say their name especially in this hallowed hall—but Meng ignored them and barrelled ahead. 'My father and I were not only aware of her powers, but sought to harness it. She is an asset to the House of Night, and deserves none of this treatment.'

'Any way to prove it?' Han drawled. 'That the late emperor had authorized and supported having a dangerous magical being in the palace—who, I should remind everyone, attempted to murder me last night?'

Apart from Matron, there was the mistress of the House of Night. But them vouching for him would only jeopardize their positions and potentially their lives. The only other person who could support his claim was Desert Rose, who had entered the palace with both his and his father's permission. But Meng doubted Desert Rose would want anything to do with him at all, after what he had done to her, much less offer any sort of aid to clear his name.

Han turned back to the Council members before Meng could offer an alibi. 'Our borders grow weaker each day our enemies closer,' he declared. 'We cannot sit by and watch our emperor continue his dalliance with a desert girl of unclear origins. Whomever rules the great Oasis Kingdom must have the mettle and foresight to lead us to greater victory and a brighter future.'

'And I suppose you believe you are the one who can do the job,' Meng said quietly.

'I will take up that mantle with all due solemnity and responsibility, if that's what the kingdom needs,' Han said.

'Would the kingdom place its faith in a son who had once betrayed it?' Meng retorted. If his brother wanted to play the game this way, then Meng no longer needed to hold back.

The Empress Dowager's voice cut them off. 'Enough.' She turned to Meng at last. 'Your Majesty, I believe now is not the time to dredge up the past. We have more pressing issues to deal with here.'

What could be more important than selecting the right leader to govern the kingdom? Meng wanted to ask. But the ministers were already nodding in unison, eager to move on to the next order of business.

'Are we all in favour of the interim emperor stepping down, then?'
Senior Minister Yuan asked the other council members.

Of course his largest dissident would be the first to put forth this
notion. Councillor Yuan had never believed in Meng's abilities as a
leader, much less supported his contentious rise to the throne.

This was all planned, Meng realized at last. Not just by Han, but
by everyone present, save for Windshadow and Matron. His mother
hardly seemed surprised by the turn of events, and every minister was
far too eager to agree with Councillor Yuan.

They had all intended for him to step down as soon as he had taken
over the throne, and Han had given them the best excuse for the veto.

He could make a scene. He could refuse to give up the throne.
He could put up a fight and not let his brother steal his throne. He
could contest every single one of Han's claims and persuade the
Council that the time had come to embrace magic, not fear or revile
it as they had for centuries. He could even put Han to death with just
one command.

But Meng did none of that. Even if he did, no one would respond
to his command, not the guards or the ministers, who had all clearly
chosen a side.

He was powerless. Perhaps he never had any power to begin with,
not even when he was pronounced the Sixteenth Oasis Emperor and
the entire Imperial Army bowed at his feet. An emperor was only
as powerful as the loyalty of his subjects, and he had been a mere
puppet. There was no destiny, only lies he had been fed since birth.
He had been a fool to believe that he could save the kingdom once he
became emperor.

Everything that followed slipped by in a blur. Meng was vaguely
aware of Han proposing the termination of his role as interim emperor,
and the look of despair Windshadow sent him as she shivered and
shook. He felt only a crippling sense of helplessness when the council
members cast their votes and his mother watched, grim and immovable,
avoiding his gaze.

Without his destiny laid out before him or anyone on his side, what
lay ahead now?

'Thank you for executing your duties, interim emperor,' Han said. 'But your service is no longer required.' Meng felt his hands curl into tight fists by his side. Han took a step closer to Meng and murmured, 'I appreciate you warming my seat for me though.' He turned back to the prison guards. 'Lock up the witch. I want her lucid for questioning.'

His mother rose from her seat and the ministers got ready to adjourn. Just like that—with hardly any protest but his—Meng's run as the emperor came to an end. He knew what it meant to be stripped of his position like that, what it meant for Han to be in power: it was only a matter of time before Meng experienced Yong's fate—and he was fairly certain Han would not wait a whole year before poisoning his meal, or worse.

Meng felt his fingers dig deep into his palms. This could not be the end for him. It would not be. Because what was stolen from him today would be returned someday—he would make sure of that.

He watched Windshadow being towed away. When she turned back to send him one last glance, he gave her the slightest, almost imperceptible nod.

TWELVE

Windshadow

The first thing Windshadow felt when she came to was the cold, hard floor beneath her. Somewhere in between the council session and being towed to prison, she must have passed out. Again.

She picked herself off the ground, all too aware of the lingering tremor in her limbs and pounding in her head. Her heart was still racing, and the world spun even as she righted herself. The chains around her wrists clinked, though she tried to keep her movements as small as possible. The soreness in her wrists wasn't just from the chains but the bits of ticha leaves stuck on them.

She had evaded the cleansing ritual when she first snuck into Oasis Kingdom and had been spared from every subsequent one after Meng became her guarantor. She had stayed away from ticha wherever possible. But she was unable to escape it in the end.

The stronger one's magic, the more brutal the effects of ticha would be. Regular mortals would only find it bitter drinking it as tea. But for her, it had felt like a million knives ripping her insides apart, like fire down her throat when she was pinned down by two armed guards and force-fed ticha tea. As a final means to quell her into submission, they had pressed ticha leaves against her skin and rammed ticha leaves down her throat so that she was choking on them.

Never had she been so humiliated before a host of men, each revelling in her wretched state. It was another level of cruelty that only Han was capable of, a cruelty that reignited her desire to make him pay in an equally painful way.

But how could she, now that she was rendered powerless and weak in this prison cell with no means of escape, much less revenge?

She let out a bitter laugh. How had she allowed herself to end up like this? She had only meant to surveil Han last night, find out what his subsequent plans were.

But then she witnessed him kill the messengers.

Technically, he didn't get his hands dirty, but he was there. He had watched them die. He had laid down the order for the assassins to slit the throats of all three present.

Han was good at covering his tracks. He took his dirty deeds outside the palace grounds, in a remote forest a few li east of Wuxi Market, where a running brook covered up the rustle of feet and muffled voices. In that mist-shrouded clearing, there was barely anyone around who could hear them.

Although she had never personally interacted with them, Windshadow recognized the two of the men as the messengers who reported to Meng. The third one was the errand boy who worked for Golsha, the tribesman-turned-merchant who colluded with Meng and helped him acquire the stones to the Immortal Spring.

Windshadow had watched as the captives were towed out of a creaky horse-drawn wagon with their hands tied behind their backs.

Han's three henchmen threw a black hemp bag over each of the captives' heads and led them down the slope from the side of the road towards the brook. One of them—who Windshadow guessed was Golsha's errand boy—shook uncontrollably and buckled when they came to a stop.

Han, in his carriage, gave a dismissive wave of his hand. Without a word, the three assassins unsheathed their swords and swung them down in unison.

The choked gurgles of the captives made Windshadow almost gag. She had killed her fair share but never this way, never this cold.

A breeze that had snuck through the forest ran through her. She couldn't be sure if it was the chill in the night air or the realization of what Han was doing that made her shiver as though she was in her human form.

Han was getting rid of people who had worked with or for Meng, likely after he had got enough information about Meng's recent activities from them. How much did he already know, and what else was he planning to do? Who else was on his hit list?

He had spotted her just as she was about to slip through the trees, ready to rush back to inform Meng. But with alarming precision and speed, Han reached into his robes and flung out a hand.

Water droplets pelted her, ice cold yet burning hot. A debilitating sensation coursed through her instantly. She felt her magic slip out of her grasp and leave her body, like a fire put out by a wintry breeze.

A gnarled tree branch snagged on her clothes, foiling her attempt at escape. She glanced down and found herself caught halfway in her human form, neither fully flesh nor air. A wave of pain washed through her just as she noticed the bits of crushed wet leaves sitting on her translucent skin.

Ticha.

She would swear, but her voice died in her throat as pain closed in on her. Even struggling made her body scream in anguish.

It wasn't difficult for Han to capture her after that. With a wave of his hand, he instructed the guards to load her onto the wagon, and she was picked up by two pairs of rough hands that bound her wrists together behind her back. They dumped her where the three captives had sat before they were killed, where the air reeked with the lingering stench of their fear.

She put up a feeble fight against her bonds. *Meng needs to outlaw ticha in this kingdom.* That was her last thought before she caved in to the pain and darkness.

But there was no chance of that now. In a heartbeat, Meng had been completely stripped of power and authority. And she had woken up in a filthy prison cell only to be towed back here after the hearing.

Her body was still aching in the aftermath of last night's assault. If only she could be free of these ticha-littered chains around her wrists, she would be able to regain her strength and then her power. With a day's rest, she might even be able to shift form again and escape.

But now she was as good as mortal. A weak one.

The prison guards had laid her next to the straw mat on purpose and left a bowl of water by the bars so that she would have to crawl over just for a sip of water. Her pride kept her from doing so until she could no longer bear it.

As she inched over, a noise in the distance made her stop. It wasn't the obnoxious footsteps of the guards who relished doubly in torturing her, but the rustle of someone who was trying hard not to be noticed.

She was aware of every shift in the air and every ripple of the wind, which was how she knew she had a visitor before spotting him in the gloom of the hallway. He lingered in the shadows, as though buying time to observe her, but she could feel his gaze on her the whole time. A gentle heat spread through the cell, offering some reprieve from the slick chill dripping off the walls.

'I know you're there,' she rasped. 'Show yourself.'

He was a lone figure in a black tunic emerging from the darkness. He carried no torch, but his face was illuminated by the small flame hovering above his palm.

The Fire Elemental took a step closer to her cell, staring down at her with a pitying gaze. 'You're betting on the wrong horse, my Elemental sister,' he murmured.

'I'll take my chances, just like you did with the First Prince.'

He stooped to level his gaze with hers. The flame died to a low ember between them, just enough to light up the planes of his face. 'Who will become the new emperor very soon. You, on the other hand, will be withering away in this cell thanks to the lily-livered one who can barely fight his own battles.'

He was baiting her, trying to figure out her relationship with Meng and the extent of her loyalty to him.

She ignored his remark. 'What's in it for you?'

This time, a gleam appeared in Lazar's eyes. 'I don't suppose I need to remind you about the prophecy.'

He need not. The prophecy was constantly at the forefront of her mind, urging her every step ever since her tribe knew what she was and pinned all their hopes on her. But she was no saviour, least of all theirs. She was here to save herself; sometimes that was all a person could do in one lifetime.

'Might have heard of it,' she replied as nonchalantly as she could.

'A war is looming on the horizon. And when Oasis Kingdom defeats its enemies and reclaims the desert, I shall be at the emperor's side, ready to claim my position as keeper of the Immortal Spring.'

'So glory,' she sneered. A snort escaped her. 'How mortal your desires are.'

When would the greed and stupidity of these men end? When would they get it through their skulls that magic never belonged to them—that it was only because the Immortal Spring was blocked; that the balance of magic between the realms was disturbed; that their laughable struggle for power and glory would ultimately come to nothing in their fleeting, tumultuous lives?

But then that would make her a hypocrite for secretly desiring that power for herself too, if only so that no one would trample on her or attempt to control her ever again. She would be a hypocrite for giving in to her powers and turning herself into a weapon so that she might become the worthiest of all, no longer discarded or unwanted or a tool for men to wield.

Lazar was no mortal man either, even if his desires were as base as theirs. If she had a chance to restore the Immortal Spring and come face-to-face with the gods, then so did he. As long as they were both in the running, there could only be one winner between them.

'Scorn all you wish, azzi,' Lazar said, unfazed. 'But we all know this is the path laid out for us, and I intend to fulfil my destiny.'

Some days, the word 'destiny' gave her purpose, made her feel like she existed. Some days, it felt like an ever-tightening noose around her neck. It was hard to bolster her confidence when she was locked up in a cell, every fibre in her still on fire from that blasted herb.

'Well, I hope your gamble works out for you,' she replied.

He watched her, head cocked, as though debating whether to finish her off right then. It would be easy, given her current state, where she could barely call up a breeze. She was in no position to offer an alliance either, for what good was she as a prisoner?

He raised the hand cradling the flame, slow and uncertain. She braced herself for the attack. But before the flame in his palm could grow any bigger, the sound of footsteps shuffling in the distance made them both freeze.

Lazar disappeared in a blink, melting back into the shadows just as Meng came into view.

'Nice of you to stop by,' she muttered, disguising her relief.

Meng put a finger to his lips and pulled out a single key from his sleeve. 'Hurry, we don't have time,' he murmured as he crouched to meet her at eye level. Windshadow remained where she was, still observing him. He gestured impatiently for her to raise her hands. She did so with much hesitation, and he reached through the bars with the key.

It wasn't until he had successfully unlocked her chains that Windshadow believed it.

Meng was going rogue.

'Why are you doing this?' As sentimental as Meng had become—no thanks to Desert Rose—it seemed inconceivable that he would risk his life and reputation to break her out of prison because he had grown attached to his assassin. What use did he have for her in whatever he planned to do next?

'Because there is much more that you and I can accomplish together,' he said.

There was no uncertainty in his voice this time, and something in his voice or the look in his eyes won her over. Underneath that steely conviction was a sort of wild abandon she sometimes felt in herself. It was the look of someone who had nothing left to lose.

Meng had been betrayed too, by the people he had come to trust—his advisors, his mother. He had been completely abandoned today in the hall, when Han and the ministers ambushed him and the Empress Dowager sat by and let it happen. Despite everything Meng had done for his mother, all she did was discard him once her other son returned.

Windshadow straightened and shook her chains loose. It wasn't over for her, nor was it for Meng. This was just the beginning for both of them—Meng to take his throne back, and her to get back in the running for the spring.

'Can you stand? Walk?' Meng asked as he began to unlock the gate.

As soon as Meng brushed the ticha leaves off her, her magic surged back like an old friend. Not quite enough to whip up a storm, but at least she was no longer close to passing out again. She picked herself off the ground with Meng's help. He placed a hand on her back and waited until she had completely regained her bearings before letting go.

Was she strong enough to take them both out of here, the palace and Oasis Kingdom? What happened if she failed?

'So what's our plan?' she asked, peering down the hallway for a sign of Lazar. Had he left? Did he know what they were about to do? 'Now that you've successfully abetted a criminal, you will be wanted for treason, emperor or not.'

Meng shot her a wry look. 'Or not.'

A clang resounded in the distance, followed by the low rumble of voices. The prison guards were here on patrol again. If they were planning to escape, it was now or never.

'We're going to make some new friends,' he said in answer to her question. 'In the northwest.'

She understood immediately. There was nothing left for either of them here. Meng knew it too. It was time to find new allies and make the ones here regret ever stripping them bare and trampling on them. Lettoria would be a good place to start—they were powerful and remorseless.

Besides, she had long heard about the Metal Elemental that the Lettorians had taken in and put to good use. Now she could finally verify those rumours and eliminate that contender.

But first, she had to return to herself.

She raised a hand and drew on the skeins of air, catching the tail of every passing breeze, every breath released, and trapping it in her palm. With each wisp of wind she pulled close to her, a new spark of life leapt up within her. The stray straws on the ground rustled around her, stirred up in a tiny frenzy as the gust grew stronger. Soon, she was standing in the eye of a small whirlwind.

She held out a hand to Meng, who hesitated just for a moment before taking it. A cry made them both jump, but they held on.

Lazar's voice rang out in the darkness down the hallway. 'The prisoner is escaping!' Footsteps began pounding down the hallway not long after.

She had never done this before, not with someone else in tow or in her current state. It was a huge risk to them both—particularly Meng, who was mortal—but now was the moment to throw caution to the wind. They only had one chance to make it out in one piece.

'Hold on tight,' she said.

Then, with all the strength she could muster in her, she gathered her mortal body and took to the air, sweeping Meng off his feet. To any onlooker, it would seem like Meng was floating, flying. But they were clinging on to each other; she could feel the warmth of his hands on her invisible skin, the sturdiness of his back under her invisible hands.

A few feet away, still half-concealed by the dark, was Lazar, ready to aim pure fire at them. Windshadow swerved out of his way and careened down the hallway, past the guards who were too slow to react, much less capture them or notice Meng in the midst of it.

The last thing Windshadow saw before she rounded the corner was Lazar diving back into the dank recesses of the prison.

They had a fair distance to go before freedom was theirs, but as they emerged from the cold, wet dungeon and the first gust of spring night air hit them squarely, Windshadow felt the swell of vindication under her wings and a vindictive pride that germinated well inside her.

She was a storm of spite and fury, and she was on her way to make the men who had humiliated her pay.

The Gold Kingdom

Once making up the north-western part of the Hesui Empire ruled by the Damohai, Lettoria goes by many names. The Gold Kingdom. The Land that Gleams Under the Sun. Country of the Brave and Mighty.

Lettoria is indeed a formidable nation that flourished from international trade, much like Oasis Kingdom. Separated only by the merciless Khuzar Desert, the two kingdoms have gone in opposite directions towards their disparate fates. Unlike its eastern counterpart, Lettoria is an unabashed proponent of magic—almost notoriously so. Where Oasis Kingdom shuns it, Lettoria wields it like a weapon.

Yet, the Gold Kingdom's past is all but glittery. Before Lettoria embarked on its eastward expansion across the Aenic Sea, the north-western land beyond the Khuzar Desert belonged to the Zukans, once famous for their ferocious bronze warriors. But civil strife tore the Zukan kingdom half asunder, making it easy for Lettoria's King Althar I to seize it, murder its rulers and rebels alike, and subjugate its people to Lettorian rule after taking over the land.

In his historic speech given from his castle in Helnia, the capital of the newly conquered metal-rich land, King Althar I voiced his grand aspirations for his expanded kingdom.

'Let this be the land where everything glitters in gold, where birds soar towards the sun rather than hide from it,' he said. 'We shall be our own makers, lords of our own land, industrious and free.'

He kept true to that promise. Within just two decades, Lettoria became one of the superpowers of the west. Its emblem, the golden eagle, became the symbol of freedom, strength, and entrepreneurship. Over time, more Zukans came to embrace the new philosophy and rulers.

But the Althar ambition was boundless, and it passed down from generation to generation, with each successor's greed multiplying by the last.

Then came King Falco, the thirteenth king in the Althar line, who had inherited the family's obsession with gold but not quite its principle of hard work. 'Why spend a decade digging for gold when you can find the being that creates it?' he once asked.

Thus began his search for the Metal Elemental, despite little evidence that the fabled saviours of the Damohai exist, and the quest for these half-immortal beings continues to this day.

Ruined is the world when magic lands in the wrong hands—even more so when it falls into the hands of inept men whose greed is limitless. For now, it is small comfort that their hunt for the descendants of the gods remains futile.

—Excerpt from 'Travels of the Lost Poet', by Zhang He

THIRTEEN

Wei

Grief was not foreign territory. Wei had experienced its depths multiple times. When his mother was imprisoned after being framed for regicide. When his brother Yong was murdered. When his Snow Wolf Sect brothers died helping him barge into the palace last winter. Even when his father died.

Yet, none of it felt this sharp or cut this deep. The fact that he had brought his mother into this. That despite his best efforts, he had failed to save her in the end—or his brother and his friends. It seemed like anyone he came close to was doomed to suffer the same fate.

If grief was a blade, then his was worn thinner with each loss he faced until it was now keen enough to slice through bone. He carried that extra weapon with him now as he rode hard towards Lettoria alongside Desert Rose.

Lettoria.

Wei's knowledge of the Gold Kingdom was mostly limited to what his tutors had taught him growing up, back when he still took their word as the unblemished truth. By the time he was old enough to realize the half-truths and outright lies, he was already making his way towards the Palamir Mountains and cutting off contact with most of the world as he trained with the Snow Wolf Sect.

Even then, it was hard to miss the news about its rapid development in technology and warfare. It was unnatural, the speed at which its military might grew. Oasis Kingdom was far behind it. The day the two kingdoms came head-to-head, there would be no way for Oasis to claim victory unless it embraced the magic it had always despised, the magic that Lettoria was already exploiting.

Good, Wei thought spitefully. After everything he had done, Meng deserved to suffer defeat at Lettoria's hands. Even until now, a part of him wished to believe his half-brother wasn't that cruel; he had always been the opposite of Han. But perhaps Wei had never truly known him, or Meng had grown into someone he barely recognized over the years.

Regardless, Wei would make him pay for everything he had taken from him. He had wanted no part of that power play—for the throne, for territory, for control of the Immortal Spring—but it seemed like Fate always had a way of thrusting him right into it.

His mother knew it too. 'You will not cower under these sands with me when you are meant for bigger things,' she had said on one of those evenings when they had dinner together. 'You belong out there, Wei, and I will not have you here hiding in the dark with me.'

Exacting revenge was probably not what she meant by bigger things, but right now it was the only thing on his mind.

He stashed aside his thoughts and turned to Desert Rose next to him. They hadn't spoken much since they left Ghost City, but she had just lost someone dear to her too, along with her home and half her tribe. He could tell how badly she wanted to stay with her tribespeople and help them relocate to somewhere safe, but couldn't. She too had a destiny to fulfil.

He couldn't stay put either, not when she was about to venture into unknown territory, potentially coming face to face with the very people who had chased her out of her tribe and tried to kill her. Not when there was so much more to do.

So they rode on in silence, bound together by their shared grief and resolve for what they had to do. The sun beat down on them, a companion and a punishment. Around them, the ground rustled like a restless sea, urged by drifting winds. But being out here on the move again was somehow comforting, and Wei was grateful to have Desert Rose by his side.

Days and weeks slipped by, each very much like the last. Wei and Desert Rose fell into their usual rhythm of telling each other the stories they knew, then making up their own, in part to keep their own thoughts at bay but also to escape reality. When night fell, they would set up a makeshift camp or seek temporary refuge in a desert town or roadside inn, one keeping watch as the other slept. Like his, Desert Rose's sleep was never restful.

The closer they reached Lettoria, the more the Lettorians caught wind of their impending arrival. Rumours about the wolf prince of the East and his desert companion drifted for miles before Wei and Desert Rose reached Lettoria.

Before long, the sands dissipated to make way for rockier roads. The desert rolled away in the distance, and the still, dry air grew laden with the smell of old snow on fresh pine leaves. The first sign of vegetation sprouted through the ground, and the roads grew crowded as Wei and Desert Rose arrived at the markets and towns on the periphery of the desert.

They arrived at the golden gates one late afternoon when the sun cast its thick rays across the ground and dragged out their shadows. But in the distance, the light hit differently. Wei had grown up in a palace, so he was used to unnecessary opulence. But even this sight made him pull to a stop.

Gold, pure gold. A shimmering gold wall stretched beyond what the eye could see, almost blinding in the sunlight.

Travellers had spoken of the Gold Kingdom almost as a fabled land, so unreal it seemed, and Wei could now understand why. To be carved of gold and situated right between a desert and the world's harshest mountain range was so inconceivable that it had to be a land blessed by the gods.

Only it wasn't the gods that Lettoria had on its side. It was the magic that it had stolen from the gods.

Unlike Oasis Kingdom, Lettoria was receptive—even welcoming—of visitors. It had no magical barrier or wall to keep out those with magic in their veins.

When Wei charged home last winter following the news of Yong's murder, he'd had to fell a slew of guards and dodge countless arrows and swords. This time, there was no dramatic entrance, no barging through gates or drawing of blades. They simply approached the gates of Lettoria like expected guests.

Of course, he wasn't complaining about the much more peaceful method—only the possibility that they were walking straight into the tiger's den.

They kept their eyes peeled for guards and sentries poised to shoot them. Every inch of him was tense, ready to attack at the first sign of trouble.

But everything was unnervingly … normal.

A gentle wind rippled past, urging them forward. Wei exchanged a look with Desert Rose. She gave him a decisive nod, and they proceeded in tandem.

Up close, the gates were much taller than Oasis Kingdom's, the highest point spiralling towards the azure sky, and the burnished carvings of lions and eagles became more apparent. The stone walls were draped with royal blue and gold banners spaced evenly apart, each bearing the Lettorian insignia of an eagle's head under a pair of swords.

The air rustled in anticipation. Travellers milled around them, chattering in excitement as they joined the queue to enter. There was no separation between visitors and citizens; everyone filed into two rows that moved at equal speed and had their belongings checked and identification recorded before being waved through the gilded gates.

Wei and Desert Rose inched closer to the checkpoint, where they had to surrender their names and purpose, as well as the fake visitor's passes they had acquired under the table at a desert inn. Upon stating his identity, a uniformed guard stepped out from seemingly nowhere and saluted at Wei.

'Prince Zhao Wei of Oasis Kingdom,' the guard greeted.

'Please call me Wei. I have given up my father's name a long time ago,' he managed in stilted Lettorian.

The guard nodded. 'Prince Wei. Those won't be necessary.' He glanced at the fake passes. 'The king has been awaiting your arrival.

Please follow us to your carriage. It will take you and your companion straight to the palace.'

Wei glanced at Desert Rose, who, having understood no part of the exchange, shot him a sceptical look.

'Are we being invited or captured to the palace?' Wei asked.

'Fret not, it is an invitation,' said the guard, leading them to a spacious gilded carriage drawn by a pair of horses. The uniformed horseman tipped his hat at them and waited for them to settle in before taking off.

They wound through picturesque streets lined with vivacious blooms. The capital city of Lettoria was a riot of colours and sounds. Bustling marketplaces, a parade square where children played and housewives convened, lively fountains, and winding cobblestone paths. Townsfolk gathered along the streets, peering curiously at their carriage as they passed. In the distance, blockish buildings belched steam and black smoke against a setting sun, stark against the conviviality of the town square.

There was no trace of the old Zukan kingdom that Lettoria had colonized. After so many centuries of Lettorian rule, Zuka was no more than a thing of the past.

Still, everything here in the capital looked positively idyllic. Where was the strife, the suffering, the resentment brewing in the underbelly of this gleaming kingdom? Was that reserved only for dark, quiet alleys or far-flung areas out of sight from visitors?

Why would a kingdom forged in gold need to go to war with Oasis Kingdom? What more could it need?

As they left the city centre behind, the gleaming spires of the palace came into view. Perched atop a verdant hill bathed in golden sunlight, it watched over the city like a stern but benign parent. Before it was a massive stone arch dressed in royal banners of blue and gold.

They were led past a sprawling, well-manicured lawn and then through massive double doors guarded by a pair of carved gilded eagles after dismounting their rides. Next, it was down a wide and long hallway where the walls and ceilings were covered in elaborate paintings of fair-skinned, flaxen-haired men, women, and babies—much like the

Lettorians—illuminated by warm candlelight. A hush trailed after them until they emerged into a cavernous hall. At the end of it sat King Falco on his gilded throne.

King Falco did not look a day older than forty, if his thick brown locks, ruddy complexion, and sturdy physique were any indication. He appeared far more amiable and relaxed than Wei's father had ever been, all warmth to his father's coldness.

As Wei and Desert Rose made their way down the royal-blue carpet that stretched towards the throne, the king straightened with a satisfied—almost triumphant—smile. 'I have been waiting for the day you step through my doors, Rogue Prince of the East.'

'Is that what they call me here?' As an afterthought he added, 'Your Majesty.'

'You are known by many names here, many of which are favourable,' the king replied.

'My names back home aren't.'

'That's because your people could not appreciate your daring to go against the grain—or your desire to challenge the safety within your walled kingdom and explore the gifts that the world has to offer.'

'By gifts, you mean…'

'Magic, of course. That which the gods left us.' He quirked a brow at him. 'You are unlike your—shall we say—more conservative people. And you deserve more than what your kingdom has given you … and taken from you.'

Wei's surprise rendered him at a loss for words. How did the Lettorian king know so much about him?

'I have been paying attention to you for a while now. I believe we can find common ground in terms of our goals.' He straightened. 'But we are getting ahead of ourselves. Welcome to Lettoria.' He gestured at Desert Rose. 'You and your servant are welcome to—'

'She's not my servant; she's my friend. And I ask that Your Majesty holds her in equal regard.'

'I apologize for my presumptuousness.' He regarded Desert Rose. 'What is your friend's name?'

'Geriel, Your Majesty,' he said, without missing a beat. It was the alias she had instructed him to give the king before they arrived. 'Her name is Geriel.'

King Falco turned pensive, as though he was trying to discern which tribe she belonged to. *Geriel* was a name common enough that revealed nothing about her origins. She could hail from any tribe in Khuzar Desert, or even any of the nations that surrounded the desert.

'Geriel. What is your last name?' King Falco asked her in heavily accented Oasis language.

Desert Rose shook her head. 'I was born an orphan.'

'Surely you must belong somewhere. No tribe?'

Wei turned back to the king. 'Your Majesty, my friend grew up a desert nomad and has no kin to speak of. I am by far the closest friend she has.'

'What, then, is a desert nomad's purpose in the Gold Kingdom?'

'My desert *friend* is here as my companion and confidante,' Wei said. 'You can trust her as much as you trust me.'

King Falco leaned back on his throne with his hands clasped and watched them both with a hint of suspicion. For a moment, Wei thought he might have overestimated the king's generosity towards Oasis Kingdom's rogue son. Perhaps he had less credibility than he thought he did.

But the king let out a laugh at last.

'Very well,' he said. 'I would like to hear your agenda for being here then, Prince Wei. But the day is spent, and you have both travelled far. So get some rest for the evening, and in the morning we can discuss how our alliance might work. If you have no alternative accommodations, you are both welcome to stay in the palace.'

Wei exchanged a look with Desert Rose, who had somehow understood the king's invitation and gave him an almost imperceptible nod.

Not only had he presumed their purpose, but King Falco was also offering them room and board. All for the faith he had in Wei's cause. If only he knew it was vengeance that drove him more than anything else—though perhaps he did not care about Wei's motives, only his goals.

Either way, this was a far warmer welcome than his father would have given him, were he still alive.

Wei turned back to the king. 'Thank you, Your Majesty. We would appreciate that.'

FOURTEEN

Desert Rose

Desert Rose stood before Wei's room, peering down the hallway for the sign of a maid tailing her. They had been taken to their separate guestrooms and had their dinner delivered to them. But unaccustomed yet to her new environs and unsure if her food would be poisoned, she had abandoned her dinner and stolen over to Wei's room.

She was alone, as far as she could tell. The silence was unnerving. Desert Rose couldn't help but imagine a thousand listening ears on the walls around her.

She knocked on the door. 'It's me.'

'Come in,' Wei called from within.

He was nowhere in sight when she entered. The room remained almost pristine, as though he hadn't settled in at all.

'Where are you?' she asked.

His voice came from behind the door next to the dressing table, close enough to make her jump. 'Changing room. What's the matter?'

She perched against the dressing table. 'Doesn't all this unsettle you the slightest?'

The sense of unease had followed her everywhere ever since she stepped foot into Lettoria, and not being able to pinpoint why unseated her further. Here in this foreign land led by a king whose reputation of greed and ambition, whose history of buying over desert tribes, preceded him, every move she made felt like walking further into a trap.

The sooner they found the Metal Elemental, the sooner they could leave.

'Everything here unsettles me,' Wei replied, his voice muffled under his clothing, but it sounded a lot lighter than the feeling in her chest. 'But maybe we're just not used to this place.'

'It's not just the environment. Falco didn't even hear your reason for being in Lettoria before offering us a place to stay and warm food to eat,' she said, eyeing Wei's tray of food also untouched on the ornate marble table.

'My Snow Wolf Sect master used to say the path of least resistance leads towards peril,' Wei said. 'He's just keeping us close so he can observe us.'

'Well, at least we made it to the king's close quarters.'

'If we don't get gutted in our sleep,' he joked, stepping out of the dressing room. He had shed his dark blue travelling robe for a billowy white cotton tunic, well-fitted trousers, and black calf leather boots.

She stared. 'You look … different.'

Unfamiliar was the word she had in mind, but she didn't utter it. It was just garments, after all.

But it wasn't just the clothing. Something had changed in him. She felt that change within herself too, with each loss she suffered. His loss was fresh and raw, and she knew his purpose here in Lettoria wasn't merely to accompany her but to exact revenge on Meng, on his own kingdom.

He flashed her a smile, one that reminded her of last winter when she invited him to journey with her back to her tribe for refuge. The disquiet in her dissipated. He was still Wei. Her Wei.

She froze. Where did that last thought come from?

He glanced down at his outfit, then shrugged. 'It's quite comfortable.' He glanced at her. 'You're not changing?'

'Maybe in a bit.' She rose from the dressing table and stepped out onto the balcony.

They were in the heart of spring now. A balmy wind curled around her, carrying the scent of magnolias. At her feet, the garden downstairs was in full bloom. A carved stone fountain bubbled merrily in the middle. Under different circumstances, she might have felt calmed by the tranquillity here. But she was here for a reason, and every moment she was here put her on edge.

'It's a lot to get used to,' Wei said, coming to her side. 'But while we're here, we need to blend in and gain Falco's trust if we want him to reveal where he keeps the Metal Elemental.'

'And?'

'And what?'

'What else are you here for?'

He did not reply.

'You want to defeat Meng and take over the throne? I thought you're not interested in ruling.'

'I'm not.' He leaned back against the balcony railings on his elbows and cast his face up to the night sky. Overhead, the first sprinkle of stars had appeared across the inky expanse, accompanied by a gleaming sickle moon.

When he spoke again, his voice carried a hint of wistfulness. 'You have your destiny laid out for you. The rest of us have to find or create our purpose. My mother was the only family I had left, and I admit a part of me wanted the throne, if only just to give her a safe home.'

'And now?'

He fell silent again, but his anger rippled almost palpably through him. 'If revenge means dethroning my brother, murderer of my family, then I will do it. And I will abolish all the laws and systems that made victims of us.' A beat passed, where he seemed to return to himself. 'Do you think it's a fool's mission?'

Desert Rose flashed him a wry smile. 'I think a restless soul like you would probably take some getting used to sitting on a cold, hard throne. But if this is what your heart is set on, then I will support you as you have supported me in my own quest.'

He stared at her, an ocean of words in his eyes. But he only said, 'Thank you.'

'Thank you for being here with me.' She reached for his hand and grasped it.

His gaze fell to their clasped hands, and she remembered how grateful he had sounded when she asked him to come home with her after the Spring Ceremony uprising. Wei never revealed it, but she could tell how much he missed his Snow Wolf Sect companions, his brother Yong, and now his mother.

'I know you didn't come all the way here for me,' she said. 'But I'm glad you're here anyway.'

Ever since they left Oasis Kingdom—and perhaps even before that—he had been a companion and confidante, her partner and an equal. He gave her no pretty words or lofty promises, only his solid presence whenever she needed a friend and an ally. He was there to pick her up when the lie about her father's death felled her. He was there to offer the unfurnished truth when Meng fed her lies and she didn't know whom to trust. He was there to reassure her she was human when her unnatural magical abilities made her question who she was.

Only now did she realize how accustomed she had grown to Wei's presence next to her every night after an entire month of travelling together, and how much she appreciated having him by her side in a strange new environment.

'In some measure …' Wei raised his gaze to meet hers. 'I did come for you.'

She blinked, not sure what to make of his confession. They had never uttered things like this to each other, only showing their care through gestures like keeping watch while the other slept, offering a shoulder when the other needed it, and leaving the last scrap of rations for each other. There had been moments where they both read something more in each other's eyes, but neither of them had ever taken a step closer.

And a step was sometimes all it took.

'You…' The word came out like loose sand.

Moonlight fell upon the planes of his face, the face she had grown familiar with over the past few months. She remembered the first time she had stood this close to him, in the quiet alley in the Capital after they ran from Bataar. He had smelled like the desert, like home, and until now she still didn't know if the ache in her chest had been from homesickness or something else.

He leaned closer now. She found herself doing the same, until she caught a clear whiff of that musky scent again. She closed her eyes, imagining being back in camp with her tribe sitting around a bonfire during the White Moon Festival. Next to her, Wei offered her a bowl of spiced mulled wine ….

The next thing she felt was his lips on hers, gentle and tentative. Her breath caught. His hand cupped her face, and her lips parted. They pressed closer, just like they had last winter, drawing warmth from each other. His embrace felt familiar, yet also like unexplored territory. On his lips, she tasted the salt of his grief as they tugged gently on hers.

When they pulled apart, neither of them knew where to look. The air felt warm and thick, as though summer had snuck up on them while they weren't noticing. From the garden below, the scent of magnolias wafted up on a breeze. The sound of their ragged breaths chased away the peaceful silence.

His hand slipped from her face, but neither of them took the first parting step.

'I should … return to my room,' she murmured at last, when it was clear that her racing heart would not settle as long as she was in such proximity to Wei.

He nodded and took a conceding step back.

Heart racing and face on fire, she sped back into her room and shut the door behind her. She leaned against it, drawing in deep breaths. Why was she this rattled? She had always been physically close with the clan boys, wrestling with them and riding behind them on horseback.

But none of that left her feeling as vulnerable and heady as being in the same room as Wei. Had he kissed her out of gratitude, friendship, or something more? And what about her own feelings?

It was a relief to be alone. Her room was spacious and cool, steeped in a musky floral scent threaded with that of fresh sheets, which helped to clear her head. She was about to reach for the candle by the door to light up the rest of her room when she heard the whistle of a blade cutting through the gloom.

She swerved just in time for the weapon to swipe past her ear. In one smooth movement, she grabbed her attacker's arm, wrenched it behind him, and aimed a kick at his back. With him sprawled on the ground, she reached for the candle and held it close to his face as he turned over on his back.

'It's good to see you again, Rose,' Bataar said, panting underneath her.

But she couldn't say the same to him. Her last two encounters with her tribemate—who had turned out to stab her in the back—had transpired in him trying to kill, injure, or capture her. The Bataar lying before her now was far from the childhood friend she had grown up with and trusted.

'What are you doing here, Bataar,' she spat, still not lifting her weight off him.

'Welcoming you to Lettoria.'

'And how did you know I was here.'

'News of the rogue prince and his desert companion reached the palace long before you arrived. Now, will you allow me to speak in less discomfort or shall I do it in this manner?'

After their last encounter, he would know better than to attack her with his usual weapon. Bataar might have taught her how to fight, but she possessed a different sort of weapon now, one that belonged to only her and was far more powerful than any steel blade he carried.

Slowly, she eased off him. He rubbed his chest where she had dug her knee into him and sat opposite her on the dressing table stool.

'Is Blackstone here? And the other clan leaders? Where's the rest of the tribe?' she demanded.

'King Falco has put us up in a guesthouse not too far from the palace.'

'You speak of him like a friend,' she sneered.

'There are no friends in politics, only allies.'

Desert Rose raised a brow.

Bataar snorted. 'You didn't think we would actually align with the Oasis Emperor, did you? That man was a tyrant.'

'So the coup, the alliance with the Oasis Emperor, the revolt at the Spring Ceremony … what were they all for?'

'To weaken Oasis Kingdom, of course,' he said. 'One enemy out of the way means less competition to find the spring.'

Of course it was for the Immortal Spring. They still hadn't given up on their quest to find it.

'How long have you been in Lettoria?' she demanded.

'Just before the Spring Ceremony.'

In other words, before the mayhem they had instigated the shouren to create at the ceremony. The clan leaders had left the beast-people to fend for themselves after sending them to their deaths.

'We never promised them protection,' Bataar said, as though he had heard her thoughts.

'Only your support. And you fled like cowards when they could use your help. What happened to Qiu, her husband Yang, and their impulsive brother ready to throw himself into that suicide mission?'

'Half of them were eager to fight for their cause even before our words could galvanize them.' He shook his head. 'In any case, their fate is no longer our concern.'

'How easily you abandon others these days. Have you also forgotten about the people—*our* people—you left behind?'

'We are not leaving them behind," Bataar said fiercely. 'As incompetent as you may think my father to be, he is not foolish—or callous—enough to lead half the tribe to our death.'

'I do not think your father incompetent, just corrupted by the notion of power.'

'Like you are?' Bataar retorted.

'Stop talking in circles, Bataar,' she snapped. 'Say exactly what you mean.'

'We know what you are, Rose. I told the rest about your little water display in Yeli Forest. And I know why you're here.'

Desert Rose felt the familiar rush of trepidation. Bataar knew, her ex-tribemates knew. They could blow her cover anytime and expose her to King Falco if they chose to.

She beat down her worry and gave him the most nonchalant look she could muster. 'And what do you think is my purpose here?'

'You have a prophecy to fulfil, don't you?'

She made no response, neither confirming nor denying it.

Bataar went on regardless. 'King Falco keeps the Metal Elemental well protected, out of sight from all. It would be near impossible to hunt him down, what more to kill him. But we know where he's kept.'

It was pointless to feign ignorance at this point. Despite herself, she said, 'And where's that?'

'The northernmost tower. The circular one with black stone walls. None of us have managed to get near it because of the high security around the area.'

She folded her arms and looked him in the eye. 'Why do you want to help me?'

'Because, contrary to what you think, we actually do want to help you defeat the other Elementals and find the spring together. Then we can have the power to stop all these warring nations from using us and destroying our home. Aren't you tired of seeing our sacred desert being torn apart by these kingdoms, these emperors who try to buy out tribes to gain more territory?'

She *was* tired. She was tired of seeing her tribe—and many others in the desert—being caught in the crossfire, being persuaded to pick a side, being chased out of their homes after rivers had been poisoned and the land had become too inhospitable to support life.

'The Metal Elemental is Lettoria's biggest secret weapon. Remove him and Lettoria becomes a severely maimed horse.' Bataar rose from the seat and took a step towards her. 'You see, Rose? We're on the same side. Help us, and let us help you. We can put an end to all this war and rebuild our tribe.'

Hearing Bataar mention the tribe made all her rage surge back. Half the tribe was still hiding underground in Ghost City, and her father had to trade his soul for the safety of his people—all because this bunch of traitors decided to overthrow him and take matters into their own hands. If they truly cared for the tribe, they would never have split it apart. After how they had conspired with the late Oasis Emperor, how could she be sure that whatever ruse they were keeping up now was genuinely in the best interest of the tribe? How could she trust that the people who had betrayed her father weren't doing all this for their own benefit?

'We're on the same side?' she echoed. 'Is that why you laid Devil's Fire in my tent?'

'We knew you'd survive that. It was to keep other people out who had no business in your tent.'

'Do you really expect me to believe that, Bataar?'

He only shrugged. 'Believe what you will, Rose.'

'You will not make a fool of me twice, Bataar,' she said. 'I would sooner surrender my soul to the Ghost King than join you bunch of turncoats.'

His jaw tightened. He made no further move towards her. 'Still as stubborn as before. Perhaps King Falco would be interested in hearing your reason for infiltrating his palace then.'

'Don't you dare,' she snapped, lunging towards him.

He was ready for her this time. In one lightning-quick move, he grabbed both her wrists and shoved her against the wall, knocking the air out of her lungs.

'We both have our reasons for being here,' she rasped. 'You stay out of my way, and I'll stay out of yours.'

'It's only a matter of time before the king does a little digging on your background, Rose. And I'll bet he won't take too kindly to you once he learns you're here to murder his precious Elemental.'

'Not if you keep your mouth shut.'

The glint of a blade caught her eye as the tip of a knife rested against Bataar's neck. Desert Rose peered past his shoulder to find Wei with his gaze fixed on her tribemate.

'Step away from her now before my blade goes any deeper.' Wei warned.

Bataar, still at knife-point, sneered without turning around. 'Are you Rose's keeper?'

'It doesn't matter who I am. Right now, you two are causing a commotion and the maids are coming.'

Bataar hesitated for a beat, then eased up on her. Only then did Wei release him. 'Very well.' He stepped away from her. 'Guard your back, Rose, against the true enemy.'

Then, with a parting glare at Wei, he slipped behind the muslin curtains before the balcony and disappeared into the night.

Desert Rose and Wei stood close to each other, watching him leave until there was no trace of Bataar left.

'Delightful as always, your tribemate,' Wei remarked, breaking the silence.

'Thank you for that. We might have come to blows if you hadn't made him stop.' She turned her attention to him, realizing only then that they were standing in the dark. She lit another candle and set the first one down by the dressing table. 'Why did you think to come to my room?'

'I just … wanted to make sure you're settling in fine,' he muttered, uncharacteristically hesitant.

Had what happened earlier changed something irrevocably between them?

'I'll see you in the morning,' he said before she could find a reply, and ducked out through the door. She stood in the middle of the candlelit room, alone with the strange mix of emotions that Wei had left in her.

She spent the better half of the night dreaming about her father roaming in Ghost City for all eternity, waiting futilely for her return, and the remaining hours tossing and turning in bed.

When first light slipped through the windows, she was already awake and dressed, ready to meet the maid who appeared at the door with a tray of foreign breakfast things. Desert Rose stepped aside to let her enter.

The maid left the tray on the study table and folded her hands before her with her head dipped. 'The king has requested that you meet Sergeant Vicardi, the army instructor, after breakfast.'

Desert Rose frowned. 'Why?'

'He understands that you trained at the palace as one of the emperor's guards, and would like to assess your abilities.'

'Why?' she asked again. 'Does he intend to recruit me into his army?'

'I beg your pardon, Miss—I know nothing about the king's plans for you.' The maid dipped her head again. 'I will return when you ring the bell to indicate you have finished your breakfast, and then escort you to the training grounds.' She retreated from the room.

Desert Rose shut the door behind her and eyed the tray of food on the table accompanied by a small golden bell. Such hospitality for people he had met merely hours ago.

Even after breakfast, Bataar's words tailed her to the courtyard, where the maid took her leave after bringing Desert Rose to Sergeant Vicardi.

Like the training grounds at the House of Night, the courtyard here was a clean, functional square with ample space for training and sparring. A gilded statue of an eagle stood guard at each of its four corners.

The sergeant, a strapping, fair-haired man with piercing blue eyes, stood in the middle of the square, where several groups of two to three male and female soldiers were sparring with one another, not unlike the way Shimu made them train in the House of Night. Except unlike the assassins-in-training at the palace, the students here were decked from head to toe in gold-plated armour. Yet, they moved nimbly, lunging at each other with ease as they brandished their gold-hilted swords.

'It looks heavy, but Lettorian gold is lightweight and still stronger than any metal nature has ever forged,' Sergeant Vicardi remarked next to her, making her jump. He paid no mind to her reaction, keeping his eyes trained on his students.

Desert Rose observed him out of her periphery. He seemed completely unsurprised by the presence of a desert girl, so completely out of place in this grand compound. In fact, he spoke fluent Dugurian, albeit with a crisp, foreign accent that suggested he had been stationed at the borderlands before.

Finally, he turned to her. 'I understand you were an assassin-in-training at the Oasis Palace.' He cocked his head. 'What reason does a desert girl have for pledging allegiance to the Oasis Emperor?'

What sort of intelligence did Lettoria possess to have learnt that about an unknown desert girl just a day after she arrived? Had they been tracking Wei and her way before they entered the kingdom?

Desert Rose picked her words with care. 'I consider my time at the Oasis Palace a means to an end. I only attempted to get closer to the emperor to negotiate for my tribe's safety and freedom.'

He continued to appraise her. 'Might your purpose for being in Lettoria stem from the same reason then? How can we be certain you won't betray us the way you turned your back on Oasis Kingdom?'

She forced herself to look him in the eye. 'The last Oasis Emperor is partly responsible for the current state of my tribe. There is no allegiance lost there. Now I vow only to free my tribe from the wars between kingdoms, and if that means I have to choose a side, then I will pick the one I have less enmity with.'

The sergeant narrowed his gaze at her. Around them, the familiar clang of swords took her back to her days training with the other girls at the House of Night. Back then, Shimu had been just as distrustful of her, a desert girl who had no business at the palace.

'Very well,' Sergeant Vicardi said at last, gesturing at the armoury on their left. 'Then pick your weapon.' He paused, his brows sliding up. 'Or, do you already have your own?'

FIFTEEN

Meng

Meng took one hand off the reins and rubbed the sleep from his eyes. It had been almost three straight days of travelling, and every inch of his body was protesting vehemently.

Windshadow had barely managed to get them out of the Capital before morphing back into her human form. She had taken them to the edge of a quiet town and promptly turned back into a girl, sprawled on the ground as though the wind had spat her out. After an hour of rest, she was back in form and prepared to steal food and supplies from the locals, an act Meng protested against soundly. She, of course, had ignored him and stolen enough rations—clothes, food, daily essentials, and even a desert horse—that would last them two weeks, by which time they would be halfway to Lettoria.

The further they rode into the desert, the more everything from the past three days caught up with him, along with a sense of mounting dread. *What have I done?* He was starting to realize that his act of breaking Windshadow out of prison and leaving the kingdom—for enemy territory, no less—had been partially driven by resentment for the way he had been treated by the imperial court.

He had never been one to act out of spite. He was not like Windshadow or even Desert Rose. But maybe they weren't quite so different after all when pushed to desperation.

Oasis Capital had long receded into the distance behind them, and Meng was sure his brother had put out a warrant for his arrest by now.

Can he do that, if I haven't officially handed over the title to him? Can he arrest the emperor?

But a part of him already knew his brother could. Not only was Han backed by the majority of the Council, the Empress Dowager, and High Advisor, but he was also the most persistent person Meng knew when it came to eliminating his enemies. He had attempted to single-handedly overthrow even their father, the legitimate Fifteenth Oasis Emperor. What qualms would he have about an interim emperor like Meng? Blood meant nothing to him.

The day was golden and blistering now, and as far as he could tell, he and Windshadow were but two specks of sand in Khuzar Desert. The vastness threatened to overwhelm him, but Windshadow relished in it. Her spirits—and energy—had improved now that they were back in her natural habitat, and Meng had the sense that she would have remained in her element form and torn across the desert straight for Lettoria had she not been saddled with a mortal like him.

But, as it were, they needed each other. As a desert girl, she had no justifiable reason for entering Lettoria on her own—much less get close to the king and the Metal Elemental—and he had no bargaining power without Windshadow.

Behind him on their mount, Windshadow spoke for the first time since they set off that morning.

'Question: how confident are you of winning over the Lettorian king?'

'King Falco is shrewd, no doubt,' he replied. 'But we have forged ties even before I took the throne.'

'And you think he'll trust you enough to reveal his secret weapon to you and help you overthrow Han, when there's nothing in it for him?'

There was talk of steel armies in the west, where Lettorian troops seemed to have steel in their bones on top of indestructible weapons and armour. Meng didn't know how true the stories were, but his past visits as a foreign ambassador in Lettoria had shown him things he never thought possible—beastly metal engines and other ingenious contraptions that fed on steam and coal. He would be a fool to underestimate the secret might of the Lettorians. It was true that the Lettorians had more of an advantage, but that didn't mean Meng, now an independent agent, had nothing to offer.

'There is plenty in it for him, if he's inclined to believe,' Meng replied. 'One murdered emperor, succeeded by two princes vying for the throne. That's enough to weaken a kingdom and leave it vulnerable to its enemies. We're providing Lettoria with enough inside information for them to launch an efficient attack and undermine Han's rule, but not enough to hurt Oasis Kingdom where it hurts. And that's where you'll come in. Find their secret weapon—eliminate the other Elemental—and cripple Lettoria from within so that we're on equal footing.'

'So you're using my agenda to fulfil yours.' She sounded more impressed than annoyed.

He shot her a wry glance over his shoulder. 'Hasn't our relationship always been mutually beneficial?'

They travelled largely in silence after that. Meng would observe the desert girl when she wasn't noticing and try to find a soul beneath that apathetic exterior. If she felt any guilt whatsoever for everything she had done so far, she displayed none of it. Once she no longer had use for him, she would most likely not hesitate to kill him if she had to.

But for now, at least, he was safe.

* * *

King Falco was already in the Grand Hall to receive them when they arrived, thanks to the private messenger Meng had sent to notify him of their arrival. It was a gamble to let even one person know about their presence in Lettoria. After all, if word got out too soon, Han would undoubtedly thwart his plans sooner than he could speak with the Lettorian king.

There was also the question of whether the king would deign to see them, now that Meng was no longer the emperor, not even an esteemed prince, only a fallen one who had abetted a prisoner's escape. Back home, he was a wanted man now.

'Well, well. Look who the wind blew in,' King Falco said as Meng and Windshadow strode down the hall. Sunlight spilled through the tall glass windows, throwing them into stark relief.

Meng came to a stop and bowed. 'Greetings, Your Majesty.' Next to him, Windshadow gave a reluctant bow.

King Falco chortled. 'Am I to receive every son of Oasis Kingdom? The rogue prince and his desert companion two days ago, now you and your desert companion.'

The rogue prince. Wei was here, with Desert Rose? Meng felt something inside him unclench—she was safe—but that was almost immediately followed by a pang of jealousy.

'Word of your eldest brother's … manoeuvrings has reached us,' the king said, as though he had heard his thoughts. 'Unfortunate business, being overthrown by your brother.'

'My brother claimed legitimacy using underhanded means …' Yet, hadn't he done the same, but in a different way? *You're a hypocrite, Meng,* he chided himself mentally.

'Whatever the case, the power of a king is determined by his ability to keep order, and you have completely lost your power.'

Meng flinched under the sting of his words. If the Lettorian king viewed his inglorious defeat this way, what then did his mother think of it?

His mother who had used him, Meng reminded himself. He no longer owed her his allegiance when she had only regarded him as a seat-warmer for her other son all along.

'I have no interest or stake in your domestic power struggle,' King Falco said. 'My sole concern is what you can offer me, and how we can forge an alliance that benefits us. I suppose you're here to propose one so that you might reclaim your seat?'

King Falco might seem like a friendly woodsmith, but he was anything but simple. Meng reminded himself that this was the man who had not only colonized the north-western territory with quick, devastating battles, but also won over the most powerful tribes in Khuzar Desert and managed to make an Elemental serve him.

'My purpose is indeed to forge a stronger alliance with Lettoria so that we can take down the usurper while avoiding a war,' Meng said.

The king chortled. 'I appreciate your intent to avoid war, but there is no hope of that happening with your brother on the throne. He is readying his troops as we speak and has already killed a team of my spies. He wants war, and I will not be a sitting duck. I will only have by my side those who are ready to fight. And seeing as you are no longer in any position to bargain, I assume you are here to offer your services.'

'As I recall from our last conversation many months ago, Your Majesty has been seeking the Immortal Spring.' He drew out a pouch from his waist belt and gave it a little shake. Inside, the pebbles clacked against one another. 'This is an heirloom passed down through the Dugur tribe. Its last recipient was the tribe leader, Scarbrow.'

The king leaned forward, his interest now piqued.

Meng poured out the contents of the pouch onto his palm. 'I'm told these are the stones from the Immortal Spring, passed down from the Damohai themselves.'

Everyone who knew about the spring would also know the story of the Damohai, the direct descendants of the Sky Princess and Earth Prince. Though now a scattered people without the prophezied Elementals to lead them, they were the rightful guardians of the Immortal Spring. But that didn't stop power-hungry kings like Falco and Meng's father from attempting to seize control of it.

'Where did you get this?' King Falco's gaze was transfixed on the stones.

'From a clansman by the name of Golsha, who was unfortunately killed not long after he acquired this for me. It is unclear whether Scarbrow knows the location of the spring, but this is a major lead that can take us closer to the spring.' He deposited the pebbles back into the pouch and tucked it back securely in his belt.

'We have a deal then,' King Falco said without missing a beat. He glanced at Windshadow. 'As for your companion… She hails from the desert too?'

'She is a highly trained imperial assassin and can be of use in your personal guard.'

The king raised his brows. 'Or a weapon to be held against my throat when the moment is ripe.'

'You have my word that will not happen.' He sent Windshadow a look, which she countered with the ghost of a smirk, almost as if she understood what they were saying. He turned back to face the king. 'I promise to hold up my end of this alliance.'

A slow smile spread across King Falco's face. 'Then I look forward to a fruitful partnership with you, Prince Meng.'

SIXTEEN

Windshadow

Curse this godsforsaken thing, Windshadow thought as she squirmed in her new uniform. She stood alone in the dressing room next to the armoury at sunrise, wondering how all this was going to take her closer to the Metal Elemental.

She wasn't here as a guest; she knew that very well. She was here only as long as she and Meng proved themselves useful. And the only use Falco had for her, after witnessing her with a sword, was in the military. If he knew what other abilities she had, would he make her serve him too?

She adjusted her breastplate, resenting the way it prevented her from shifting into her element. Every piece of her new training armour was plated in gold and sat snugly against her body. It was impressive, sure—lightweight and flexible, yet tough as a dragon's hide—but donning another set of uniform and once again training with the enemy's troops felt like taking two steps back.

The gold was no ordinary metal; it could only be forged by one person. The sooner she found and killed the Metal Elemental, the sooner she could get out of here and be on her way to find the others.

Outside, the day was already beginning with the clang of swords and brisk scuffing of feet around the courtyard. But she wasn't meant to join the other soldiers yet. Instead, she stepped out into the armoury, surveying the gleaming weapons hung on the walls and racks. In the middle of the room was a table covered in scrolls and a lone cup filled with what appeared to be tea. Clear and pale orange, seemingly innocuous. She gave it a sniff. The tea contained only a faint whiff of ticha—almost unnoticeable—but it was enough to recall the anguish it had brought upon her before.

'Don't drink it,' a voice—all too familiar—said from behind her. Windshadow turned, already knowing whom to expect.

And there she stood. Her desert azzi and old ally from the House of Night, dressed in a uniform not unlike hers, only without the metal armour.

'I've had enough experience with ticha to recognize it,' Windshadow replied.

Even here in Lettoria, the herb was used to filter out magical folk. They might be out of Oasis Kingdom now, but they were still regarded with caution here. Lettoria appeared to embrace magical beings, but it clearly had defences against them too. It might not outright employ raw ticha as a weapon or torture instrument, but brewing it in tea meant the Lettorians knew how to incapacitate their magical abilities.

Windshadow smirked at Desert Rose. 'Glad you're alive, azzi.'

But Desert Rose clearly didn't share the same sentiment. Despite her well-intentioned warning, she hadn't forgotten how Windshadow had betrayed her, pushing her to deliver the fatal attack on the emperor just as Meng arrived at the scene with his mother and palace guards. Windshadow could have told her it was a mere coincidence that everything had happened all at once, but Desert Rose wasn't the sort to believe in coincidences.

She glowered at Windshadow, but she clearly didn't hate her enough to see her suffer the effects of ticha. *Once a bleeding heart, always a bleeding heart,* Windshadow thought.

'I suppose you drank yours,' she said, flinging the contents of her cup out of the window and setting the cup back on the table. Desert Rose didn't reply. 'That's your problem, azzi. You're too trusting.'

'Blame the ones who deceive, not those who trust.'

'If you're waiting for an apology, I'm going to have to disappoint you,' Windshadow said. 'I'm not sorry for what I did. I did what I had to in order to survive. You would do the same too, if you were in my shoes.'

'You said you wanted peace for our tribes, peace in the desert,' said Desert Rose. 'How is any of this helping your tribe at all?'

Windshadow snorted. 'I'm not naïve enough to believe that would be possible with wars led by greedy men. The only way to bring peace to the desert is to become the last Elemental standing and unlock that cursed spring—'

Desert Rose shushed her, but she was done caring what the gods thought. If they could allow the desert to fall into its current state, then they had no right to fault her for a little blasphemous remark.

Sergeant Vicardi entered the room. If he had overheard them, he showed no sign of it. He only surveyed Windshadow's cup, then peered at her face.

Windshadow raised a brow. 'Thank you for the tea, Sergeant. It was delicious.'

The sergeant frowned, clearly expecting a different response. 'Pick your weapon and go out to the courtyard. You two will be sparring partners.' In his Lettorian accent, the Dugurian word for sparring sounded almost like *dancing*.

A smile slid up Windshadow's face. *Just like old times.* She was certain she could defeat Desert Rose without a weapon—after all, she had done so before—but she grabbed a sword hanging on the wall anyway and gestured for Desert Rose to lead the way.

Out in the courtyard, there were at least five pairs of soldiers duelling with each other. Windshadow could tell that these were no ordinary guards. Their method of combat was less regulated, more spontaneous, swift, and unexpected, which meant they were trained against more sophisticated assailants.

'So you're doing all this—helping Meng become emperor, training at the House of Night, coming to Lettoria—to become the last Elemental?' Desert Rose asked once they were out of Sergeant Vicardi's earshot. 'You knew all along that you're one of the five?'

'Do you remember that time you asked me about the first time I discovered my powers?'

Desert Rose nodded.

'That skin-hawk attack changed my life and my position within my tribe,' she said. It had been a long while since she thought about her tribe. Her time with the Lijsal people was not one that she revisited out of nostalgia.

Desert Rose's brows pulled together in confusion. 'You said the other children stopped picking on you after they saw what you could do—'

'Get into position!' Sergeant Vicardi barked from the edge of the courtyard.

Desert Rose shifted into a combat stance, her hands weapon-free. Windshadow was tempted to forego her weapon too, but revealing her powers in a place like Lettoria—where an Elemental was made to serve a mortal king—could only mean enslavement for her. She raised her sword, locking eyes with Desert Rose, then lunged without warning.

'Before my tribe knew about my powers—before they placed its future in my hands—they only saw me as the strange, quiet girl who didn't quite belong anywhere in the tribe,' she said as Desert Rose dodged her blade. 'After the attack, where they saw me rip that skin-hawk apart, they realized what I was and what I could do for the tribe.' She thrust her sword at Desert Rose again, aiming for her chest. 'You're no stranger to territory wars between the tribes, I'm sure.'

Desert Rose danced around her sword again. She could attack at any moment with her powers. But of course, she didn't. She wasn't the sort to attack first unless she had no other choice. That was her second biggest flaw, in addition to being too trusting.

'My tribe was another one that wanted to rule the desert,' Windshadow went on, relentless in her attack on Desert Rose, who remained on the defensive. 'And when they knew they had an Elemental among them, they placed all their hopes in me. Suddenly, I had value; I was an asset to the tribe—the biggest asset. I was the one who would find the spring and bring glory and power to the tribe.' She whirled around and nearly caught Desert Rose in the chest. 'No one ever asked me what I wanted. They just thrust that role upon me and expected me to serve the tribe without question. Do you know what it's like to live under the weight of your entire tribe's expectations?'

Hatred was simple, direct. It was something you could hold on to, something that could sustain you. It didn't make for much of a life, but at least it kept her alive. She felt it course through her all over again, rustle and snap inside her like a creature made of the strongest gale. She yearned to rip off her metal armour and shift into her element. She was the wind. She could kill someone with a gale. Together, she and Desert Rose could raise a storm that would take down this palace. And she alone could take down Desert Rose and be rid of one Elemental. All she had to do was take off her armour and shift into her truest form.

The other soldiers had stopped duelling to watch them. Sergeant Vicardi observed them by the sidelines.

She had a choice: kill Desert Rose on the spot, or wait until she found and killed the Metal Elemental before moving on to Desert Rose. It was rarely a good idea to reveal herself too soon, but what if things were different here in Lettoria? What if revealing her abilities would give her special privileges that could speed up her mission here?

Desert Rose was beginning to pant from the effort of dodging Windshadow's blows, but still she refused to use her powers in a courtyard full of strangers.

That was her third failing. She didn't see her powers as a gift or a weapon, but a curse she had to live with.

Windshadow retreated to a safe distance and broke free of her armour, casting it aside along with her sword. Stripped of that cumbersome metal, she was free to slip into the air, become one with it, wield it like a keener blade.

There was a collective gasp as everyone witnessed her dissolve into the air. Good. Even in a kingdom that exploited magic, there was still some reverence for it.

From her higher vantage point, she watched Desert Rose drop her stance and straighten, glancing wildly around her.

Windshadow careened towards her, shifting back into human form just before she crashed into her opponent. They tumbled to the ground and rolled for a few paces before she sprung back on her feet.

Desert Rose righted herself and hissed, 'Enough. Are you trying to get us both killed?'

She smirked. 'In case you haven't noticed, this is not Oasis Kingdom. Displaying your natural abilities won't get you stoned to death.' She raised a palm, gathering the air into a flurry around her. 'Come on, azzi. Let's give these mortals a good show.' She flung out her hands, letting loose a gust of wind that ripped through the courtyard and knocked the soldiers and Sergeant Vicardi off their feet.

Desert Rose threw up her hands at last, emitting a jet of water at Windshadow. But it was a half-hearted attempt to fend her off. Windshadow had seen what she could do. Together, they had once destroyed a dragon made of storm and fury in the White Crypt. Together, they could kill the Metal Elemental and make King Falco quail at their feet. They didn't have to play nice with these mortal rulers when they were the ones who could make the rules.

'Enough,' Sergeant Vicardi bellowed, stalking over to them after gathering the shards of his dignity. He narrowed his eyes at Windshadow and Desert Rose, but his fear hovered almost palpably in the air. 'You two, follow me.' He turned to the other soldiers and snapped, 'The rest of you, get back to training!'

Everyone leapt back into action, but their gazes trailed after Windshadow and Desert Rose as they followed the sergeant out of the training grounds towards the main hall, a turreted stone building surrounded by a sprawling garden.

'Windshadow,' Desert Rose murmured all of a sudden as they cut through the palace grounds, keeping a few paces behind the sergeant. 'What is it that you truly want?'

No one had ever asked her that. For as long as she could remember, vengeance was all she knew, and survival was what she was good at.

She shrugged. 'I want to find the spring and be the last Elemental standing, but not for the sake of my tribe. Not for anyone else but myself. After that, who knows?'

'You're willing to destroy yourself just to be the surviving Elemental?'

A mirthless laugh escaped her. 'If I'm destined to burn out like a fierce flame, then I would like to make the most of my time here. What's the use of being half-immortal if I can't enjoy my magical abilities?'

Windshadow could tell there was more Desert Rose wanted to say but was too distracted by where they were going to pursue this conversation. She in turn offered nothing more.

They found the king in the middle of the herb garden, inspecting the rosemary shrubs.

'Your Majesty,' Sergeant Vicardi greeted. 'We've discovered two more.' He gestured at Windshadow and Desert Rose.

King Falco lost interest in the rosemary at once. He threw his head back with a laugh. 'The Oasis sons certainly know how to pick their assistants.' He peered at both of them with a hungry glint in his eyes. Windshadow fought the urge to spit in his face.

'Well,' he said, once he had gathered himself again. 'Let's put you two to good use then.'

SEVENTEEN

Desert Rose

This could be a trap, Desert Rose thought as she stole across the rock garden outside the southwest tower that evening. She pressed close to the shadows, wincing when the crunch of gravel under her feet grated against the silence of the night.

She had trusted Bataar before and he had trampled on that trust, helping his father and the other clan leaders overthrow her father. He was the reason her father's soul was now trapped in the Ghost City. She would be a fool to trust Bataar again, especially when this could very well be his ploy to have her captured for breaking into a high-security area where the Metal Elemental might or might not be residing.

But she had to know. This was her only lead, even if it did come from Bataar. It beat sitting around waiting for King Falco to use her to fight his war. The sooner she could kill the Metal Elemental, the sooner she could leave Lettoria.

Home. It felt like a world away now, in this stone fortress with its blind corners and dark hallways concealed underneath that gleaming facade.

She skirted past the bailey and over a moonlit pond. Obscured by the misshapen shadows of poplar trees, she saw the circular stone building with blackened walls that Bataar had mentioned. Before the looming wrought-iron fence stood two pairs of guards. In the darkness, possibly more.

This remote corner of the palace felt like a world removed from the opulence out front. No one would guess that a supernatural being who could spin gold lived within these grimy walls. Desert Rose eyed the lone raven perched on a tree branch above her, willing it not to give her away as she scoured the gloom for a way inside.

A cold, slender hand wrapped around her mouth from behind, and she was pinned against a tree before she could react. She reached for her dagger tucked in her waist belt as she struggled to break free. Then her attacker came into view.

'Hello, azzi,' Windshadow smirked, taking her time to ease off her. 'Night-time stroll?'

Desert Rose straightened and stepped away from her. 'You followed me?'

'Let's just say I'm here to give you a hand in whatever you're planning to do.' She nodded at the guards. 'You know things will be easier with my help.'

After this morning's altercation and Windshadow's confession, she couldn't tell if the other desert girl was a friend or foe. On the one hand, she empathized with Windshadow's reason for all the things she had done. But that didn't mean she should accept her help.

'I did what I had to in order to survive,' Windshadow had said this morning. 'You would do the same too, if you were in my shoes.'

Would I? Desert Rose wondered. A part of her was certain she wouldn't go to the extent Windshadow had—allying with a foreign prince to overthrow an emperor, then framing someone else for the murder—but another part of her wasn't sure if her conscience would overpower her desire to save her tribe.

'I'll distract them,' Windshadow said now. 'You sneak in through the back.'

She didn't give Desert Rose a chance to protest, dissolving into a cool breeze that swirled into a mighty gust around the guards. The poplar leaves danced in fury on the ground; more fell from the trees.

The guards gave a shout and tailed Windshadow as she flickered into her human form, leading them away into the eastern corner.

Desert Rose scurried around to the back, where she found the window with bars wide enough for her to wriggle through. Her feet hit the damp ground with a tiny splash. Windshadow joined her just after her eyes adjusted to the darkness.

'Dramatic decoy,' Desert Rose muttered. 'What did you do to them?'

Windshadow shrugged. 'Two of them are scouring the vicinity; the other two are standing guard in case the "evil wind" returns. That should keep them busy for a while.' She nudged her arm. 'Let's move.'

They crept along the dank, narrow passageway in a single file, Desert Rose in the lead. She didn't like the thought of Windshadow tailing her, of having her back exposed to a blade she could easily pull out and ram into her spine. But Windshadow had had many chances to kill her if she had known a long time ago that they were both Elementals, and yet she hadn't done so.

Desert Rose glanced behind her. Windshadow was watching her like she could hear all her thoughts.

'I know all about being your tribe's last hope, by the way,' she said in response to Windshadow's question that morning. 'I know about holding their fate in your hands and the fear of letting everyone down. Why do you think I'm here?'

Windshadow snorted, nudging her along again. 'Well, that's very noble of you. How lucky of your tribe to have you.'

'Is there nothing and no one that you live for?'

'Sure. Myself.' Desert Rose glanced back at her once more, but Windshadow was unapologetic. They descended a flight of stairs dimly lit by a lone torch in its bracket. 'I'm not like you, azzi. I didn't have a tribe that adored me, or a father who loved and protected me from any harm. I had to survive on my own, and I'm terrific at it.'

Desert Rose felt a pang in her heart. Underneath that thorny exterior, Windshadow had nothing in the world but a steel heart that she was eager to protect.

'Yet, you still care about your tribe. There are still people there that you love and miss,' she said. 'Otherwise, you wouldn't have gone all the way to Oasis Capital to join a rebel faction to assassinate Emperor Zhaode, or gone to every length to help Prince Meng get on the throne. Deep down, you want to protect your tribe. You just love it more than it seems to love you—'

'Enough,' Windshadow snapped, coming to a halt. 'Stop acting like you know me inside out. You know nothing about me.'

Desert Rose only looked at her sadly. 'Why is it so hard for you to admit that you have a heart, Windshadow?'

'Quit looking at me like that,' was her only response.

Desert Rose let a pause lapse between them. 'If it came down to you and me in the end … would you do it?'

Windshadow remained silent until Desert Rose gave up waiting for her response and pressed on through the gloom.

'Yes,' the other girl said at last. 'I would.'

Desert Rose smirked. 'Liar. If you wanted to, you would have by now.'

Windshadow lifted a brow. 'Don't be so sure. I could just be biding my time. Remember: the moment you let your guard down around an Elemental, you're as good as dead.'

They fell silent after that. Darkness closed in on them the deeper down they went. Desert Rose was about to suggest turning back until she spotted an opening up ahead illuminated by a warm golden glow. It was hard to tell which part of the tower they were at now, after all the winding passageways and neverending stairs. But the opening led to a cavernous space filled with more kinds of weaponry and armour Desert Rose had ever seen in her life. Displayed on the towering circular walls were ornately carved shields, swords, machetes, blades, knives, daggers, axes, bayonets, halberds, sabres, and spears in various fashion, along with many others she did not know the names of.

In the middle of the space was a gleaming cannon, its burnished body aglow with lamplight. Next to it, on a wooden bench before a long work table, a wiry-looking young man in a chainmail tunic sat with his back facing them, hunched over the sword he was forging.

Desert Rose edged closer, careful to stay beyond the reach of lamplight. She watched him trace his fingers down the blade with utmost dedication and care, almost transfixed. The blade gleamed brighter and became keener under his touch.

He didn't need crude tools or fire; his magic flowed from him and became infused with everything he touched. He had made all this. Every blade and spear and spike. He was a one-man weapon workshop, and he served the king of Lettoria. He was Lettoria's secret weapon.

Desert Rose shared a look with Windshadow. It was now or never. It would be quick. She wouldn't even have to think twice; she couldn't afford to. Her father and tribe were waiting for her in Ghost City.

She inched forward, heart drumming in her chest. Her hands shook as she raised her dagger. She tightened her grip on the hilt, drawing courage from its weight, and the way it dug into her palm. Behind her, Windshadow watched, ready to leap to her aid— she hoped.

She could do this.

Her eyes squeezed shut as she brought down the blade, waiting for the impact of it piercing into his neck. It connected—but not with flesh. A clang reverberated in the chamber.

Her eyelids flew open, just in time to see the boy whirl around with the newly forged sword in his hand. With a practised move, he knocked her weapon out of her hand and now her knife lay useless a few feet away.

Windshadow stirred up a gale between her palms and flung it at him. The contained orb hit him squarely in the chest. He stumbled backward but recovered soon enough. Up close, he appeared even younger, perhaps of Qara's age. Yet, there was a keenness in his demeanour that chased away the innocence in him.

He chuckled. 'Are you two planning to defeat me with a knife and a little breeze?' His accent suggested he was from one of the northern tribes that lived below the Palamir Mountains, perhaps the Hu'an.

With a casual sweep of his arm, he sent his sword hurtling straight at Windshadow's chest. Desert Rose aimed a jet of water at the weapon before it could reach her, but Windshadow knocked it aside before the water struck the metal.

'Very good,' he remarked. 'The king figured it was a matter of time before one of you came looking for me, but what an honour to have two Elementals here tonight. I do love a fair fight; it's no fun duelling with mortals and their paltry weapons.'

'The weapons you forged,' Windshadow sneered. 'How's it like being King Falco's lackey?'

She was stalling for time for Desert Rose to make her move.

Behind the Metal Elemental, Desert Rose reached for her knife again. He spun around just as she raised her blade, and with a flick of his wrist, something whizzed through the air and struck her dead centre in the chest. She let out a strangled gasp and glanced down.

A tiny dart, not unlike the one Bataar used on her last winter, was wedged in, just deep enough to penetrate her skin.

'You're no stranger to bloodweed, I suppose?' said the Metal Elemental. 'It grows particularly well near oasis towns. But, more remarkably, it becomes twice as lethal when combined with my metal.'

A burning sensation began to spread across her body. She tried to reach for the dart and yank it out, but her hands had gone numb. She was on the ground before she knew it, her legs having given way. The air closed in on her as tremors juddered through her.

Windshadow knelt next to her. She plucked out the dart, pressed down on the wound, and grasped her hand. 'Stay with me, azzi.' She turned and shot the Metal Elemental a glare. 'Help her, you godsforsaken bastard.'

'She just tried to kill me,' he snapped. 'Besides, you didn't ask very nicely.'

Whatever else Windshadow said was lost in the fog of pain that descended on her. Desert Rose could feel herself writhing on the ground, her body turning inside out to battle the venom. How long more did she have to live? Was this how her story would end? What would happen to her father, her tribe, Wei?

The pain seeped into her bones and ripped through her body, vicious as a sand hound's bite and twice as relentless.

A scream tore out of her.

EIGHTEEN

Wei

King Falco reminded Wei of a skin hawk. Hungry, unpredictable, and biding its time.

Wei sat across from him in the dining hall, where a luxurious dinner spread was laid out between them on the long table. The guards who had stood by the doors had already been ordered to leave, so he and King Falco sat alone in the high-ceilinged hall large enough for Wei's unease to join them at the table as an unwanted guest.

'And how has the palace been treating you?' the king asked as he took a sip of wine from his goblet.

'My companion and I are well taken care of, Your Majesty,' Wei replied, measuring his tone. 'Thank you for your hospitality.'

King Falco watched him over the rim of his wine goblet. 'I have heard about your ... personal tensions with your home kingdom, how you left for the mountains when you were sixteen. So why should its fate concern you now?'

He shouldn't be surprised that King Falco had looked into his background, of course. No sensible ruler would allow the son of his enemy to enter his kingdom without first learning of his intent. But just how much did he know?

'Circumstances have changed, and so has my position. After my father's corrupt rule, I'm afraid my brother is following in his footsteps. My mother has recently been killed in an attack launched by the imperial scouts.'

'And you believe your brother is going after all potential rebels, you being one of them?'

Wei nodded. 'As much as I have denounced the kingdom as my home, I cannot let it fall under the wrong hands, particularly in those of my mother's murderer.'

King Falco set down his goblet and raised a lofty brow. 'You want to become emperor then?'

Ever since he could remember, Wei had been lured by life beyond the palace, beyond the magic-resistant wall of Oasis Kingdom. He had always envisioned himself being free of the shackles of the imperial court, of his wretched title, and even more wretched birth star prophecy that made him hated by his father and, by proxy, the entire court. When he turned sixteen, he couldn't wait to escape, even if it meant leaving Yong and his mother behind.

But he had also seen Desert Rose and Qara being welcomed home with the amount of jubilation he had never personally experienced. That was where Desert Rose belonged. That was why she had constantly yearned for her home when she was in the Capital. She was surrounded by love and acceptance in her tribe.

Where did *he* belong? Where else could he touch ground now that his family was gone and he had left the Snow Wolf Sect?

'I'm not interested in ruling the world,' he answered at last. 'But I see no other way apart from getting on the throne myself.'

'But has Oasis Kingdom ever been your home?'

Oasis Kingdom had once been a home, but that was a long, long time ago. Back when he and Yong were small enough to fit into their mother's lap, back when they could wheedle her for stories about the great unknown, back when he didn't understand how cruel a father could be, how a brother could hate him enough to threaten his life.

But the one thing he had learnt from Desert Rose was that everyone could be the maker of their own destiny. And—even though he hated to admit it—one thing he had learnt from Meng was that the way to win was not to resist, but to rebuild.

'It might not have been, but it can become one,' he said.

The king mulled over his answer. 'How confident are you in defeating your brother?'

It was near impossible. Not only did Meng now have the backing of the imperial court, the military, and his mother, Wei was also disadvantaged by his ill-fated prophecy spun by the High Advisor Mian, who had sowed seeds of resentment—and even hatred—in Wei's father towards his own flesh and blood from the moment Wei was born. How would the imperial court—and the people of Oasis Kingdom—ever accept a rogue son, a wanted rebel, as emperor?

'Confidence comes from knowing the enemy, and I like to believe I know him well, having grown up with him,' Wei said.

King Falco nodded in agreement. 'You would know your brother's nature best, but you can't protect everyone on your own. Together, though, we can defeat Oasis Kingdom. You are skilled in martial arts and well versed in battle. And with your inside information, we might even claim victory before anyone draws a sword.' He leaned forward, his gaze pinned on Wei. 'So join me. We overthrow your brother, make you Oasis Emperor, and our two kingdoms live in peace from thereon.'

It sounded like a reasonable proposition. After all, hadn't he come all this way also to seek an alliance with King Falco? But something in him held him back, and he knew better than to ignore his gut instinct.

The king was watching him, his stare as hungry as a wolf in winter. An urgent knock came at the side door in the corner of the hall, sparing Wei from having to answer.

'Enter,' King Falco commanded.

A page scurried through the door, panting as he knelt before the king. 'I beg your pardon, Your Majesty. There's been a disturbance in the northwest tower.'

'Explain.' Any trace of geniality was gone from the king's demeanour.

'They found the two desert girls in the northwest tower ...'

King Falco rose from his seat at once. Every muscle in Wei tensed. What was in the northwest tower? What was Desert Rose doing there?

The king glanced at Wei. 'Come.' His order sounded like a threat.

They abandoned their dinner and hurried down the halls, their shadows slipping in and out between the glow of torches along the way. This was the first time he was witnessing a crack in the king's composure. Whatever was in the northwest tower had to be of utmost importance to him.

They took what was clearly a shortcut, heading down mostly shadowed corridors free of scurrying maids and servants. Moonlight peered in through narrow windows carved through the thick stone walls, throwing their path into brief relief.

A scream ahead—the voice all too familiar—made his heart lurch. He quickened his footsteps, nearly running ahead of King Falco.

They stepped through a heavy-set wooden door into a circular chamber with towering walls covered in a full arsenal of weapons. In the middle of it, a boy wearing chainmail armour sat on a bench before a long table, sharpening the sword in his hand as he considered the girl writhing at his feet.

'Rose!' Wei rushed forward and propped her up against him. He gathered her icy hands in his, but she seemed completely oblivious to everything around her.

'Just as you anticipated, Your Majesty,' the boy said, like a son in hopes of scoring his father's affection. 'But we have two Elementals instead of one. The other one is here somewhere.'

King Falco turned to Wei. 'It seems your companion made an attempt to kill my Metal Elemental.'

The Metal Elemental. Of course. He would be the one forging all these weapons, locked up in a tower. How had a mortal king managed to make an Elemental serve him? Had he also guessed their intentions from the start and laid this trap to lure Desert Rose here?

'Your Majesty, there must be a mistake,' Wei said, struggling to keep his voice calm. 'My companion meant no harm.'

King Falco shot him a sharp glance. 'Chryso wouldn't have deployed the venom if he didn't feel that he was in danger. You dare deceive me about your intentions, Rogue Prince? Right now, your friend has poisoned metal running through her veins. She won't last half a day.'

Cold fear slid down his back. 'Please. There has to be a way to save her.'

'There's an antidote, of course. But I don't see any reason to offer it to a trespasser who attempted murder in my territory.' He chuckled, but when he spoke again, he no longer sounded like the amiable king who had received them in the Great Hall. The coldness in his voice was new, but not out of place, as though it had merely been lurking beneath the surface all this time. 'Did you think you could walk into my kingdom, live in my palace, and try to destroy my secret weapon behind my back? You underestimate me, Rogue Prince.'

He should have known better than to believe that the king of Lettoria would welcome him without any defences, that he would offer room and board without a price. The Metal Elemental had been lying in wait for them all this while, and King Falco had likely been planning this from the moment they stepped through the kingdom gates.

The words were out of Wei's mouth before he realized it. 'I'll do anything. Please save her.' Desperation snagged at his voice like a rusted hook, but Wei couldn't care less about that now. King Falco had the upper hand here, and the only way forward was to play his game.

The king raised his brows. 'Have you made your decision about our earlier conversation?'

What would joining arms with King Falco look like now that Wei no longer had his trust? It would no longer be a partnership; it would be conditional servitude. But perhaps King Falco had never been interested in a partnership to begin with.

In his arms, Desert Rose let out a scream, jolting him back to the present. Wei pinned her arms by her side before she could claw at herself.

'I'll do it,' he blurted in the midst of holding her still. 'Please just give her the antidote.'

'Very well. I hold you to your word. You know what happens if you double-cross me, Rogue Prince.'

Wei nodded. Dread sat in the base of his gut like dead weight.

King Falco gestured for the pair of guards who had accompanied them here. They approached Wei and lifted Desert Rose from his arms. A part of him was reluctant to let go of her—could he really trust Falco's word?—but there was nothing more he could do now. He let them tow her away, his helplessness once more a noose around his neck.

King Falco, already disinterested in Desert Rose, turned to the Metal Elemental. 'The other desert girl is here, you say?'

'I've barred the exits with this'—he revealed the iron fillings in his palm, then flung them around him—'so we'll find her in no time.'

Out of thin air, a shifting breeze materialized into a girl who fell to the ground in an unceremonious heap. She lay sprawled on the floor, incapacitated by the Metal Elemental's iron powder.

Wei recognized Windshadow, the desert girl who had trained with Desert Rose in the House of Night. The one who had murdered Yong to help Meng ascend to the throne. The one who had pushed Desert Rose's hand and framed her for his father's murder. She looked no different from the last time he had seen her in the palace—lithe and lethal, her gaze almost feral as she calculated her next move.

She had been working for Meng back in the palace. So either she was here spying for him, or she was a free agent now and here to kill the Metal Elemental. Either way, it gave him some sort of pleasure to see her in this state, after everything she had done.

King Falco circled her, observing her the way one would a captive animal. 'Had your fun?'

Windshadow hissed, a sound like the rustling of sand in a looming sandstorm. But she could only remain where she was, glowering up at King Falco and Chryso.

'I'm not in the habit of wasting Elementals,' the king said. 'So as of today, you are to join my army and offer your services.'

Windshadow scoffed. 'Be your puppet, and then what—let Metal Boy kill us once you've achieved your goal?'

'If you're lucky, you get to kill him.' A slow smile spread across his face. 'Yes, he's told me about the prophecy. Perhaps, once the whole business with the Immortal Spring is over, the last Elemental standing might consider a peaceful life in the Gold Kingdom.'

Windshadow snorted.

King Falco's demeanour hardened. 'Or, perhaps you would prefer to have Chryso kill you on the spot now.'

If she were smart, she would accept this offer at face value. And Wei knew Windshadow was the sort who would do or say anything to survive.

'I accept your terms,' she said, but rebellion was already stirring in her eyes.

'I will leave Chryso to show you the ropes then.' He shot the Metal Elemental a loaded glance before turning to Wei. 'Come. We have much to discuss now that you are on board.'

But as they left the tower, Wei's thoughts circled back to Desert Rose. Had they managed to purge the venom? What would happen to her? He longed to see her and be by her side, but his hands were tied now.

'They will no doubt attempt to kill Chryso again,' King Falco was saying to him. 'I want you to keep a close eye on them and report anything amiss to me.'

'I'd like to first make sure that my companion is in good hands,' Wei said.

The king flashed him a smile. 'Of course. But I hope that she will not be a distraction for you as we prepare for battle. You understand what must be done, don't you?'

Wei made no response. He recalled his time in the Snow Wolf Sect when one of his first training was to kill an entire wolf pack to escape the bitter cold of the mountain. But each time he came face to face with a beast, he hadn't been able to do it. Something had always stopped his hand.

'Kindness can be a fatal flaw,' his sect master had said. 'You will always be at the mercy of others if you are unable to set your heart in stone and do what needs to be done. To survive, sometimes you need to kill or be killed.'

His first thought had been that he hadn't left his father's bloodstained kingdom to enter a bloody battle with wolves. Later, however, he realized that the rules of survival in the palace were no different from those in the wild. If he wanted to protect those he loved, he had to play the game even if he didn't care to win. He had made the mistake of turning his back on the power struggle his father had seeded amongst him and his brothers, the 'destiny' he was cursed with at birth, but his leaving Oasis Kingdom had only resulted in his brother and mother being murdered.

And this time, it was Desert Rose he couldn't protect because he was powerless to do so. He would not make the same mistake again. If complete loyalty to King Falco—or at least the appearance of it—was what would keep Desert Rose safe for now, then that was what he would commit to. He had done it before; he could do it again. He would set his heart in stone, this time not just to survive, but to protect the one he loved.

King Falco was watching him, waiting.

'I understand,' Wei said at last.

A smile slid across the king's face. Now that he had everyone right where he wanted, he slipped back into his affable demeanour. 'You are still a son of Oasis Kingdom. I cannot make decisions on behalf of my country on your word alone, but I promise you no harm will come to your companion as long as you keep to your end of the deal.'

Wei made no reply. There were men like Han and his father who did not disguise their cruelty and greed, but it was the ones like King Falco that he had to guard against—the ones who could rob you clean while pouring you wine over dinner.

That evening, Wei stood at the balcony of his room, mind racing and feeling oddly bereft.

Just last night, he had stood here with Desert Rose, giving in at last to the pull in his heart, the one that sharpened every time he looked at her and heard her rare laughter. And, by some miracle, she had seemed to feel the same way. His hands were bound now, his voice silenced. Every move of his would be watched by King Falco, and any step he took out of line would mean death for Desert Rose.

Every part of him ached to go to her—if he could just hear her voice, know that she was okay—but he was at the mercy of King Falco now. They both were. The king could easily charge her for attempted murder and brand them both enemies of the kingdom unless Wei followed his rules.

Wei felt his fists clench, his fingers digging into his palms. *This is only temporary*, he told himself. As soon as he unseated Meng and took over the throne, this arrangement with King Falco would end.

In the distance, a shadowy speck loomed towards him, a dark spot against the indigo sky. It was a risk for Sunrise to be here. This would have to be the last correspondence for now.

Sunrise dropped the scroll into his outstretched hand and perched on the ledge, watching him. Only upon unfurling it did Wei realize that the scroll was streaked with blood. At least a week old, by the look of it.

Matron's typically tidy handwriting was a nearly illegible scrawl this time.

Castaway ascends throne. Red Circle cleansed for a bloody dawn. Crown-bearer advances through sand kingdom. Final letter before heads roll.

Wei reread the last line, feeling sick to the stomach.

Everything was happening at frightening speed. Not only was Han back in the palace, but he had also seized the throne and begun his bloody campaign, cleansing the palace and getting rid of anyone who was still loyal to the last two emperors. Matron had likely been executed by now—Matron, who had brought him up like a second mother, the only person to risk her life by visiting his mother while she was imprisoned and bringing her food and medicine. Who had unfailingly sent him letters all these years he was away from Oasis Kingdom to keep him apprised of everything that happened within it.

Yet another person he cared for had been sacrificed in this power struggle.

Crown-bearer advances through sand kingdom.

Han had wasted no time in mobilizing the army too; they were cutting across the desert towards Lettoria. It would take about a month—weeks, if they moved quickly—to reach their doorstep.

He rolled up the scroll and attached it back to Sunrise's talons. 'Stay with Zeyan,' he whispered as he stroked the hawk's head. 'Don't come back.'

He released her back into the sky, where she circled twice before grudgingly taking her leave.

Wei watched Sunrise recede into a speck in the distance. A dormant rage rose inside him. How many people had Han murdered by now? Was it too late to stop him? What was Meng's fate now that Han had taken the throne?

It felt like a long time ago that Wei had cared about Oasis Kingdom and considered it his home, albeit a miserable one. Sometimes, he even dreamed of a better future for it, promising to undo the legacy of his father and his ancestors.

Perhaps it was time, at last, to make good on that promise.

NINETEEN

Meng

Sleep was impossible here in enemy territory.

Despite King Falco's reception towards him, Meng knew he was living on borrowed time. Now that the king knew he had the stones to the Immortal Spring, it was only a matter of time before he found a way to acquire it from him, whatever the method. He had lain awake for most of the night with the purse of stones tucked under his pillow, thinking about the altercation in the northwest tower Windshadow had told him about.

Thinking about Desert Rose.

Windshadow had mentioned that Desert Rose was injured, but she did not go into any detail before she disappeared to tend to her own wounds. Just how powerful was the Metal Elemental to render them to this state?

At the crack of dawn, he leapt out of bed and got dressed.

Outside, the first rays of sunlight were just starting to peek out from behind the mountains as Meng hurried across the palace grounds. A deep sense of uneasiness trailed at his feet like an unshakeable shadow, growing heavier with each step he took.

The northwest tower was a looming stone building bordered by a thick forest behind it. Meng followed the sound of voices down the draughty hallway until he came to a high-ceilinged chamber gleaming with an impressive array of newly forged weapons.

King Falco stood behind a work table in the middle of the chamber, surveying a topographic military map. Next to him were Wei and another boy slightly younger than Meng, toying with a silver dagger as though he was drawing comfort from it. He had the features of someone born in the desert, though he wore a chainmail tunic embossed with the royal insignia.

The Metal Elemental.

The boy turned in his direction as though he had heard his thoughts. Meng ducked behind the wall, hoping he didn't have supernatural senses like Windshadow.

King Falco clapped his hands once, bringing the Metal Elemental's attention back to him. 'We have no time to waste. The Oasis Emperor has begun to advance. His troops are already stationed at the Yancheng outpost, and will likely pass through Yarshe Valley, thirty miles east of Turga. We need to attack before they reach the desert town, before they get a chance to restock their rations and advance even closer to us.'

'This is just a preliminary attack meant to distract us,' Wei said.

Us? Wei and the Lettorian king were 'us' now?

King Falco nodded in agreement. 'Which is why we need a two-pronged approach. Distract and attack.'

'Taking down the Wall would be the surest way to undermine Han,' Wei said.

Meng tried to quell a rush of outrage. What was Wei suggesting? How could he offer such intel to the enemy?

Despite himself, he stepped out from behind the wall and blurted, 'Taking down the Wall would be the destruction of Oasis Kingdom.'

Everyone turned to look at him. There was nothing but hatred in Wei's eyes as he glared at him, while the Metal Elemental merely regarded him as a trespasser and eavesdropper.

'How kind of you to join us, Prince Meng,' King Falco said, as though he was expecting him all along. 'I'd love to hear your thoughts too.'

'There's no need to destroy innocent civilian lives when we can defeat Han without a battle,' he said.

Wei shot him a deadly stare. 'Innocent lives. Since when did you care about that? Not when you killed my brother or my mother, surely.'

His mother? Yong, he could understand. But Meng had never arranged for Wei's mother to be killed.

Wei turned back to King Falco. 'The citizens aren't faring any better behind that Wall. Besides, it's the fastest way to dismantle Han's campaign. The Wall is the strongest protection Oasis Kingdom has against magic. Once Han loses that first line of defence, we've already won half the battle. We might not even have to attack any further.'

Again with the 'we'.

'But it would bring chaos to Oasis Kingdom,' Meng argued.

Under any emperor's reign, the toppling of the Wall would guarantee the people's revolt. They could easily destabilize—even overthrow—the ruling emperor. Except this was Han they were speaking of. He had already disposed of those in the imperial palace and the army to ensure that he would have only utmost loyalty within his ranks. How would he quash a civilian uprising with the Fire Elemental by his side?

Meng massaged his temples. What was he doing, helping to plan an attack on his home kingdom with the enemy? 'I don't suppose you have any intention of bringing the Wall back up?'

'One issue at a time, Prince Meng,' said King Falco. 'Like Prince Wei said, the Wall must go. It's the most efficient way to cripple the enemy. We weaken their troops that are already out in the field, and deliver another blow at their doorstep. Chryso.' He turned to the young man, who set down his dagger and straightened. 'How is the battalion coming along?'

'Exceedingly well. They can be dispatched tomorrow if needed.'

'Excellent.' King Falco gestured to Meng and Wei. 'Come. Let's take a look.'

Chryso led the way out of the chamber through a nondescript opening at the back. Meng and Wei tailed him, as well as the king, who appeared to be in high spirits. It was a strange feeling, walking side by side with Wei for the first time in his life, almost as though they were allies. Almost as though they were brothers.

They emerged into a sprawling courtyard behind the tower, hidden from plain view. In this remote periphery of the palace, hardly anyone would be privy to the sight that lay before them now.

Dressed in full armour, soldiers of uniform build lined up in rows of ten, each spaced two feet apart. There was something unnatural about them, from their vacant gazes to their unnatural stillness and homogeneity, as though they were all carved from the same mould. They stood absolutely still, neither a twitch here nor a fidget there, neither statue nor human.

Meng gaped, unable to find the words. Next to him, Wei was equally silent.

'Every war costs us our men, and that seems like a flagrant waste of resources. So, with Chryso's help, I've found a way to build an indestructible army. I call them the Ferros, the Iron Guards.' He patted one soldier on the shoulder, beaming with pride. 'Every one of them has steel built into their bones, steel forged by the one and only Metal Elemental.'

That explained it. The king wasn't just using the Metal Elemental to forge stronger weapons; he had gone one step further to mine the Elemental's magic and build an army of superhumans.

What mortal army could go up against one like that?

'Do they have any weaknesses?' Wei asked before Meng could. If he was fazed by the king's secret project, he showed no sign of it. 'With metal in the body, these soldiers won't last a day in the desert.'

King Falco nodded in grim approval. 'Which is why we will attack from the north. It will take us longer to reach Oasis Kingdom, but the journey will be less treacherous and we can make use of Yarshe Valley upstream.' The king laughed. 'Emperor Han thinks he can take the battle to my kingdom to minimize his losses. What will he do when half his men have been poisoned by the river running down from the Palamir Mountains?'

'Poisoned?' Meng echoed.

The king ignored him, addressing Wei. 'The Water Elemental will join the military expedition in Yarshe Valley.'

Wei's fists tightened by his side as he cast a glance at Meng. Something passed between them. Water Elemental. This was someone Wei was concerned about.

Desert Rose. King Falco was sending her to do his dirty work. He had known what he was doing all along by letting them all enter his kingdom. He hadn't welcomed them as friends or even potential allies, but as pawns in his game of chess.

'Will she recover in time to make the trip?' Wei asked, his fists still balled, though he kept his voice light.

Recover. Just how badly was she injured? Meng stared at Wei, hoping for an explanation, but his brother's attention was fixed on the king. From what little Meng knew about him, however, the more Wei tried to hide his emotions, the more he was actually struggling with them inside.

'She is recovering well, last I was told. The mission is hardly dangerous,' King Falco went on before Wei could protest. 'She will be fine. In the meantime, I would like you and Chryso to accompany the troops through the mountains.'

Wei did not respond immediately.

'Would you rather have the Water Elemental out on the battlefield? I understand from the Air Elemental that Emperor Han has a rather formidable Elemental on his side who is bent on surviving the prophecy.'

So the two war-hungry leaders of the largest kingdoms in the world now each had Elementals working for them. Given Han's insatiable hunger for vengeance and power, Desert Rose would either be killed or captured to serve him.

Wei's jaw tightened. 'I'll do it.'

The king gave him a dismissive wave. 'Off you go to prepare, then. The troop is departing the day after. Chryso, bring Prince Wei to meet Sergeant Vicardi.'

Meng caught the look Wei shot him as he turned to leave with Chryso, a glimpse of worry trapped in it.

The king waited until they had left the chamber before speaking again.

'Your Air Elemental is quite the assassin. Not two days in my territory, and she and the Water Elemental have already attempted to kill my metal boy.' He sent him a look that dared him to deny his statement. Meng said nothing. 'This alliance can only work if we both honour it.'

'I was not aware of her plans, Your Majesty,' Meng said.

'Don't lie to me,' the king snapped. He recomposed himself after a beat. 'An Elemental with her capricious spirit won't be able to sit still for long, so I've assigned her a task. In the meantime, you and I should discuss what to do about those stones in your custody.'

'Before that, I'd like to visit the Water Elemental,' Meng said.

A flicker of impatience flashed across the king's face, but he waved a permissive hand. 'Very well. She's resting in her room upstairs.'

Meng turned to leave, keeping his footsteps measured until he was out of King Falco's sight. A storm of anxiety churned in his gut. They had only been here for two days, and their cover was blown. He should have known Windshadow had an agenda of her own; she had never been one to sit around patiently for opportunities to roll by. What he hadn't anticipated was her going against their plan so soon. And now, one by one, they were all becoming the king's puppets. Even Wei. Even Windshadow.

And Desert Rose...

His footsteps quickened as he ascended the spiral flight of stairs. In this remote part of the palace, there were hardly any comings and goings, no servant or messenger, so it took him a while to find the room that Desert Rose and Windshadow were sharing.

The room was mostly utilitarian, adequately furnished but uncarpeted. Desert Rose lay asleep in a bed near the ajar window that let in a warm breeze and gentle sunlight that spilled across her face.

He went over to her and perched lightly next to her on the bed. Her complexion was devoid of its usual flush; under the pale morning light, she looked almost drawn. The gentle rise and fall of her body indicated some stability in her immediate condition, but it wasn't until Meng took her pulse that he realized something was wrong.

Her pulse plodded at an irregular rhythm, feeble and erratic. Meng drew back his hand, staring at her wan face.

She hadn't sustained a common physical injury from combat. She had been poisoned, and there was still some left in her body. He could feel it plodding through her veins, foreign and heavy like molten steel.

She stirred, eyelids fluttering open. His heart thudded in his chest as he leaned closer to her. Recognition dawned on her face as soon as her gaze focused on him. Meng found himself locked in her eyes. Her brows pulled together.

After all those months of regretting how they had parted ways and yearning to arrive at this moment—though not quite in this particular setting—he was now bereft of words. He struggled to offer something—a conciliatory platitude, a smile—but every word and gesture felt like a clumsy mockery of her, as though whatever he did now only served as a reminder for what he had done to her last winter.

Say something, you fool! Anything, his mind urged.

'How are you feeling?' he blurted.

'Delightful,' she croaked as she tried to rise. He helped her up, then busied himself with pouring a goblet of water from the bedside table.

She glanced around. 'Where am I?'

'The northwest tower,' Meng said, placing the goblet in her hands.

She seemed to recall their history then and fell into a stony silence as she took a sip from the goblet, avoiding his gaze. A long moment stretched between them.

'Why…' they said at the same moment. Meng gestured for her to speak first.

'Why are you here?' she asked quietly. This time, her voice sounded much colder.

'I heard you were injured. I wanted to see if you were recovering well.'

Her smile was bitter. 'If I'm still alive, you mean.'

'I never wanted you dead.' The words came out more emphatic than he intended.

'Then why did your scouts tail us to the Darklands and ambush us there?' she demanded.

Meng blinked. 'I never ordered any ambush.'

'So you admit you sent the scouts after us. Drove us into a corner.'

He sighed. 'I know whatever I say now cannot erase what happened last winter, but …'

But what? What exactly was he hoping for? He was not entitled to her forgiveness after how he lied to her, used and betrayed her—the way his mother had done to him. He knew now exactly how it felt to be betrayed by someone he trusted.

She was waiting.

'I never intended to hurt you,' he said. 'I had my reasons back then.'

Her gaze remained averted. 'Your intention does not matter, nor do your reasons. Your actions do.'

She was right. He never meant to hurt her, but he had. He had made every conscious decision that led them to that moment in the astronomy tower. There was no going back to how they once were, sitting side by side in the imperial library telling each other stories, nursing steaming cups of tea to keep out the winter chill. The thought made him ache inside in a way he never thought possible.

'I was wrong. About everything. I know it now,' he said at last. 'And I would do it all differently if I could.'

The aftermath of his apology was another stretch of silence now filled with his own ragged breathing. Her face was still turned away from him, so he couldn't make out her expression.

'What can I do to earn your trust again?' he asked quietly.

She let out a slow sigh. 'It's not up to me to tell you.'

There was nothing more to say, at least for now. So Meng left the room without another word, a heaviness sitting in his chest, regret and longing bitter on his tongue.

It wasn't until he was outside the room that he realized he hadn't asked her how she had been poisoned.

A thought crossed his mind. What if the poison wasn't completely purged? What if it had been deliberately buried inside her? Enough had been drawn out to keep her alive, but there was also enough left in her that could be activated anytime. The dosage had to be carefully measured. If that were true, then it meant that King Falco was holding

Desert Rose hostage. That this was how he had gotten Wei to play his game.

As though his thoughts had summoned him, Wei appeared before him. It was clear that he had been hovering outside the room, eavesdropping through the ajar door all this time.

Fresh hatred brimmed in Wei's eyes, renewed since they last saw each other back in the Capital. Meng had, after all, hired Windshadow to get rid of Yong under his mother's orders. But now, Wei looked as though he was ready to murder him on the spot.

Meng shut the door behind him and eyed his brother. Would he really attack him here in this hallway, with Desert Rose just behind that door? 'You have never cared for the throne,' he said, picking his words with care. 'Why are you here helping King Falco attack Oasis Kingdom?'

'Maybe I have reason to want the throne now, even if it can't bring my mother back.'

Meng stared at Wei. 'Your mother is…?'

Wei shot him a withering look. 'Drop the act, Meng. You know what you did. Pretty smart to ambush us all at the Darklands. My mother never cared for becoming Empress Dowager, just so you know. All she wanted was a peaceful life in the palace.'

Meng frowned. Ambush at the Darklands? This was the second time he was accused of ordering such a thing. 'I never ordered the scouts to kill you or your company, much less your mother, despite all the advisors' warnings.'

'Well, thank you for your benevolence,' Wei sneered.

'It wasn't me,' Meng insisted. 'Think about it. I was dethroned three weeks ago. I arrived in Lettoria two days after you. How could it have been me who ordered the attack?'

Hesitation flitted across his face. Wei narrowed his eyes at him. 'Are you saying it's Han then?'

Could it really be their older brother? Even if Han had taken over the throne immediately after Meng was overthrown, it would still take some time for the scouts to execute his new order to kill Wei and his mother. The timeline did not add up.

'I cannot say for sure.' A pause lapsed between them. 'Are you really going to help Falco take down the Wall? I know you don't give a damn about our kingdom, but those are our men you will be attacking.'

Wei had always been a stranger to him, his actions unfathomable, but he never thought Wei would choose to be an enemy of Oasis Kingdom.

'Those are men who have pledged loyalty to Han, who have killed Matron,' said Wei. 'And don't tell me what I give a damn about.'

'Are you so desperate for someone's approval that you're seeking it from the enemy?'

Wei did not miss a beat. 'And are you that ill-versed in political strategy to not see that this is the only way we can defeat Han? The enemy of our enemy is our friend—for now, at least.'

Meng felt something in him unclench since he entered this stone tower. Never had he imagined that he would one day be standing on the same side as Wei, fighting against a common enemy. Despite being born on the same night, they had gone on to meet vastly different fates. It was a miracle they had even arrived at this point, but this truce was unlikely to last.

'How is she?' Wei muttered, interrupting his thoughts. He was glancing at the closed door, looking torn between charging in and turning away.

'You can ask her that yourself,' Meng said.

Wei shot him an annoyed look.

'Desert Rose is still poisoned,' he said quietly.

'What?' The sharpness in Wei's voice made Meng flinch.

'Her blood isn't completely cleansed. There's still enough poison buried in her body that can be activated anytime. One decision from the king can determine her fate.'

Wei's jaw tightened. 'I knew it. He's using her to keep me in line.' He swore. 'He's always one damn step ahead.'

'I don't understand. She said she doesn't believe in destiny. Why is she going to all this effort to fulfil the prophecy?'

'Her father's soul is trapped in the Darklands. The only way to free him and her tribe is by fulfilling the prophecy.'

The other half of the Dugur tribe. The ones who had chosen not to follow the clan leaders after they overthrew Scarbrow. Desert Rose had told him about the coup last winter. Given how close she was to her tribe, the betrayal had to have cut her deep. Yet, she was not giving up on restoring it.

'She'll die trying to eliminate the Metal Elemental,' Wei went on, staring at the door again. 'I came here partly to help her in that mission, but Falco is now keeping a close eye on me so I can't stay by her side. If anything happens to her...'

Meng understood. 'I'll help her.' If she would accept his assistance. 'I'll find an antidote ... or something, anything.'

Wei gave a grudging nod. 'Whatever you do, don't alert Falco. Best not to let Rose know too. She'll want to take matters into her own hands, and it's too risky with the venom still inside her.' He turned to leave, adding as an afterthought, 'Be careful.'

Meng wasn't sure if he meant that for him, but he blurted, 'You too,' before he realized what he was saying.

Wei paused for the briefest moment, as though he wasn't expecting that, then nodded once and headed down the stairs. Sometimes, Meng wondered if Wei would make a better emperor than any of them.

The Fallen Empire

Many historians disagree on the details of the dissolution of the Hesui Empire. There have been so many accounts from various sources—both legitimate and unofficial—over the past few centuries that the truth has grown muddied along the way.

Some say it was attacked on multiple fronts by various aspiring despots—the settlers of the west (now known as Lettorians and Sorensteins), the ethnic tribes of the south, and the Yan people of the east (now known as the Oasis people)—who had all colluded in taking down Hesui. Others claim that the entire empire had originally fallen into the hands of the First Oasis Emperor Zhaoshun, who had commissioned a team of alchemists to develop a concoction that could temporarily disable the Hesui people's magic.

However, the earliest historical records show that Zhaoshun's unscrupulous attack had helped him conquer Hesui, and the western settlers had invaded much later. Through raid after raid of border towns, the westerners encroached closer to Oasis Kingdom. Out of desperation to safeguard the Capital, the Oasis Emperor had no choice but to cede the western parts of the empire to the likes of Lettoria, Sorenstein, and Mayweather. That explains why Oasis Kingdom has been at war with Lettoria and Sorenstein since its founding, and why it still has not given up on one day reclaiming those lands.

The southern region, particularly along the Bay of Baghria, was soon overrun by vicious pirates. Lettoria and Sorenstein took control of the land and formed the Southern Colonies, which includes N'yong, Bahagia, and more.

And in the centre of the once great empire of Hesui lay the Khuzar Desert, now still a contentious territory that no emperor could lay claim to, though that did not stop them from exploiting it. But Oasis Kingdom has largely adopted a protectionist approach with its Wall, while the other countries have attempted to conquer the various desert tribes that, though not as mighty as a whole nation, have been fiercely fending them off.

So the desert remains a wind-battered wilderness and hotbed of magic governed by no mortal ruler—for now. Kingdoms may rise and fall around it and emperors may come and go, but it would be a mistake to think that the desert is as dead as the last empire it was once a part of.

Whichever version of history one is inclined to believe, one thing is clear: the story is far from over, and the fate of these kingdoms is as ever-shifting as the sands of the Khuzar Desert.

—Excerpt from *'Land of Sand and Song: Tales from the Khuzar Desert'* by Lu Ji Fang

TWENTY

Windshadow

Windshadow lingered at the corner of the room she shared with Desert Rose, waiting until the brothers were gone before shifting into her human form.

Her desert azzi had sunk back to her slumber after Meng left, leaving Windshadow to pack her essentials in silence. She considered waking Desert Rose, but Windshadow had never been good with goodbyes.

Of course, there was still a good chance she would make it back. But it was anyone's guess what surprises lay in store on this trip to the Palamir Mountains. 'A separate mission,' the king had said. 'One that requires your special skills.'

'You have someone you need assassinating?' she had drawled.

He gave her a look, as though disappointed that she was still attempting to play innocent. 'I have a special mission for you, Air Elemental. I've received intel that Emperor Han has sent a secret troop to attack from the Palamir Mountains, and I would like you to intercept it. If our calculations are correct, they will reach in a week.'

Intercept. 'Why me? Why not your metal boy?'

'Chryso and Prince Wei will be busy at the frontline, and the Water Elemental has her own task to accomplish once she's recovered. Prince

Meng will remain here as my second strategist. That leaves you to help me get rid of the threat approaching from the Palamirs.'

'I'm here to assist Prince Meng, not partake in your wars.'

'And Prince Meng would ultimately benefit from your assistance to Lettoria. Whatever agreement you have with him, we can all achieve our aim of finding the spring if you prove to be an asset to me in the meantime.'

Of course he was after the spring. Every ruler in the region sought the Immortal Spring for the promise of riches and longevity, the cure for all mortal ills and woes. He who controlled the spring could rule the world—or bring it to its knees.

But any mortal who thought he could control the Immortal Spring was a fool. Windshadow was almost disappointed to think that she was almost impressed by the Lettorian king's scheming.

Whatever King Falco had in mind wasn't as simple as defeating Oasis Kingdom and knocking Han off the throne. It wasn't just political power play, and it certainly wasn't to forge a lasting peace with its neighbours.

'I have no interest in being anyone's asset,' she said. 'I serve only my own purpose.'

The king dipped his head, almost respectfully. 'We can always find a way to align our goals. For instance, I can assist you in becoming the last surviving Elemental.'

She raised her brows. 'And you would sacrifice your precious Metal Elemental and give up on the water one to help me succeed?'

'Consider it bidding on the best horse. I look upon you most favourably.' He beamed, as though expecting her to fall to her feet in gratitude. She remained unmoved.

'Or, I could just as well eliminate them on my own instead of relying on you.'

He only laughed. 'You forget you are but one Elemental, who has been captured once by a mortal king. If you choose to be against me, I can very easily invest my efforts in helping another Elemental succeed.'

Desert Rose murmured in her sleep, jolting Windshadow out of her thoughts. She went over to the window and closed it slightly.

Her desert sister was looking much better than yesterday, though her pallor hadn't completely subsided.

Windshadow wondered if Desert Rose would be disappointed in her sudden departure again. It seemed like she always abandoned her at the most inconvenient timing, right when she needed a friend. But could they ever really be friends? With only one Elemental to remain, they were destined to be rivals.

She tucked a dagger into her waist belt and another into her left boot. There was little to pack, since she and a small troop of Lettorian soldiers would be travelling light in this guerilla-style mission.

As a final measure, she scribbled out a note—*Palamir looms, we meet on the battlefield*— addressed to no one in particular. It could be for Meng or Desert Rose; Windshadow didn't particularly care. She folded it up and tucked it under a half-empty goblet on the bedside table. With one last glance at Desert Rose, Windshadow slipped out of the room.

* * *

The Palamir Mountains was a week's ride from the gates of Lettoria, shorter if Windshadow shifted. But with twenty soldiers in tow, there was no way she could transport all of them, especially not a day after the Metal Elemental's attack in the tower; her body still felt like it was rebelling against her. There was no choice but to remain in her mortal form to conserve her energy until they reached the Palamirs.

On a late afternoon three days later, the mountains loomed in the distance, first revealing its jagged snow-dusted peaks, then its sprawling body. The trek up the mountain involved wending through an alpine forest and the going was slow, hampered by the fog that grew denser the deeper they went. They could only rely on the scant specks of sunlight to guide them along. The horses became more jittery with every step forward, stamping their hooves and bucking, eager to turn back.

After a lot of taming and wrestling with the reins, they emerged at an outcrop, where they paused to take stock of their surroundings. But while the sparsely vegetated ground was strewn with hoof prints, there was no sign of anyone here.

'Wait here,' Windshadow told the soldiers. 'I'll go and scout the road ahead.' The general, a young man just a few years older than her, started protesting. Windshadow shot him a withering look. 'Unless you can do a better job of keeping silent and undetected.'

She slipped partially into her second skin, turning her lower body into vapour. She trailed over rocks and undergrowth, buoyed by her magic as she forged ahead. It was tempting to shift completely; she felt much quicker and stronger in her elemental state. But she needed her upper body to be corporeal for potential combat. Having her lower body blend in with the mist was enough to take her around swiftly.

The Lettorian troop couldn't have arrived so soon. It would take even the most seasoned mountain-dweller two days to navigate his way around this maze—more in this fog. Palamir Mountain was known for its wolf population, but they hadn't encountered one so far. Was that about to change?

Ears pricked, Windshadow inched forward, ready to attack at the slightest rustle. Something crackled in the distance ahead—a fire? Closer to her, a lone gust of wind howled as it ripped through the desolate space. The horses reared and stomped behind her just as a dart whizzed past her ear.

A whinny from one of the horses pierced the silence. Windshadow whipped around to find the beasts being felled one by one. Flames erupted from the gloom, bright scarlet and gold, just shy of reaching her. The soldiers screamed as the fire ate them up.

Windshadow's mouth went dry. There was only one reason a freak fire could appear out of nowhere and keep burning despite the fog.

As the fog dissipated in the clearing, so too did the anguished screams of the men, though their echoes lingered. Windshadow remained where she was, peering at the lone figure tangled in the last wisps of fog.

'Fancy meeting you again here, azzi,' Lazar drawled, toying with a flame hovering above his open palm. He seemed unconcerned about the charred bodies lying at his feet.

Windshadow cursed inwardly as she shifted fully back to her human form. Gods, she was starting to tire of being one-upped by these cocky Elementals. She was here to wipe out their troop, not serve as kindling.

'I didn't think the Lettorian king would fall for this trap Emperor Han laid out for him. But not only did he fall for it, he even sent you.' He took a step closer to her, the ball of flame still dancing above his palm.

Windshadow reached for the dagger tucked in her waist belt. Even if the blade forged by Chryso didn't kill him, the crushed ticha leaves smeared on it would cripple him and buy her enough time to escape.

Of course, she wasn't going to escape. This time, she was not going to flee from him like a scared animal. She was an Elemental as much as he was; they were both in the running for the spring. She could finish him off once and for all and be rid of one pesky Elemental.

'It's adorable you think I came here because King Falco wanted me to, and not because I just want to get rid of your smart mouth,' she said.

She stepped to the side, sizing him up. He did the same, mimicking her footwork. They circled each other, slow and keen, waiting for the moment to attack. A part of her almost looked forward to it.

She whipped into a furious gale just as he set himself ablaze. Flames rippled from him like a second skin that had come alive. She dived towards him, ignoring the unbearable burn of his unearthly fire. He had to have a weak spot, somewhere she could break in and shred him to bits.

But neither of them seemed to do significant damage to the other. His fire only grew bigger with every move she made, stoked by the fury of her draught, while she became more ferocious upon every contact with his flames, as though his power was unleashing hers wholly. She hadn't felt this way when she duelled with Desert Rose or Chryso, as though she was being sustained—no, amplified—by another power, growing many times stronger the more she engaged with it.

And a part of her relished that power. It made her feel alive. For the first time since she discovered her magic, she had met a worthy match, and it was giving her new life. Did Lazar feel it too?

They continued hurling themselves at each other, each time sparking an even larger flame until it became clear that their fight was pointless.

At last, Lazar retreated and shifted back into his human form. The flames dissipated almost instantly, revealing a young man once again. Windshadow followed suit, shifting out of her element.

He sighed. 'We shouldn't be fighting each other, azzi. We should be joining hands.'

Windshadow did not reply.

'We're the Damohai, the chosen ones,' Lazar went on. 'Why should we sacrifice ourselves for these mortal kings' ambitions? What power do they even have over us? Our destinies are far bigger than these petty territorial wars.'

'Our destinies are to die for the restoration of the balance between the realms,' she said flatly.

'Do you really think the gods will let us die? This is just a test, a trial we have to pass in order to ascend to the heavenly realm and be among our kin once again.'

Windshadow let out an exasperated laugh. *This boy is flat-out insane.*

'In case you've forgotten how the story goes,' she said, 'we descended from an illegitimate child of two celestial beings, a child who was rejected from heaven and went on to procreate with a mortal woman. We're half-bloods.'

'So you're content to let destiny play out and not get anything out of it?' He shook his head, looking almost dismayed. 'And here I thought we were the same kind.'

I am nothing like you, was her first thought. But she found herself unable to utter the words. They were more alike than she liked, at least by way of their ambitions.

'If your life's goal is to ascend to the heavenly realm,' she said instead, 'then why join Emperor Han and involve yourself in this mortal war? Why not just focus on finding all the Elementals?'

'Because the Earth Elemental—the most elusive one out of us— is in Oasis Kingdom.' The information made Windshadow snap to attention. 'Emperor Han wanted to seize the throne. It makes sense to team up with him.'

'How do you know the Earth Elemental is in Oasis Kingdom?'

He shrugged. 'I have my sources.'

She would be a fool to trust him. He would much sooner kill her in her sleep than join hands with her for more than a day. But it was easier to make a friend of an enemy, at least until the other Elementals were no longer in the running.

Except for Desert Rose. The thought flashed across her mind. She beat it down before it could take shape. Friend, azzi, or whatever she was, Desert Rose was destined to only be her enemy in the end. Windshadow would do well to remember that. She and Desert Rose might make a good team, as they had in the White Crypt during the trials, but she and Lazar were formidable. Together, they stood a far better chance of defeating all the other Elementals.

Lazar was watching her, his gaze keen as a freshly sharpened blade. 'We're stronger together, and you know it.'

As much as Windshadow hated to admit it, he was right. Together, they were much stronger. Strong enough to make an entire kingdom burn. To make mortals quail at their feet. To shape the fate of the world.

'And if you think those kings are only after territory and resources, then you are far too naive, azzi.' Lazar shook his head. 'They're working together to find the spring and unlock it, and it starts by gathering all the Elementals on the battlefield to fight it out.'

Windshadow narrowed her eyes at him. 'Why would they work together? They've always been enemies.'

'You of all people should know that enemies can become allies if they share a common goal. Once they've found the spring, they'll go right back to tearing each other's throats out for possession over it. And who will they use to unlock it?' He jabbed a finger at himself and her. 'Well, I'm not about to let myself become their sacrifice.'

She rolled her eyes. 'People have searched for the spring for years. They're not going to find it in time for the battle ....'

'Are they not? I understand that one of the Oasis princes is in possession of the Elder Stones.'

Prince Meng. Falco had indeed been eyeing it ever since they entered Lettoria. She wouldn't be surprised if he had asked for the stones by now, or perhaps found less civil ways of acquiring it.

Windshadow froze. The Fourth Prince she first knew—the one who had engaged her to help him get on the throne, who didn't reveal a shred of sorrow at the First Prince's death—would never do it. That Fourth Prince knew how to draw a line between his duty and desire; he would never allow his feelings to get in the way of his goals.

But Prince Meng, now vindicated from his mother's expectations, was soft with sentimentality, willing to follow his heart rather than his head. There was no telling what he might do with the only leverage he had if he learnt of Falco's plan to sacrifice the Elementals on the battlefield.

Before she knew it, she was charging down the path from where she had come.

'Where are you going?' Lazar called out. He pointed over his shoulder. 'The battlefield is that way.'

'You said it yourself, we're going there to become sacrificial lambs. Why would I go that way?'

'It's our *destiny*,' he said, as though she was slow. 'We win the race or we *die*.'

'To hell with destiny. It will not make a plaything of me.' If Falco didn't have the stones, he wouldn't have the spring. She could only hope she wasn't too late to stop Meng from doing something as stupid as handing them over in exchange for an antidote for Desert Rose.

Lazar was incredulous. 'So you're going back to Lettoria? We have this one chance to take over the spring and wipe out those foolish mortals.'

'Not every battle takes place on the battlefield,' she replied. 'I'm going to stop a foolish prince instead.'

TWENTY-ONE

Meng

Meng stood before the Lettorian king in his private chamber, steeling his resolve. The king was reclined in his velvet couch, surveying him with polite interest.

It had been a day since Desert Rose left for Yarshe Valley, three since Wei left for Danxi Plains and Windshadow for the Palamir Mountains. He had sat around in the palace for that long, feeling completely useless since he neither had magical powers like the girls nor battlefield experience like Wei. The only advantage he had were the stones he was holding on to. The ones that held crucial clues to the Immortal Spring.

Despite the lavish interior of the chamber, the plush carpet under his feet, and the high-backed chair he had been invited to sit in opposite the king, Meng had to control himself from squirming. With everyone else he knew gone, he was now alone in Lettoria not as an Oasis ambassador or an esteemed guest, but merely as a refugee with something the king wanted.

The Lettorian leader had proven himself untrustworthy and scheming thus far—how could Meng trust him on anything else? But this was the only leverage Meng had, the only way he could help.

'A trade,' the king repeated, clasping his hands before him on the desk.

Meng nodded, keeping his demeanour as calm and confident as he could. He was the one with the stones. He was in a position to negotiate. Even if his proposition was not the sort he had ever made. Not as Fourth Prince, at least.

Giving up the only clue he had to the Immortal Spring—all for a girl. He could hear his mother's voice in his ear, chiding him. *Foolish boy. Of what use is a sentimental heart to the ruler of a kingdom?*

But he was no longer the ruler of his kingdom. He never truly got the chance to be one before the throne was taken away from him. Now, he was branded as nothing but a traitor, just like Wei. He had trusted in his mother's plan and done everything she had ever asked of him, only to be betrayed by her in favour of Han. What good was his residual loyalty to the one who had turned her back on him after using him?

His decision might seem foolish and sentimental, but at least he was making it on his own now. This time, unlike all those times he had ignored its calls, he would listen to his heart.

'Fine,' King Falco said, pulling him out of his thoughts. 'And what would you like in return?'

'The antidote,' said Meng. 'To the venom still buried in Desert Rose.'

The king seemed more impressed than surprised that Meng knew she was still poisoned. He made no denial of what he had done. Instead, his expression twisted into one of amusement as he leaned back in his chair. 'You're willing to give me the stones to save a desert girl's life?'

Consider it atonement, Meng thought. He had dragged her into this mess when he helped her enter the imperial palace, already planning to recruit her for the House of Night the way he had with Windshadow. He had made use of her desire to find her father and save her tribe to advance his own political agenda. She was right to despise him and never trust him again, but this was the least he could do for her now.

The aim now was to secure the antidote. After that, he could decide how to get those stones back.

He nodded.

'A fair trade,' King Falco agreed. 'Very well then. Follow me.'

Meng rose from his seat after the king and followed him towards the wall behind the mahogany desk, where a floor-to-ceiling gold-framed portrait of King Falco was hung. The king pressed on the carved talon of a stone eagle statue next to it, and the wall split apart from behind the painting with a low rumble, revealing another chamber within.

'Grab a torch,' King Falco said. Meng reached for the one perched in a bracket above the eagle statue and followed him into the dimly lit chamber.

No bigger than the king's main chamber, this one was lined with mahogany racks upon which sat an assortment of various treasures—bejewelled sculptures forged from gold, polished ivory tusks and crisp jade carvings, precious minerals and crystals in velvet-lined boxes and glass cases, leather-bound tomes, burnished weapons, and many more items that Meng could tell held their own in worth and value.

They came before a large square table at the end of the chamber. A map was sprawled across it, pinned down on all corners by lion-shaped paperweights carved from brass. Despite its worn edges, the map was carefully drawn, with all topographical details accounted for. Lettoria constituted the top-left portion; Sorenstein right below it. Directly opposite of them was Oasis Kingdom, bordered by the Palamir Mountains in the north, Danxi Plains in the middle, and the Southern Colonies below.

And right in the middle, surrounded by all the claimed territories, was the Khuzar Desert.

A group of men shuffled into the chamber. Apart from the vizier, King Falco's right-hand man, none were Lettorian. Meng recognized the three Dugur clan leaders from the one time he visited the desert and attempted to rally the tribes behind Oasis Kingdom. Accompanying them was a trio of what appeared to be shamans, dressed in their tell-tale patched robes and amber-coloured woven hats.

'Thank you for joining us, gentlemen,' King Falco said, ushering them closer to the table.

Blackstone, the most menacing-looking one, gave Meng a curt nod. 'We understand you have something of ours, Prince Meng. The stones belong to the tribe, and we would like to assume rightful ownership of them again.'

Meng distinctly remembered Golsha, the ex-tribe member who had acquired the stones for him, telling him that the stones were passed down from chieftain to chieftain for safekeeping. Now with the Dugur tribe split and Scarbrow's whereabouts a mystery, the stones had no owner.

He turned to King Falco. 'As discussed, we have a trade. I would like the antidote before I hand over the stones.'

The king shot him an easy smile. 'Of course.' He reached over to a carved wooden box on one of the shelves and pulled out a porcelain vial. 'This is all I have, so carry it well,' he said before tossing it to Meng.

Meng had just managed to tuck the vial into his breast pocket when King Falco called for the guards. Almost immediately, a pair of them burst through the door of the chamber, hands on the hilts of their swords.

'Search him,' the king ordered.

The guards pinned him to the table at once. Panic seized Meng, but it was futile to struggle against the thick burly hands running through his robes. They seemed to know what they were looking for, and quickly found the nondescript hemp pouch that contained the stones to the Immortal Spring.

Despite finding what they wanted, the guards continued to pin him to the table. Meng cursed inwardly. Why did he keep allowing Falco to be one step ahead of him?

Upon a nod from King Falco, Blackstone seized the pouch from the guards and poured out its contents onto the map. He gestured at the shamans, who took their places around the table.

The three shamans closed their eyes and bowed their heads simultaneously as they extended their hands over the map. As one, they began chanting in a language Meng was unfamiliar with, their low, droning voices filling up every corner of the secret chamber. It sounded like the language in which Desert Rose had read *Duru-shel Minta*, the ancient rhyme about the war of the realms.

The stones rattled and shook, emanating a strange glow as though roused by a supernatural force. The chanting crescendoed, its echo almost hypnotic. Meng felt his heart drum harder with each passing moment.

And then, all at once, the stones shot towards the same point on the map and fell still.

The Darklands.

Once upon a time, the Darklands was a sacred burial ground for the old kings of the Hesui Kingdom. Surrounded by desert canyons, it was protected by the natural landscape. After the kingdom was torn apart, it was abandoned and consumed by the desert over the years. Now, it was merely brought up in campfire tales as a fabled place where the souls of wronged or corrupt men who died out in the desert roamed eternally. Yet, according to the stones, the spring was located in that barren wasteland where no one had ever made it out alive.

One of the Dugur clan leaders, whose name Meng had forgotten, gasped. 'That's not possible. The Darklands is unholy ground.'

'Only the stories made it so,' one of the shamans said, his voice quiet with reverence. 'It was once a sacred burial ground for kings and nobles.' He peered closer at the stones. 'The spring appears to be near it, not inside it.'

King Falco's eyes were gleaming. 'To the Darklands, then.' He turned to the advisor. 'Immediately.'

The advisor nodded once and left to make the arrangements.

Meng's arms were starting to ache from being pinned behind his back. He nudged the guards to loosen their grip, but neither of them budged. The motion drew King Falco's attention back to him.

'Arrest him,' the king ordered. 'I want him securely locked up in the prison below the northwest tower. The Elementals are not to be interrupted at the battlefield.'

This time, Meng struggled—hard.

It was futile. King Falco, the clan leaders, and the shamans only watched mutely as the guards towed him out of the chamber. They continued down what seemed like a never-ending flight of spiral stairs, where the light receded into a pinprick when they arrived at the bottom.

A jangle of keys. The screech of a metal gate. And he was thrown unceremoniously into the grimy cell. The gate clanged shut before he could scramble back to his feet.

It felt doubly humiliating to have escaped the prison back home only to end up in another cell here. What sort of emperor could he make when he was gullible enough to be unseated by his brother *and* outsmarted by the enemy?

The vial of antidote pressed against his chest, offering meagre comfort. What did it matter that the antidote was in his hands now that he was behind bars? King Falco was going to awaken the spring with help from the Elementals, and there was nothing he could do to stop him. And Desert Rose, without the antidote, would be nothing more than a sacrificial lamb on the battlefield.

Meng recalled an old saying Golsha once told him. *He who controls the spring owns the world.* With control of the spring, Lettoria's might would be limitless. When that time came, conquering Oasis Kingdom would be a walk in the garden.

He had failed utterly—as a son of Oasis Kingdom, as the Sixteenth Emperor, as Zhao Meng. It had taken one bad decision after another to arrive at this point, and this was how his story would end. He would die an ignominious emperor, a traitor to his kingdom and his heart.

Meng closed his eyes and leaned against the cold dank wall, letting the darkness consume him.

The real victory is to win without fighting.

—The War Handbook, by Lu Cao

TWENTY-TWO

Desert Rose

The venom took two days to be purged from her body. She would have healed sooner if it weren't for the ticha, but by the time she felt well enough to leave her room in search of someone—anyone—she felt almost completely restored.

It was almost peaceful here in the northwest tower. In other circumstances, she might even enjoy the tranquillity. Instead, a sense of unease gnawed at her as she tried to recall what happened before she passed out. The Metal Elemental's poison dart striking her right in the chest. Windshadow pulling out the dart and demanding for the Metal Elemental to save her. Windshadow dissipating just as King Falco arrived with Wei. Their muffled conversation before the pain overtook her.

Not only had she put Wei in a precarious position with the Lettorian king, but also Windshadow and Prince Meng. She shouldn't be concerned about the latter two—after all, they had betrayed her before.

What can I do to earn your trust again? Meng had asked.

That was the thing. Wei had never once asked her to trust him. Yet, implicitly, she did, even if she had been wary of him when they first met. It was people like Meng and Windshadow who asked for her trust before destroying it.

A part of her still couldn't help but wonder about their fates now that she had failed to kill the Metal Elemental.

Desert Rose got out of bed and changed into the fresh set of Lettorian-style garments someone had laid out for her—a cotton blouse and fitted riding pants, along with a coat embossed with the Lettorian insignia.

Aside from Meng, there had been no other visitors. Windshadow was nowhere to be found, possibly hiding somewhere to save her own hide, again. A part of Desert Rose wasn't even surprised, though another part struggled with the disappointment of being abandoned yet again by her.

And Wei. Where was Wei? She hadn't seen him since they …

She pushed the memory to the back of her mind, ignoring the unease creeping up her neck as she slipped out of the room. Dawn was just breaking, a soft light on the horizon peeking above the trees. There was no one in sight. The north-western tower was deserted, almost abandoned.

Maybe not quite.

She heard the periodic shriek of a blade being sharpened as she arrived at the ground level. And there, hunched over his worktable, was the Metal Elemental—Chryso, she vaguely remembered someone saying—forging a new weapon with unwavering focus. With his back facing her, he seemed oblivious to her presence.

She inched towards him, hands raised, hoping her power wouldn't fail her at the critical moment.

'King Falco had me inform you that you'll be setting out to the Yarshe Valley in two days,' he said, unperturbed by her arrival. His fingers ran down the length of the sword, letting its rings echo around the chamber. 'Your very first mission for Lettoria.'

She dropped her hands. 'I have no interest in partaking in his war.'

The Metal Elemental set down the sword and turned around to shoot her a flat stare. 'He expected you to say that. He also said you'd come around as soon as you learned that your mission will help Prince Wei in his.'

She snapped to attention. 'Wei?'

He turned back to the blade he was forging. 'He's on his way to Oasis Kingdom as we speak. I set off today with the second contingent. What you do at Yarshe Valley will give us a leg up at the frontline.'

Was Wei really going to help King Falco attack his home kingdom? She understood his desire for revenge—after all, she had sought hers too with the Oasis Emperor when she thought he had orchestrated the coup against her father. But surely Wei knew there were other ways to overthrow a ruler without engaging in head-to-head combat. Why was he putting his life on the line for King Falco?

And he'd left without saying goodbye. That stung the most.

She had to get to the bottom of this. This was not the Wei she knew. Perhaps the Metal Elemental was lying to her. But what would he get out of this?

'What about the rest of them?' she asked. 'Where's Windshadow?'

'Off ambushing some troops in the Palamir Mountains. Prince Meng will stay by King Falco's side as a second strategist.'

In just a week, King Falco had managed to corral them into his war strategy. And now they were all gone, each on their assigned mission. Everything was happening too quickly. Something felt amiss, like a shift in the air signalling an impending desert storm.

'I'm coming with you,' she said. It seemed foolish to be alone with someone who had shot her with a poisoned dart, but she needed to find out what was truly going on. And right now, the Metal Elemental seemed to be the only way for her to get some answers.

He chuckled. 'Oasis Kingdom has a Fire Elemental on their side, according to Windshadow. Trust me, you'd much rather be at Yarshe Valley than on the battlefield.'

The battlefield. Wei was going to be fighting the Oasis Army. To fight Han in person.

Realization struck Desert Rose. King Falco wasn't helping Wei attain the throne; he was sending him to his death. To him, Wei was no more than a weapon and a pawn. And Wei, bent on taking the throne now, was charging to the battlefield blindly.

'You said my mission at Yarshe Valley will affect Wei,' she said.

He nodded. 'You'll be raising the water level in the Yarshe River.'

She frowned. 'That's it?'

He smirked. 'Not too difficult, is it? But by raising the water, you'll be helping to delay—even deter—the Oasis Army from advancing beyond the Red River downstream, giving us a significant advantage in our attack.'

Us. Our. Here was a desert boy who had aligned with Lettoria's purpose. Why would he—an Elemental with phenomenal powers—stay in this godsforsaken place to serve a king to whom he owed no allegiance?

'I don't understand,' she said. 'Why are you doing this? Are you truly content to hole up in this tower and serve a war-hungry king? Don't you have a tribe waiting for you back home?'

He shot her a look. 'I don't know how your tribe handles these greedy, war-mongering nations, but mine was willing to sacrifice me in exchange for their safety when they knew Falco was searching for magically gifted people to join his secret army.' He let out a bitter laugh. 'My brother was the only one who protested, so the Lettorians took him with me.'

'You have a brother?' She had assumed he was a lone orphan just like her and Windshadow.

He paused, looking like he regretted revealing too much. 'Foster. At first, I was relieved to have him along, but I soon realized he was just Falco's way to ensure my obedience.'

Desert Rose felt a pang of sympathy for him. His circumstance was no different from hers—a once-united tribe split apart by western forces like the Lettorians or Sorensteins to become pawns in their war. Lettoria might appear to be more benign than Oasis Kingdom, but sometimes those who painted themselves as the saviours caused the most unimaginable destruction under the pretext of righteousness.

'So he's here?' she asked. 'Your brother, I mean.'

'He's in the Lettorian Army, and I make him armour and weapons.' A note of bitterness laced his voice. 'He is safe there for as long as I remain loyal to King Falco.'

'Why don't you both just escape?'

He shot her an exasperated look 'You think we haven't tried? King Falco is no fool. He keeps us separated at all times. The only way I know he's alive is through Sergeant Vicardi bringing me his armour for fortification. I know it's his by the mark I carved on the breastplate. And this.' From his pants pocket, he pulled out a dirty bronze coin with a square carved out of its middle.

A tracker. Typically forged by tribe shamans harnessing the desert's magic, it was mostly used by parents to keep track of their children in the Khuzar Desert, where one could disappear in the shifting sands if careless. Her father had placed one on her until she came of age at sixteen.

'He has one too,' Chryso went on. 'But the last time he tried to sneak into this tower to find me, he was thrown into prison for a week.' He went back to furiously forging his blade, this time with more determination than before. 'Falco promised that he'll set us free after the battle at Danxi Plains, once we've defeated Oasis Kingdom.' His voice was quiet, as though he had little faith in the king's word but was trying to convince himself of his impending freedom anyway.

Desert Rose watched him pinning all his hopes on his weapons like a lifeline, the quiet desperation in his eyes not unlike the one she felt after leaving Ghost City, and the pang in her chest grew.

'I'll find him,' she blurted.

Chryso snorted. 'Sure you will.'

'I promise I'll find a way to get you both out of here. I just need you to look out for Wei on the battlefield.'

Chryso narrowed his eyes at her. 'Are you trying to strike a deal with me?'

'It's better than the one King Falco made with you,' she said, her heart beating fast. 'Do you really intend to serve him for as long as he keeps your brother hostage?'

He had no reason to trust her, another Elemental that he should want to kill, nor did she trust him to keep Wei safe. But if they could put their misgivings aside, Wei wouldn't be heading into a suicide mission against Han who had an Elemental by his side, and Chryso and his brother could be free of King Falco.

Chryso considered her for a long while, his wide dark eyes illuminated by the glint of weaponry all around them. She could see him calculating the cost and returns of this negotiation.

At last he said, 'His name is Nurlan.'

* * *

It took them a week and a mere stop at a small town on the border of Khuzar Desert before they arrived at the stretch of streaked sandstone peaks, beyond which lay Yarshe Valley.

The journey with the four soldiers was largely uneventful and mostly tense—Desert Rose exchanged barely ten sentences with them along the way, though they watched her like hawks, as though bracing for the moment she would use her powers on them to escape. She had no doubt their pockets were filled with emergency ticha to restrain her if that happened.

But now that they were here at the foot of the hills, their shared exhaustion and wonder at the view before them dissolved the tension among them. A magnificent sunset fell upon the row of jagged hills. Aglow, the crimson stone bodies burnt amber and red, stark against the snowy backdrop of the Palamir Mountains in the distance.

They came to a stop at the base of one of the mounds, where a small cave had been carved into the rock face.

'We'll take a rest here before nightfall,' the leader of their troop said as he dismounted from his steed. 'In the morning, we will go over this hill and through the forest. We should reach the river by late afternoon.'

As they settled into the cave and started a fire, one of the soldiers came over to offer Desert Rose some herbed flatbread and refill her waterskin. She accepted it with a murmur of thanks and settled into a corner to rest.

The last time she was out in the mountains, she and Wei, along with his sister and her family, had fled an uncontrollable fire on Yeli Mountain. Mountains made her feel suffocated, as though she was being walled in, but Wei had made it easier to breathe back then. Was he on the way to Oasis Kingdom now? Was he really prepared to come sword to sword with the Oasis Army, his own people?

She fell into a troubled slumber punctuated by the distant call of wolves and filled with images of Wei's bloodied body on the battlefield, her father's spirit trapped in the Ghost City for eternity.

Throughout her patchy dreams, the river on the other side of the hill—at times ferocious, at times calm and reassuring, like a benevolent beast—beckoned to her.

At dawn, she started awake at the call of a thrush, panicking for a moment at the unfamiliar surroundings before noticing the soldier who had given her food the night before. He crouched before her as though about to wake her up, and straightened when she sat up.

'It's time to leave,' he said, handing her some salted bread and water. His gentle demeanour despite his rough-looking exterior reminded her of Wei.

They set off just as the sun began to peek out from behind the mountain range. Guided by pawprints in the mud and Desert Rose's senses, they made their way to the river.

Fed by the snow-peaked Palamir Mountains, the Yarshe River was nestled in the nook of a sprawling deciduous forest. It was at least ten paces wide and flowed with the fervour of a valiant army. Mist trailed down from the mountains, shrouding the valley in an ethereal cloud.

'Watch out for wolves,' the troop leader said to the other three soldiers as they dismounted from their horses. 'This place is infested with them. Shoot any that you see.' He nodded at Desert Rose. 'Do what you have to do.'

She considered the river. Could she really do this? What would happen downstream if she went through with it?

One of the soldiers—the one who offered her food in the morning—gave her a hand. She hadn't managed to catch his name, but he was the only one who showed any concern for her welfare this whole journey. She held onto him as they made their way down to the river bank. The others kept an eye on them from behind, bows poised to take down anything that interrupted them.

'Be careful,' said the soldier. 'I've seen what Elemental magic can do to you.'

'You've seen it?'

'My brother possesses abilities of his own. A power larger than he can wield. It is both a blessing and a curse, from what I see.'

Realization settled in her. 'You're Nurlan.' Older and rougher around the edges, with an air of that solemnity that was the complete opposite of Chryso's flippancy, he was certainly not how she expected Chryso's brother to be.

Nurlan blinked in surprise. 'You know me?'

'Chryso told me about you.'

A sad smile curved around his lips. 'That's just the name King Falco gave him. His real name is Ruslan.'

In the distance, a hawk let out a wild shriek that sounded like a warning. The horses stamped their hooves, eager to leave.

'Hurry up,' the troop leader called from behind.

Nurlan helped her find her footing on a rock right next to the river. The grass was slick, and reeds bowed to the force of the river. Desert Rose tried to calm her racing heart and focus on the water at her feet, drawing on its strength. It was wilful, untamed, but she had a lot more control over her element these days.

The plaintive howl of a wolf made her jump, breaking her focus. She glanced around for a sign of predators. The trees were still. Yet, nothing was serene. The animals were getting restless. Was it because of her power? She was here disrupting the lifeblood of this forest, after all.

She turned back to the river, pushing aside her misgivings. She had to do this, for Wei. It was the least she could do to protect him if he was going to throw himself head-first into battle.

She closed her eyes, forcing herself to be alone with the water. Every sound faded into the background. As the water began to respond to her, the familiar tingle rushed to her fingertips, and a buzz spread through her body. It was joy; it was ecstasy—a heady lightness that could take her up to the heavens, something she had never felt before ever since she discovered this elemental affinity.

Someone gasped behind her. She ignored it, still revelling in the sensation of her power flowing through her.

Somewhere close by, another cry of an animal echoed through the valley. More joined in, crescendoing into a cacophony backed by the roar of water.

She opened her eyes at last.

A wall of water almost twice as tall as her was gushing past her, crashing over the rocky riverbed and starting to flood the banks. Her outstretched hands trembled, partly from exertion and partly from the staggering sight.

Shouts rang out around her, breaking her reverie. She whipped around to find a pack of wolves stalking towards the soldiers. The men had their bows loaded and poised to shoot, but it was clear they were outnumbered.

'Stay here,' Nurlan told her. Gripping his sword, he charged towards the wolves before she could protest.

She stepped back from the bank, reeling from the strain of accomplishing the feat. That was when the pain struck her, bringing her to her knees. All these months of practising had made the blowback from using her power more manageable, but she had never attempted something as complex as this ever since she conjured a water platform to flee Oasis Capital.

Bile rose in her throat. She began to shake uncontrollably. Something was amiss. This went beyond the regular dizziness and exhaustion. Her body felt like it was revolting against her, ripping itself up from within.

She gasped for air, clawing at the grass until a low, ragged snarl caught her attention.

She looked up to find herself staring straight into the golden eyes of a grey wolf. It watched her, hackles raised and teeth bared, ready to lunge at her. Her body was too weak to even hold itself up, much less reach for the stray sword lying just three feet away.

Next to them, the river continued gushing, its roar drowning out the voices of the soldiers. Would they even hear her if she called for help?

She lowered her gaze and inched away, conveying no harm, but the wolf only crept even closer. In the distance, the anguished cries of the soldiers rang out along with the shrieks of horses.

The wolf pounced.

On reflex, she squeezed her eyes shut and threw out her hands, gathering every last shred of energy in her to create a water barrier between them. But she felt only the weight of the animal on her, its coarse fur brushing against her skin, its hot, rancid breath fanning her neck. She braced herself for the attack.

Something whistled through the air. Then came the unmistakable sound of an arrow striking flesh and bone. The wolf whimpered and toppled over. Desert Rose cracked open her eyes to find an arrow wedged in its skull. She sat upright, glancing around wildly for her rescuer.

Less than ten feet away stood Wei. He rushed towards her and helped her up. 'I leave you for a few days and you raise hell.'

'Wei,' she rasped, still struggling to catch her breath. Her nausea had only gotten worse. 'What are you doing here?'

'I'll explain later, but right now we need to get you away from this river.' He peered at her face, noticing her distress. 'What's wrong?'

A second wolf, dark as night, stepped out from the thickening mist and appeared behind Wei.

'Look out!' she cried.

Wei spun around just as it leaped at him and sank its fangs into his shoulder. He let out a cry as he tumbled to the ground with the animal. Desert Rose pulled out her knives from her waist belt, ready to return Wei the favour, but with him wrestling with the animal, there was no way to ensure she would strike the right target.

Neither beast nor man gave in. Wei's blood stained the grass as they rolled down towards the river bank. Desert Rose could only watch, helpless in her debilitated state. She could quell the water and subdue it to minimize the impact on Wei. But this time, her body fought against her magic when she tried to call upon it. Where magic used to fill up every vein and vessel in her like a warm balm, it now burnt and stung. Something was awfully wrong.

When at last Wei managed to throw the wolf off him, an arrow shot out of nowhere and struck the beast square in its chest. It fell into the river with a heavy splash and was immediately carried away downstream.

Nurlan dashed over to her. He set his bow down on the grass and tried to pick her up, but she pointed at Wei lying by the river bank.

'Help him, please,' she said. Nurlan nodded, then went to collect Wei.

She got up on shaky feet, letting out a sigh of relief when she saw Wei stand up with Nurlan's help.

There were no more wolves in sight, as far as she could tell, but it was impossible to guess how many more were lurking in the forest. Almost all the horses were dead, save for one stuck by the river it was unable to cross, and so were all the soldiers.

Desert Rose tried to calm the beast, stroking it until it was no longer jittery. She ripped off a portion of her outer skirt as Nurlan helped Wei over, then bandaged his shoulder as quickly as she could, ignoring the way Wei was watching her, worry etched on his face.

'Find a safe place to hide,' Nurlan said, handing her the reins to the horse when she was done. 'The nearest cave from here or something. I will catch up when I can.'

'No,' Desert Rose said. 'We go together.'

'This horse cannot bear all of us,' Nurlan said. 'I'm under orders to protect you at all costs. Go and seek shelter. You're both in no state to—'

'When will you ever learn to put yourself before others, brother?' another voice cut in.

Another horse in Lettorian chainmail armour broke through the fog. Its rider's gaze was fixed on Nurlan as he pulled to a stop before them.

Nurlan gasped. 'Ruslan. What—how did you...?'

The Metal Elemental pulled out the tracking coin, flashing his brother a wry smile. 'Are you hurt?' Nurlan shook his head. 'Then let's go.' He offered his brother a hand, but Nurlan did not budge.

'Surely you couldn't have come here on Falco's orders. He wouldn't—'

'Of course not. But there was no better chance to come and find you.'

'Oh, Ruslan,' Nurlan sighed.

Ruslan shook his proffered hand, insistent. 'Come on, we don't have time. Let's at least find a safe place to hide for now.'

Desert Rose and Wei shared a look. Whatever they needed to catch each other up on would have to wait. Wei helped her up the horse, then hoisted himself behind her and took the reins.

'You're injured,' she said. 'Let me ride.'

'I'm fine.' The bandage around his shoulder was already soaked in blood and his jaw was clenched against the pain, but he nudged the horse into action and rode single-handedly.

'I don't want you dying on me before we get out of this place,' she said, taking over the reins from him. 'Hold tight.'

He hesitated for a moment. The horse lurched, jolting them forward. Wei flung his good arm around her waist on reflex. He muttered an apology but was reluctant to withdraw his arm. She held it there. The warmth of his hand on her waist took her back to that evening on the balcony, and she was glad she had her back to him now so he couldn't see her face on fire.

'We ride south,' Nurlan said as he steered his horse closer to them. Behind him, the Metal Elemental shot Wei a loaded look, the recognition that they had both abandoned their posts to be here. 'The forest is less dense there and we can probably find a cave to spend the night.'

Desert Rose nodded. The setting sun spilled its last rays between the peaks of the Palamir Mountains in the distance. There was no chance of them leaving this valley before nightfall. The forest was still restless, rustling and swaying as the mist thickened into fog. Save for the dead body a few paces away, the other soldiers who accompanied her were nowhere in sight.

As the effects of her power began to subside in her, so did the raging river. The water returned to its original cadence, splashing along as though it hadn't experienced a major supernatural disruption at the hands of an Elemental. Yet, a sense of discomfort continued to nag at her.

They cantered down the river, the brothers taking the lead. Every little sound made them tense up, but they only rode faster, keeping their eyes peeled for predators. The sense of foreboding trailed after them, a silent companion. She had done something to the river that felt unnatural, and her body was feeling its effects too.

She wanted to ask Wei how he had managed to find her, what the repercussions were for what he had done, and what sort of deal he had made with King Falco. But when a pair of wolves—one russet and one grey—stepped out from behind a tree, all her questions were left abandoned.

The wolves pounced at them in tandem.

Desert Rose yanked on the reins to swerve the horse away from them. 'Take the reins,' she told Wei. 'I'll use my magic to—'

'No,' he said at once. 'You need to stop using your magic for now or you might die.'

'What?'

But he was too busy unsheathing his sword to explain further. He pulled her close to him and swung his blade out at the russet wolf as it made another dive for her. The wolf collapsed midway through the air and landed before them with a hard thump.

The grey one attacked almost simultaneously, teeth bared. Desert Rose threw out a hand, hoping that her magic would not fail her. Nothing. No energy flow, no comforting warmth. Instead, her taking a hand off the reins only made the horse buck and whinny.

A warning shout made them both whip around. Nurlan was doubling back for them, steering his horse towards the wolf as Ruslan's blade arced through the air. It sliced across the wolf's flank before sinking deep into its chest.

The wolf crumpled to the ground with a whimper. A moment later, it fell still.

Ruslan reached down to extract his sword as Nurlan asked, 'Are you both okay?'

She nodded. The Metal Elemental watched her with an inscrutable look, saying nothing. Before she could thank him, he turned away and sheathed his sword. It would have been so easy to let her die just now—it would be one less Elemental for him to compete with—but he had saved her. Why? And could she bring herself to kill him when the time came?

She pushed the thought to the back of her mind—she would worry about the bridge when she came to it. She nudged her horse into action again, but another thought crossed her mind.

'What was that you said earlier?' she asked Wei. 'About me potentially dying if I use my magic?'

His brows formed a grim line. 'The poison is still inside you. Falco didn't have it removed entirely. If you continue to use your magic, not only can it kill you, it would also poison everything that you touch—including this river.'

She froze. 'What?'

That explained the abnormal response her body had. An Elemental's magic was supposed to work in harmony with its respective element, not against it. What she did was not harnessing the river; it was distressing it. The river wasn't working with her; it was revolting against her.

Her grip on the reins tightened. The horse slowed in response. She nudged it again to speed it up. 'But Chryso—I mean Ruslan—said raising the river will help protect you and the troops against attacks from the Oasis troops downstream.'

'He left out the fact that once your magic came into contact with the river, it would poison the river.' His voice was flat. 'It's a preemptive strike against the Oasis Army before the actual battle.'

Cold fear slid down her back.

The Yarshe River was the bloodline of the tribes, nations, cities, towns, and villages that had settled along its long winding body. What would happen to the millions of people who lived along its tributaries, who relied on it for survival and their livelihood? What had she done?

'You knew Falco was planning this and you didn't stop him?' she said.

'I came as soon as I could, didn't I?' he retorted. 'Besides, my hands are tied now when it comes to Falco. The flooding of the river will give the troops an advantage, that's for certain.'

She stared at him. 'Innocent people will die because of me!'

Nurlan turned around to glance at them.

'Will you keep your voice down please?' Wei hissed. 'Or are you trying to attract more wolves?' She kept silent, waiting for his answer. 'There are losses in every war. We need to look at the big picture.'

'The big picture,' she echoed in disbelief. 'So civilian lives are unimportant as long as you get your revenge on your brother?'

'That's not what—' He shook his head. 'Let's talk about this later.'

Something was different in him these days. In the time they had spent apart, had he become someone she didn't recognize anymore? The Wei she knew would spend a whole evening guilt-ridden about killing an imperial scout. He would even shed tears over his abusive father. Why was he being so callous now?

'Who are you?' she asked.

His gaze was unapologetic. 'Someone trying to keep you alive.'

'I hate to interrupt your lover's squabble,' Ruslan called from the front, sounding more bored than contrite, 'but we've found a place we can stay for the night.' He gestured to his left. 'Cave behind that tree.'

Desert Rose and Wei dismounted as quickly as they could, eager to put some distance between them for now.

The cave was nestled behind a dense bush next to a massive oak tree with a crown of auburn leaves. They followed the brothers inside, their weapons drawn in case it was inhabited by wolves. But the cave was empty, dry, and appeared to be a suitable abode for the night.

'Well,' Ruslan said, noticing the tension between Desert Rose and Wei. 'Too bad we don't have Elementals here who can help start a fire,' he joked.

No one cracked a smile.

'Let's go collect some firewood, brother,' Nurlan said.

'And some yarrow or Heaven's Balm if you can find them,' Desert Rose said, eyeing Wei's wound. She reached over to tighten the bandage and pressed a hand over it, ignoring Wei's gaze resting on her.

Nurlan nodded, then dragged Ruslan out before he could say anything more.

Desert Rose and Wei watched them leave, waiting until their footsteps faded into the distance before they could no longer ignore each other. They regarded each other in silence, their last argument standing between them like an unwanted guest.

'You should rest,' Wei said at last. He led her to the wall and they sat side by side against it.

A wave of weariness came over her, and she realized just how hungry and tired she was. She glanced at Wei and found the same exhaustion on his face. In spite of everything, they were together again. And in spite of everything, a part of her was thankful for that.

She reached out to touch his bandaged shoulder, wincing when her hand came away bloodstained. She ripped off another portion of her outer skirt and set about changing his soiled bandages.

'Okay,' she said. 'Tell me everything I've missed.'

TWENTY-THREE

Wei

Wei watched as Desert Rose unwrapped his bandages with careful fingers, her attention fixed on the wound as she waited for his response. It reminded him of the time they met each other in the desert, when he helped her purge sand-hound venom from her arm where she had been bitten.

They sat next to each other, their knees almost touching, and it almost felt like old times, when they would huddle close and tell each other stories from home and their travels.

But then he recalled that look on her face. For the briefest moment, she had regarded him almost like a stranger, as though she no longer knew him.

Who are you? she had asked.

I'm still me, he had almost blurted. *Still Wei. Your Wei.*

Did he still have the right to say that, now that they were no longer on the same page when it came to the war? Had things changed between them irrevocably since he left on the expedition with the Lettorian troops, when he chose to help King Falco destroy the Wall that protected Oasis Kingdom? His father had always branded him as a traitor to his people and his home, once declaring that he cared about no one but himself. Maybe he was right.

But he wasn't doing this purely to satisfy his desire for revenge, nor did he wish to see his home kingdom descend into chaos. If taking down the Wall meant that he could stop Han before his cruel reign commenced, then he would make the same decision all over again.

He told her everything. About the conversation he had with King Falco over dinner and the interruption in the northwest tower. About the plan to lure Han out to the battlefield at Danxi Plains by taking down the Wall and poisoning the Yarshe River upstream. And finally, about the king using Desert Rose's life to ensure he stayed in line, and the poison still inside her body.

It was a relief to have everything out in the open at last, out of earshot of the king's aides. Desert Rose was the first and only person he had opened up to completely—one who had witnessed him at his most vulnerable. Not even Zeyan, Yong, or his mother had been privy to the thoughts and emotions he kept a tight lid on. They had never seen him cry over his father's death, listened to his accounts of growing up with Han, or seen him beam with pride at his half-sister who had gone to live with the shouren in Yeli Mountain. Only Desert Rose had. And regardless of what her response would be, coming clean with her felt right. He watched her gather her thoughts, feeling strangely disarmed by her softening gaze.

'So you mean to say,' she said, 'that you know Falco is using you as a pawn to defeat Han, but you don't care?'

'I'm saying I have to go along with his plans for now, but I'm aware of the risks.'

She frowned in disapproval but did not press the issue. 'So what happens now? What do you plan to do?'

'I need to rejoin the troops. I can't be gone too long or they'll report back to Falco.'

She shook her head. 'Why are you putting your life on the line like this? There are other ways to take down your brother.'

'Don't you understand? As long as the poison is still inside you, Falco has all the power. He can activate the poison anytime I step out of line. So if he wants me on the battlefield, I'll have to be on the battlefield.'

'He never intended to help you become emperor though,' she reminded him.

'I know that. But I can't do anything that would make him doubt my loyalty. Coming here was a risk, but I had to make sure you were okay. I've seen what the poison can do to you. If you continued to use your powers back there, you could have died.'

Her brows furrowed in confusion. 'So you're doing all this—fighting in his war, walking right into Han's hands—just to keep me alive?'

His lips curled into a sad smile. 'Just? There is no just when it comes to you.'

Her breath caught. She turned her attention back to the bandage, fastening it mutely, though she did not remove her hands from his arm when she was done.

He only realized what he had said when the words had settled between them, but he felt no uncertainty this time. No panic to retract his words in case she backed away. It felt good to leave that statement out in the open at last, to finally release what he had known for a while but didn't dare voice.

The sound of their breathing seemed to fill up the entire cave, and the space between them grew narrower with each passing moment.

When she looked up at him again, her eyes reminded him of the sky that hung above them the night they kissed—calm, vast, and moonlit. A sky you could write the future in. He leaned in, inhaling her familiar scent. She shifted closer too, ready for his lips to find hers again. He brought his hand to her cheek, feeling the heat in her soft skin.

Someone cleared his throat, making them both jerk apart.

'Sorry to interrupt,' Ruslan said, sounding anything but sorry as he dropped the gathered wood in a pile at his feet.

Wei glared at him. 'Impeccable timing.'

Ruslan smirked.

Behind him, Nurlan shot them an apologetic look as he set down two waterskins and a pile of berries wrapped in leaves. He handed Desert Rose a pouch filled with the herbs she had asked for. 'This should be enough to clean up his wounds for now.'

Wei glanced at Desert Rose, who murmured a word of thanks and accepted the items. She had restrained herself from using her magic to produce water that could wash his wounds, now that she knew she was still poisoned.

'It's less than a week to Danxi Plains,' Ruslan said, as Desert Rose cleaned Wei's wound with water. 'We can catch up with the troops in time if we set off at dawn and ride fast.'

Wei frowned. 'We meaning?'

'Her, you, and I.'

Wei shifted in protest. Desert Rose made him sit back down. 'I thought Falco's use for Rose ended at Yarshe Valley,' he said. 'Why would he want her on the battlefield when her magic doesn't work now?'

Nurlan busied himself with starting a fire. *He knows something,* Wei thought.

'In case you haven't noticed, Falco lies,' Ruslan said. 'His intention was always to get the Elementals and his super army to fight in his war. Oasis Kingdom has robust defences and its own Elemental—sending regular men to fight would be sending them to their deaths.'

Wei winced as Desert Rose sprinkled the crushed herbs onto his wound. Everything Falco did took them one step closer to the battle at Danxi Plains. Right where he wanted them. But to what end?

'No,' he said. 'It's too dangerous. Rose doesn't have the same advantage as the other Elementals in this war.'

'Are you going against Falco's orders then?' Ruslan pointed at Desert Rose. 'She's still poisoned.'

Desert Rose paused in tying up the bandage to glare at him. 'You're the one who shot me with that dart. Can't you reverse the effects?'

'I don't hold the antidote, Falco does.' He raised his brows. 'Bold of you to ask a fellow Elemental to save your life, by the way.'

'You did once.'

He shrugged. 'Moment of weakness.' Ruslan paused. 'There's a reason why Falco wants us on the battlefield, and it's not just to fight against Oasis Kingdom.'

Nurlan shot him a warning look. 'Ruslan…'

He ignored his brother and went on. 'Falco needs us to unlock the Immortal Spring. Only an Elemental can do that.'

Of course, King Falco was after the spring too. Which ruler wouldn't be tempted by the prospect of eternal life and the cure for all mortal woes? Wei had once sought the elusive spring himself, if only to gain some leverage in negotiating for his mother's exoneration, but only fools hoped to gain control over a remnant of the gods. Falco was no fool, but he was ambitious, and ambitious men were the most dangerous of all.

'I'm not going to help some power-hungry king unlock the spring,' Desert Rose said, as fiery as the flame that Nurlan had finally managed to kindle.

'Unfortunately, we don't have a choice and Falco knows it. He knows about the prophecy, and that we have to get to the spring or die trying. So he's giving us a chance to fight it out among ourselves like dogs in a ring, and then have the winner unlock the spring. Once we do that, he'll swoop in and take over the spring for himself.' He leaned back and tossed a stray leaf into the fire. It sizzled instantly.

'Falco doesn't even know where the Immortal Spring is,' Wei pointed out. 'No one does.'

'Not yet, maybe. But he's been eyeing Prince Meng's stones—the ones he stole from a Dugur tribesman. I bet he's already gotten his hands on them by now.'

'The Elder Stones!' Desert Rose turned to Wei sharply. 'That's what Prince Meng got Golsha to steal from the tribe, from Papa. Papa used to tell me the stones held a very important clue, but he never explained further. They were passed down to him when he became chieftain. If a chieftain lost possession of them, that was grounds for him to be overthrown ….' Her gaze drifted away.

Wei recalled the conversation he overheard between Meng and the ex-Dugur tribe member last winter, where Meng revealed that he had commissioned the latter to steal the stones. In the commotion that ensued after that, Wei and Desert Rose had forgotten about that exchange, but it only showed how long Meng had been searching for the spring and the lengths he would go to find it.

Wei shook his head. 'It's too dangerous,' he said again. 'Your magic is unstable now. You saw what it almost did to you back there.'

'If she stays away from the battlefield, Falco has her blood tracked and can easily activate the antidote,' Ruslan said. 'She has at least a fighting chance if she goes, provided she doesn't use her magic.'

Wei and Desert Rose sat in stunned silence. To think Falco had managed to manipulate them so thoroughly that they were now backed into this corner. They should have known better than to trust the Lettorian king. They should have known that he never intended to make a fair deal, only use them both.

'You knew this all along,' Desert Rose said at last. 'You both did.' Nurlan at least had the decency to look remorseful, but Ruslan only shrugged.

'Every Elemental for himself,' he said.

'And you intend to help him, after what he's done to you and your brother?' she asked.

He shot her a withering look. 'I have no interest in playing Falco's game. He promised that our service to him would end after we got everyone to the battlefield.'

'You're abandoning the Lettorian army?' Desert Rose asked.

'It's not abandoning if I never belonged there. I was just a weapon Falco stole from my tribe. Besides, you and I are Elementals—we're meant for a greater destiny.'

A greater destiny. It was a thought that had sat in the back of Wei's mind ever since he learnt of Desert Rose's identity. She was destined for much bigger things, and the gap between them grew wider with each step she took towards fulfilling the prophecy.

What future did he, a mere mortal who had to seek his purpose in an otherwise aimless life, have with not just a Damohai, a descendant of immortals, but an Elemental who was destined to restore stability between heaven and earth? They were walking on different paths that would eventually lead them further away from each other.

He shouldn't have kissed her, shouldn't have given in to his feelings. He was only starting something that had no end—he would just be holding her back from her purpose, making the inevitable separation that much harder.

Desert Rose glanced over at him, almost as though she could hear his thoughts, but said nothing. She once told him that she didn't believe in the notion of destiny, but perhaps destiny would end up having its way with them in the end.

'I'm assuming you have a reason for telling us this now,' Wei said.

'Like I said, I have no interest in being Falco's pawn.' He turned his gleaming eyes to Desert Rose. 'What do you say we form a temporary alliance?'

* * *

Dawn crept up on them like a gentle woodland creature. Outside, a cool morning mist drifted in, bringing with it the scent of birch trees. Wei roused to the muffled clang of blades outside. Next to him, Desert Rose was still sound asleep, which meant the brothers were training with each other at the crack of dawn.

He considered letting her sleep. Perhaps if she couldn't catch up with them at Danxi Plains, she would miss the battle and stay out of danger—the danger of using her magic, of going along with Ruslan's cracked plan.

They hadn't agreed to anything yet. Ruslan had told Desert Rose to mull over his proposition last night, and unlike before, Wei and Desert Rose didn't make their decision jointly.

Wei didn't trust the brothers, even if they had saved their lives the day before. The only reason they did that was so they could use them when the time came—just like King Falco had been using them all along. One was an Elemental that had to kill Desert Rose or be killed himself, and the other was part of the Lettorian Army. Wherever their loyalties lay, it wasn't with him and Desert Rose.

But of course, Desert Rose didn't have much of a choice. Caught between her destiny and her duty to her tribe, she had only one path to take, at least for now.

She stirred before he could wake her. Noticing him, she sat up at once, rubbing her bleary eyes.

'How are you feeling?' he asked.

She looked marginally better than yesterday, when her magic rebelled against her. In fact, she was already raring to go, putting out the embers and gathering their scant belongings. There was a restlessness in her, an impulsiveness that he witnessed last winter after she'd been told her father was killed.

She was going to fling whatever she had left—her magic, her life— in a last-ditch attempt to save her tribe and free her father.

Outside, the brothers ended their duelling practice and returned to the cave sheathing their swords.

'Ready?' Ruslan asked.

Wei kept silent, waiting for Desert Rose's reply, hoping he had misread the reckless determination in her eyes.

She glanced at Wei and took a deep breath. 'I'm ready.'

To Wei, it felt like the beginning of the end.

TWENTY-FOUR

Windshadow

Windshadow dovetailed through the rocky mountain range and wove through the misty forest, leaving Lazar far, far behind before he could react.

Would the Fire Elemental attempt to follow or capture her? Would he report back to Emperor Han? Either way, there was no stopping her on her way back to Lettoria. Lazar would not leave Emperor Han's side until she had tracked down the Earth Elemental, which meant that joining him would be to offer herself to Han in the meantime. Frankly, she would rather die than ally with that odious man.

Palamir Mountain was a labyrinth of ragged snow-covered peaks, rocky outcrops, and alpine forests, each one looking exactly like the last. She went in circles several times before weaving through a wall of conifers and emerging into open air at last. She cursed herself for the time wasted.

It was apparent now why King Falco had dispatched her here, while also sending everyone else who could possibly help Meng out of Lettoria. It was so Meng would be left completely on his own without any backup or help, especially from her. So Meng could offer no aid to the Elementals when they took their places on the battlefield. It was to keep all of them—Desert Rose, the princes and her—apart so that they were easier to eliminate when the time was ripe.

The journey back to Lettoria was taking too long to complete in her elemental form, especially after that duel with Lazar, but she forced herself to press on.

Night crept in just after she left the mountains behind, forcing her to seek shelter. A part of her wanted to return to the desert, to become one with the dry, dusty air again, to catch a glimpse of the home she had left behind. It had been years since she left her tribe, and just as long since she settled anywhere. What would it be like for her feet to finally touch ground for good instead of always letting herself be carried away by the wind?

She pushed away that notion before it could take root. She was the wind. Sentimentality was for fools; she hadn't survived this long to let it get the best of her now.

She charged forward, harnessing all the energy she could gather from the air, and all the rage and determination she could find within her. She was the Air Elemental, and she would no longer just survive. She would triumph.

* * *

Night had fallen over Lettoria by the time she found Meng in the dungeon under the palace's northwest tower. She had drugged the unsuspecting guards at the entrance, but breaking a prisoner out of Lettoria would be a greater challenge.

There was no sign of light or life in the dank depths of the dungeon. To detect Meng's exact location, she could only rely on her heightened senses in her elemental form. But she found him at last in a tiny cell in a corner of the dungeon.

He seemed just as surprised to see her there as she was. After all, she had a larger mission to fulfil, and it wasn't in this dingy prison. But, she reminded herself that she wasn't here out of misplaced loyalty or affection—she was here to repay her debt. Many moons ago, he had saved her from execution for being part of a rebel faction. In exchange, she had helped him get on the throne. Their relationship had always been a transactional one—neither could succeed without the other's help—and her reneging on her end of the deal would only throw this dynamic out of balance.

Meng hurried over to the bars. 'What are you doing here?'

'Seemed like bad karma to leave my benefactor to rot in a foreign prison cell,' she said. Without his help, she wouldn't have survived her sentence back then, or trained at the House of Night, or learnt the inner workings of the imperial court. She also wouldn't have gotten this far in finding the spring.

And, although she was reluctant to admit it, Desert Rose was right when she guessed that Windshadow was capable of caring about something other than her own survival. Despite herself, despite all the wrongs she had suffered as a 'different child' in her tribe, she still cared about it and, along with that, the fate of her people. (Well, some of them, anyway.) And she was here now because she believed deep down that Meng was the right person to rule Oasis Kingdom, to bring peace to the region, between the desert tribes and the surrounding nations.

'It's too late,' Meng murmured, looking especially forlorn behind those bars. She hated the defeat in his voice. Hated that he had allowed this to happen. 'They're already on their way to the Darklands. To the spring.'

'Why did you give it to him?' she demanded. 'It was the only leverage you had.'

'I had to find a way to get the antidote for Desert Rose.'

She shot him a look of annoyance. 'Don't you think your guilt is getting a little out of control? You're not the one who poisoned her.'

'It's not to assuage my guilt, Windshadow. It's to *save her life.*'

Windshadow understood what he meant at last. It wasn't just guilt that wracked him; the fool was in love.

You would have done the same, a small voice piped up in her head. No, she snapped mentally. She wouldn't. She would have looked at the big picture and acted accordingly.

She responded with a withering look. 'You do realize she's an Elemental? She's destined to die either way—whether it's getting killed by another Elemental or winning the race and earning a glorified death by ascending to Heaven … or however the story goes.'

His smile was sad. 'It was worth a shot.'

'That's your problem, Fourth Prince. You let your emotions run the show these days.' She surveyed the lock. It would require considerable effort to break it.

'Even if we find the spring, there's no stopping them from finding it too, and there's no stopping the war—'

'You're a walking sack of optimism, Fourth Prince. Has anyone ever told you that?' Windshadow said, gesturing for him to step back from the gate. He obliged, flinching when she flung out a whip of wind at the lock sharp enough to break it. It fell to the ground with a clang.

Meng stepped out through the gate. 'I haven't finished. Since the war will happen, and they will find the spring eventually, we'll just have to defeat them at their own game.'

Windshadow felt a smile creep back on her face. This sounded like the old Meng. Brilliant, unpredictable, still but deep like a lake.

'It's not over yet,' she agreed. 'Not until the last Elemental falls. And maybe not even then.'

She held out her hand and he took it. It almost felt like old times again. With a deep breath, she shifted into her elemental form and swept them both out of the northwest tower. They had a spring to find, a war to participate in, and a destiny to play out.

The most efficient attack is a swift and silent one. An army of twenty can defeat that of a hundred as long as there is the element of surprise.

—*The War Handbook,* by Lu Cao

TWENTY-FIVE

Desert Rose

The journey out of Yarshe Valley ended much sooner than Desert Rose had expected.

It was much faster—and safer—to arrive at their destinations by taking to the flat open plains than through the valley, so they crossed the river again and cut through the forest from where they came. With two of them still recuperating from their injuries, the journey was slow-going, and they spent two days picking their way out of the valley after emerging from the cave.

The brothers rode ahead, bantering nonstop while navigating through the forest. Desert Rose and Wei followed their trail, decidedly more sombre as they rode side by side, each lost in their own thoughts, each aware of the danger the other would be heading towards after they left the valley. Underneath the renewed sense of purpose, there was also an air of finality that neither of them wanted to acknowledge. The possibility that this might be the last time they saw each other. The last time they rode next to each other. The last time they were able to say whatever they had buried in their hearts.

The forest grew sparser the further behind they left the valley, the canopy thinning overhead to reveal more of the cerulean midday sky.

Finally, they came to the edge of the forest, where sunlight threw the crimson-streaked cliff faces into stark relief.

She could tell Wei was just as reluctant for the journey to end so soon. The closer they got to the end of the forest, the slower he rode. At last, they came to a stop under a birch tree and dismounted.

They stood facing each other, neither of them able to find the words.

She broke the silence first. 'I will see you on the battlefield.' It sounded like a promise. 'Don't do anything stupid until I get there.' It sounded almost like a plea.

Wei flashed her his wry smile. 'I should be the one saying that.'

She matched his smile, staring deep into his eyes. His gaze roamed all over her face, as though he was trying to memorize every inch of it. Everything she meant to say dissipated into the morning mist.

He seemed to be struggling to find the right words too. What could she say to someone who had gone through life and death and grief and loss with her, accompanied her in the dark, and fought alongside her? Ever since they left Oasis Kingdom, she hadn't felt all alone against the will of the gods, against all odds in her mission to save her tribe, because he had been by her side the whole time. She realized only now how accustomed she had grown to his unwavering presence.

There was no telling what might happen once they parted ways here.

His hand shot out, but landed gently on her face, against her cheek, pulling her towards him as he leaned closer. The familiar proximity of his breath against hers, the heat in their skin, made her heart race. But this time, she relished the sensations.

This time, his kiss was urgent. There was no hesitation in it, no doubt, only conviction and a note of desperation. His lips tasted like longing and sorrow, and she wanted more than anything to remain in this sun-dappled corner of the forest, where the rest of the world didn't seem to matter, where she wasn't an Elemental burdened with a destiny and he wasn't on the path to vengeance and rebellion. Here, they could just be a desert girl and a lost prince who found each other in the wild.

They parted slowly, leaning their foreheads against each other as they collected themselves.

Wei straightened and reached for his waist belt. He pulled out a pair of double knives and spun them slowly in his hands before handing them to her. 'Here, I got these for you.'

They were exquisite, with mother-of-pearl hilts and curved Katari steel blades that fit right against each other. The carvings on them were forged in a style distinctive of the south-western region and the hilts sat perfectly in her hands.

She gripped the knives and looked up at Wei. 'I love these. Thank you.'

If only she had something to offer back. But the attack by Yarshe River had made her lose most of her belongings. She tucked the knives in her boots and untied the hemp bracelet around her wrist, the one that Anar Zel once gave her for protection.

She reached for his hand, then pushed up his sleeve and knotted the bracelet around his right wrist. 'I'm counting on this to keep you safe.'

He stared down at it, a small smile playing on his lips.

'Come on, children. War waits for no one,' Ruslan piped up from a few feet away.

Desert Rose and Wei both turned to shoot him identical dirty looks.

'Can you believe I have to be stuck on the same horse with that guy?' Wei muttered.

Desert Rose sent him a sympathetic look. 'May you have the patience to not push him off midway.'

Nurlan was already on the ground, his makeshift bag hitched, ready to go his intended way. Desert Rose would share the horse with him for a day before dropping him off at the nearest desert town. He would be a defector, but by the time Falco learnt of his disappearance, Nurlan would hopefully be back with his people and Falco would be too preoccupied with the war to hunt him down. And hopefully, when all that was over, the brothers would reunite in the desert again.

Hopefully, Nurlan had said multiple times last night when they went over the plan.

'Remember our meeting place, brother,' Ruslan called. 'Don't be late.'

Nurlan nodded, then climbed up the horse. He offered Desert Rose a hand. 'Come on.'

She got on the horse with his help and took the reins. With one final nod at Wei, she rode off, ready to dive back into the desert once again.

* * *

The journey to the Darklands was fraught with the same dangers as the last.

Nurlan had insisted on following her there even after she had dropped him off at the nearby desert town and swapped her horse for a camel while stocking up on rations. It wasn't until she reminded him that King Falco and Lettorian soldiers might be at the Darklands too that he grudgingly agreed to stick to the plan. Chaos would soon descend upon the desert, and he was the only one who could warn his people.

It had been a while since she travelled through the desert alone. The last time she did so was last winter, before she stumbled into Wei's camp with Bataar's poisoned dart wedged in her thigh. Being here alone again filled her with the same rush of fear and exhilaration, even more so now that she carried within her a polluted magic. Magic that not only made the sands stir restlessly but would also kill her if she employed it in any way. All she had left to defend herself were her two pairs of double knives.

Just like old times, she thought. Life was much simpler before she discovered her power, before she learnt that she was an Elemental. All she relied on were her knives, which never failed her. Well, except for that time at the Darklands where Anar Zel had to rescue them from desert ghouls.

Now, the tribe matriarch was not around to save her. Nor Wei and his crew, her father and her tribespeople. She was on her own, and she had to make this work.

She had little leverage with the Ghost King now that her magic was unusable, but she had made a deal with him. As long as she survived as the last Elemental and freed them all from their purgatory, she could walk away without a scratch and have her father back. But in her current condition, there was no way she would survive the war between Lettoria and Oasis Kingdom without some extra help. If the Ghost King wanted her to fulfil her promise, then he would need to lend her some assistance.

She held back a snort. Bargaining with the Ghost King. Had anyone ever succeeded in doing that and lived to tell the tale?

She would find out.

She referred once more to the scuffed brass compass Nurlan had given her before they parted ways. It was impossible to tell where she was. All around her, dunes rolled for as far as the eye could see.

Darkness closed in on her as dust in the air gathered. Beneath her, the sands skittered like a living thing. Her camel brayed, restless and anxious despite her attempts to soothe it. Silence enveloped her like a smothering cloud.

It soon became impossible to tell in which direction she was going. A frenzied chittering noise rose from the ground, as though a thousand creatures were stirring underneath. *Stay calm, Rose,* she told herself. She would not leave until she had accomplished what she had set out to do here.

Then she spotted it. Emanating from the ground a soft greenish glow, as though a rare gemstone lay buried underneath. She coaxed her camel towards it, ignoring the trail of chittering that seemed to follow her.

A few feet to her left, something sprang from the ground—a shadow that rose to inhuman heights—and a shriek ripped through the silence.

She ignored the commotion around her and got off her camel, focused on finding the spot where the sand was coarser than anywhere else. Her tribespeople had taught her the trick to finding the opening to the underground stairwell the last time she was here. Her feet roamed the ground around her until they finally tapped on a hollow spot. A pearly sliver of light peeked out from it.

Behind her, shadows loomed. Another rattle came from a distance. She let go of her camel, bidding it to flee, then wedged her foot in the gap and pushed the sliding entrance until it was wide enough to fit her.

A pair of shadows swooped towards her, their shrieks tearing through the gloom. She ducked and leapt down into the stairwell, watching them skate by overhead.

She left the entryway ajar in case she needed to make a quick exit, but the tumult ceased as soon as she descended the stairwell. The air felt still, as though the walls were holding their breath. With the tribe shamans no longer here to regulate the temperature, the chill soon crept under her skin. Her heart skittered at every sound and echo, but she kept one foot after the other, relying on the pearly light in the distance to find her way until she reached the bottom.

The cavern where her tribe had resided was now just a pile of debris, save for the area where the shamans had put up the protective dome. Where it was previously filled with warmth and light, it was now a dark, draughty space cluttered with rocks and collapsed stone edifices. Her tribemates had taken everything with them—everything that they could salvage—leaving no trace of their presence.

Soon, she found the boulder that covered the secret stairway down to the dungeon. There, the light shone the brightest, illuminating a telling spot in the ground.

She didn't have to wait long before the ghosts revealed themselves. They crowded in on her even before her feet hit the bottom of the stairs. Behind them, the Ghost King appeared just as dramatically as before, flanked by his army of souls. Desert Rose spotted the only familiar face among them. The sight of him filled her with strength again.

'Papa!' she cried, rushing towards him. But the Ghost King stood in her way before she could reach her father.

'Your promise has not been fulfilled,' were his first words to her.

'I know that,' she said, trying to hold back her irritation. 'Complications arose.'

She told him everything—at least, everything he needed to know. From King Falco's plan to the war at Danxi Plains, her being poisoned and unable to use her magic, and the whereabouts of the other

Elementals. Her father listened closely, his face growing more sombre with each revelation.

At last, the Ghost King spoke. 'You want my assistance in fighting a mortal battle.'

She glanced at her father. Even he didn't seem convinced by her plan. She turned back to the Ghost King and nodded with more conviction than she felt.

'And what streak of arrogance led you to believe that I would offer my aid to this meaningless war?' he demanded.

Why had she been so sure he would help? He could easily strike a deal with another Elemental, one whose magic wasn't poisoned. What did he care about the wars of men anymore?

Except that he did care. Once.

'You too were once a mortal king who cared about wars like this,' she said. 'The Hesui Empire was torn apart by these two kingdoms now about to wage a war over this sacred land, once glorious under your reign. Will you really sit back and watch?'

The Hesui Empire was defeated a long time ago, but surely the Ghost King still remembered the injustice. Being the last king that ruled over the empire before it fell into the hands of the first Oasis Emperor, and later the Lettorian king, his resentment had to run long and deep.

He made no reply, but his silence didn't feel menacing this time. She braved on.

'You of all people should understand why this war can make or break the future of this world. It's not just a war between two mortal kings. It's a war among us Elementals. We each have a stake in it, and we're all going to seize our opportunity to win this fight.'

Could she do it when the time came? Could she kill Windshadow and Ruslan, who, while not entirely a friend, had saved her life once and offered his aid several times?

She pushed the thought aside. She would worry about her conscience when the time came. Right now, Wei was on his way to Danxi Plains and attempting what could be a suicide mission, while she was wasting time haggling with the Ghost King.

'I made a deal with you,' she went on. 'And I will do whatever it takes to hold up my end of it. You know I will.' She snuck a glance at her father. 'So will you help me, please?'

The Ghost King watched her for a long moment. 'As soon as all the Elementals are dead, our work is done,' he said at last.

She nodded. Which side won the battle had no bearing on her. Her loyalty lay only with her tribe; as long as she survived the Elemental destiny and saved her father, nothing else mattered.

But something did. Someone. And he was on his way to Danxi Plains now—towards a certain doom. All the more reason to stay alive. How she was going to do that given the state of her magic was something she would figure out on the way to Danxi Plains.

An echo of voices aboveground made her snap back to the present. Her gaze found her father again. *Be careful,* he mouthed. She nodded, then crept closer to the entrance of the underground chamber, straining to hear more.

There were two of them—a male and a female.

She crept up the stairs and hid behind the boulder that covered the opening in the ground, keeping her breathing shallow as she observed the newcomers.

They stood not ten feet away, their backs to her as they surveyed the wreckage.

'An explosion?' the female voice said in slightly accented Oasis language. It sounded all too familiar.

'Seems like it,' replied the male. 'The burn marks fall in a strange pattern though.' His face came into view as he stepped closer and knelt down to observe the charred marks on the ground.

Windshadow came over to Meng's side and scrutinized the marks. She glanced around the chamber, narrowly missing sight of Desert Rose.

'A force field was created here. The explosion only affected its outer periphery.' She pointed out the protective circle the tribe shamans had set up that night. It wasn't big, now that Desert Rose looked at it, just enough to shield the fifty or so people huddled close together. The crumbled boulders, rocks and fallen pillars lay just beyond the circle.

Meng frowned at the damage. His attention shot to something on his left, lying under a rock. He pulled it out and dusted it off. A zalban. One of the elders must have dropped his woven hat during the migration. 'Who could have set off the explosives?'

Fresh fury kindled in Desert Rose's gut. She stepped out into full view. 'I'm sure you know the answer to that question, Prince Meng.'

The surprise on their faces appeared genuine.

'Rose…' Meng said. 'I thought you were…' He peered at her face, and having obviously noticed something there, concluded, 'Still are.'

'Still am what?' she asked, not bothering to keep the note of irritation out of her voice.

He reached into his robes and pulled out a small porcelain vial. 'This should neutralize the poison in your body.' He offered it to her, waved it insistently when she hesitated. She reached for it and unscrewed the stopper. In it was a single round brown pill.

'He traded a vital clue to the Immortal Spring just for the antidote.' Windshadow made no disguise of her annoyance. No doubt it would have made things easier for her if Desert Rose had died from the poison. One less Elemental to eliminate.

'The stones, I know. Ruslan told me.' She received a pair of blank looks in return. 'The Metal Elemental. That's his real name.'

'Antidotes usually take a few days to bind the toxin,' Meng said. 'There's no way to be sure if King Falco gave me the real antidote. You can choose not to take it if you don't trust him. Or me.'

She tucked the antidote in her breast pocket. Meng's gaze fell. It was Falco she didn't trust, but she only said to Meng, 'Thank you. I'll make my decision in due time.'

He nodded and pursued the issue no further. 'You said I'm supposed to know the answer to who set off the explosives.'

'We found an imperial emblem left behind at the scene. One of your scouts must have dropped it after they blew up this place. My tribe matriarch …' The thought of Anar Zel's undignified death made her want to throw a rock at him. How could he stand there so brazenly and play innocent?

Meng frowned. 'Like I told Wei, I never ordered my scouts to blow up anything.' Realization unfurrowed his brows. 'When were you here?'

'Mid-spring, a little more than a moon after the Spring Ceremony.' Windshadow glanced at Meng. 'Han was already emperor by then.'

Meng nodded. 'We were already halfway through the desert to Lettoria,' he said to Desert Rose.

'So it wasn't you?' Desert Rose murmured. He shook his head.

A strange sense of relief washed over her. Meng wasn't the one who set the decree. He hadn't ordered for her tribe and Wei's mother to be killed. He hadn't tailed them to Ghost City. She had misunderstood him. Perhaps he was not the person she had thought he was.

But no, he was still the person who had manipulated her and used her to advance his goals. The one who had arranged for the murder of Wei's brother. Even though he had done those things under his mother's orders, it didn't excuse his actions or decisions.

But if Han was the one who sent the scouts, then what was his motive for doing so? Was Wei his target?

'They've found the location of the spring,' Meng said, breaking into her thoughts. 'And apparently it's somewhere here.'

'Right here? In Ghost City?' Desert Rose said.

'The stones weren't particularly specific,' Windshadow said drily. 'Maybe Falco should have gotten a more detailed map.'

'He's timed it all perfectly,' Meng said, his brows furrowed. 'By the time the Lettorian Army finds the spring—'

'The battle at Danxi Plains would be over and Falco would have what he needs to unlock the spring,' Desert Rose finished.

'Not if I'm here to stop him,' said Meng.

'Because you managed to stop him perfectly from robbing you of the stones,' Windshadow quipped.

Meng shot her an exasperated look. Desert Rose had never seen him lose his patience with anyone before. 'What use am I on the battlefield?'

'No one's asking you to pick up a sword.'

Meng frowned. 'Falco intends to tear down the Wall. If I create a diversion with the spring, Wei might have a better fighting chance.'

Desert Rose could tell he wasn't fond of the idea. Meng hated the idea of chaos. If all the world was a raging river, he was a brook. And tearing down the Wall that had protected Oasis Kingdom for centuries would bring unrest, introducing an uncomfortable revolution to the kingdom.

'The Metal Elemental is on his way to Danxi Plains,' she said.

'So is the Fire.' Windshadow smiled with grim satisfaction. 'One fell swoop then.'

Something passed between them. The understanding that whatever they had been through together, whatever they once shared, they would no longer be desert sisters once they reached the battlefield. The stage had been set, and they were to fulfil their roles and play out their destinies.

You are not alone, Rose, she told herself. She had a whole army behind her, under an undead king contracted to aid her. And Windshadow, despite her ruthlessness, had a heart.

She could do this. Win the cruel game the gods had laid out for them. Survive. She would do whatever it took, for her father, for her tribe.

Ghost City wasn't always a forgotten catacomb; it was a resting place for kings and other esteemed figures in the heart of the ancient Hesui Kingdom. It made sense that it would be built around something as sacred as the Immortal Spring.

She closed her eyes and reached for any skein of water she could find in this place that was dry as a bone. The sound of trickling water seeped towards her, so soft she almost missed it. She had heard it that night too when she first arrived here with Wei and the others. Could the spring truly be here, right at their feet? The notion didn't seem so far-fetched now.

She inched in the direction of the sound, letting herself be pulled by the energies around her. It was coming from a dark, narrow tunnel behind the boulder concealing the underground chamber. They were so close. She could feel it, all the energies converging, tugging at her.

'I feel it,' Windshadow murmured, holding out a hand as though she was reading the wind.

They wound deeper, relying on the lone torch Meng carried. It flickered dangerously the further they went until it completely went out just as the swell of water reached a feverish roar, shifting like an impatient beast. On instinct, she reached for Windshadow's hand and felt the other girl hold on to hers. The energetic turmoil outside was churning up a storm in both of them. Was this it? Were they about to meet their fate sooner than they were prepared to?

A voice from the other end of the tunnel cut through the frenzy. They paused. The voice was muffled, but there was no mistaking the language and accent.

Now that their attention was broken by the disturbance, so too did the energy connection. The sound of water subsided. Everything went still and silent as before, until all they heard was their shallow breaths.

Windshadow swore under her breath. 'Damn Lettorians.'

TWENTY-SIX

Meng

The Lettorians came crashing in with their metal tools and equipment, hardly making any effort to conceal themselves, as though they owned the place. Ghost City was a burial ground for the old kings and rulers of the Hesui Empire. But of course, the Lettorians didn't care about its sacredness. This was not their religion, their people, or their history. To them, this was merely grounds for plunder. So confident that they were the only ones here, they barely noticed Meng.

It had taken them less time to discover Ghost City than Meng had anticipated. Desert Rose would probably have found the spring first had the Lettorians not interrupted her and Windshadow and forced them to flee. But the Lettorians were here, and the plan would be executed as intended, just without the girls locating the spring for now.

The Dugurians leading the way were much more reverent than the Lettorians, treading carefully through the narrow passageways in silence with their heads bowed. Meng could make out Blackstone's hulking figure behind the three shamans, and the others filing behind him. He tailed them, keeping to the shadows and leaving a good distance between him and the group led by the shamans.

The Dugur clan leaders came to a stop at the end of a particularly long passageway. There was no way to tell how deep inside Ghost

City they were now. Every corner they turned had looked like the next, save for the carvings on the wall that were dimly lit by the entourage's torches.

At last, the passageway opened up into another cavern, this one smaller than that where Meng had run into Desert Rose. Unlike the other, this circular cavern was just large enough to fit all twenty of them—Lettorian soldiers, Dugur shamans and clan members, and Meng. Overhead, the ceiling stretched far beyond what the eye could see. From the distance above came a strange blue light that pooled on the ground. The Dugurians came to a stop before it, and the shamans gathered in a ring around the light.

'Is it here?' one of the Lettorians demanded, his eyes wild with anticipation.

Meng's own heart thundered so hard he almost feared they might hear it. After years of searching, here they were, about to uncover the ancient relic of the gods that would tip the scales of heaven and earth.

The shamans ignored the Lettorian soldier and held their hands out before them, palms facing the dusty ceiling. They began chanting in unison, their voices echoing around the chamber.

But contrary to what the Lettorians expected, the shamans were not waking up the spring. Meng watched them intently. It had taken some effort to convince them to do this, but they had agreed in the end that it was for the greater good.

An ominous rumble came from the walls and ceiling. There was a definite crack of rocks that threatened to break loose around them. The Lettorians scrambled apart. Meng hung back, still watching.

King Falco was no fool, but his biggest flaw was overconfidence. *He who believes his opponent is defeated is the one who has lost.* To never underestimate one's enemy was the key lesson of Lu Cao's *The War Handbook.*

Meng might have never been on the battlefield or fought for his survival in the wilderness like his brothers, but he had studied *The War Handbook* from cover to cover. He had learnt how to forge alliances with people the enemy least expected. After all, he had served as Oasis Kingdom's unofficial ambassador for a year under his father's rule, and he had made deals with the most unlikely characters—including the beast-people of Yeli Mountains and an excommunicated Dugur tribe member—to achieve his ends.

Lu Cao therefore would probably approve of Meng making a secret negotiation with the Dugur clan leaders behind King Falco's back. After all, a good tactician knew that one should always have another thing up his sleeve, in case the most obvious plan—and the next, and the one after that—failed.

'Stay back,' Bataar instructed, though he remained close to the shamans.

The Lettorian soldiers backed away from the ring of light, retreating deeper into the shadows. As the chanting crescendoed, rock collapsed all around the Lettorians, piling high enough to obscure them from sight. Soon, their cries of confusion and anguish were silenced as they were crushed by the tumbling rocks. Meng winced, wishing he could block out the sounds of death.

After the dust settled, the only ones remaining were the Dugurians. Meng stepped out of his hiding spot at last. The clan leaders exchanged a grim nod with him. A part of him remained on guard against them, but they had come this far in their alliance and the Dugurians had kept to their word. All that was left now was the final step.

'The token, Bataar,' Blackstone ordered, gesturing at his son.

Bataar pulled out a pouch tucked in his waist belt. 'Got it from Rose on her first night in Lettoria,' he explained for Meng's sake as he shook the contents out onto the ground. Desert Rose's lock of hair lay next to the stones that they had taken from Meng, looking strangely ethereal in the pool of blue light.

Meng stared at it. 'A token?'

'If we can't get the Elementals themselves here to unlock it, then we need to at least wake it up,' Bataar explained. 'Rose's hair contains her essence. Though not enough to unlock the spring, it can help her build an affinity with it.'

'It would be much easier if Rose were here,' said the clan leader named Gaan. 'The magic would be much stronger. Or better yet, her essence.'

'Rose doesn't trust us anymore,' Bataar said. 'You know what she's like.'

'If she only knew we're trying to help her.'

'Enough idle chatter,' Blackstone interrupted. He gestured at the shamans. 'We don't have much time.'

The three shamans took their places around the circle, sitting cross-legged with their eyes closed as they began another round of chanting, this time in the old tongue they had used to locate the spring. As the stones began to rattle under the shamans' voices, the pool of light expanded and rippled, casting long shadows that danced on the walls of the cavern.

The sound of gently trickling water filled the cavern, calming. Coupled with the hypnotic blue light, it could lull a weary traveller to an eternal sleep. It had been a long journey. What would it take to have a moment's rest?

The ground issued a deep bellow, pulling Meng out of his reverie. He jumped, finding himself drifting on the verge of consciousness. Next to him, Blackstone was shaking Bataar awake while the other clan leaders cleared their groggy eyes.

Yet, the shamans did not falter. They pressed on, relentless in their chanting, until an unbearable weight settled in the air, pushing everything together and apart at the same time. Meng squeezed his eyes shut as his fingers curled into fists by his side. It felt as though the cavern might implode from the pressure at any moment.

Meng had read about the desert's qi—the unique energy that sustained it and held everything in balance, influencing everything from climate to vegetation to even people's moods—but now that he was experiencing it in its purest, most compact form, its potency both awed and terrified him.

Blood trickled down the shamans' noses and perspiration streamed down their faces. The spring's energy was too much even for these practitioners to bear, and they seemed to be bearing the brunt of it, as though they were absorbing all of the energy into their mortal bodies to spare the rest of them.

Bataar took a step towards them, but Blackstone held him back. These shamans were here to perform this crucial and final task of their lives, and they were giving it everything they had left in them. Their belief in the Elemental saviour would see them through this mission. According to Blackstone, they were prepared to die for the cause with no regrets.

One by one, the shamans toppled to the ground, spewing blood. As the final shaman breathed his last, the light on the ground died, along with the sound of running water. The clan leaders and Bataar placed their hands over their hearts and bowed once. Meng stared at the blood-stained ground, the shattered stones, and the empty spot where the lock of Desert Rose's hair had lain. This chamber had seen far too many deaths in such a short time. Even if restoring the balance between the realms was the ultimate aim, at what cost did it come?

'The deed is done,' Blackstone declared with unbridled triumph. 'Thank you, Your Highness, for aiding us in this sacred task.'

He ought to feel relieved, glad, and proud of what he had helped to actualize. But like that time he took over the throne through illegitimate means, he felt only a sense of apprehension sitting on his chest. He had helped to change the world, but all he felt was a heavy dread at an unknowable future.

The spring had awakened. And a new dawn now fell upon the desert, for better or for worse.

TWENTY-SEVEN

Wei

Wei was no stranger to the sorrows of parting.

He had been through it before at sixteen when he decided to leave Oasis Kingdom—and his family—to explore the world beyond its walls. He had travelled with worry and guilt niggling at him for not being there to protect, in his own feeble way, his mother and brother, for choosing his own path instead of submitting to the one he was doomed to in the palace.

He was no stranger to the pain of having to leave behind all that he knew and loved. But experience never made parting any easier.

Watching Desert Rose ride away from him and then turning around to go his separate way made his heart ache in a way it never had before. He glanced down at the hemp bracelet on his wrist. Had she reached Ghost City yet? Would she succeed in persuading the Ghost King to help her? Would they meet again on the battlefield?

He had learnt a long time ago not to question fate or worry about things beyond his control, but his thoughts were unbridled this time.

No time for that now. He gripped his reins harder and glanced at Ruslan riding next to him on the horse he had gotten at the last desert town. If their plan succeeded, both of them would be free of King Falco, free to build a new life for themselves.

He pushed all thoughts of Desert Rose out of his mind for now and rode harder. The end was close.

* * *

They arrived at the Lettorian camp before dawn broke.

Ahead of them, coated in the morning mist, Danxi Plains sprawled far beyond what the eye could see. Everything was still, almost peaceful, in this sleeping world. The crisp, earthy scent of dew and the evergreens from the northern mountains hung in the air.

Wei scanned the mountains, searching for a sign of his pet hawk. Had Sunrise managed to deliver his message to Zeyan and Beihe? It was a long shot, but if anything happened to him today, he trusted them to finish what he had started. Given that he hadn't heard from them since he left Lettoria, he could only act in good faith in his Snow Wolf Sect brothers now.

In the distance, about five li away, he could make out the faint silhouette of Oasis Kingdom's fortified stone walls—the fortress they were about to attack. The scouts had already advanced to the gates under the cover of night, ready to weaken the capital from its feet.

Meanwhile, the troops here were starting to rouse. The group of ten mages was already putting on their armour outside their tents, bracing themselves for the feat they were soon to perform. The Wall would take all ten of them to tear down, and they were to be protected at all costs.

Wei and Ruslan joined the soldiers as they were gathering their weapons and equipment.

'Where have you been?' Sergeant Vicardi demanded. 'I don't recall seeing you travel with us for days.'

'Special mission for King Falco regarding the secret weapons,' Wei lied without missing a beat. The sergeant made no reply, indicating that he had long known about the king's plans involving the Elementals.

These are not your people, your comrades, or your friends, Wei reminded himself. 'Temporary allies become your biggest threat once you no longer have a common enemy,' his Snow Wolf Sect master once told him.

But he rode with these temporary allies towards the battlefield now. For now, at least, they shared the same goal: demolish the Wall and overthrow Han. He would do it for Yong, for his mother, for himself, and for the life he could have had but never did.

There was no way to approach undetected. The mist provided scant cover, but the silence was thick enough for any hoof beat or the creak of armour to cut through. Wei kept his eyes peeled for the slightest foreign movement. The closer they approached, the heavier the sense of disquiet weighed on him. They were being watched, for sure, though from where he couldn't yet tell.

The first arrow shot towards them from a good distance away. A soldier let out a cry and went tumbling off his horse. All too late, the mist parted to reveal two rows of Oasis soldiers flanking them, fencing them in.

'Guard the mages!' Sergeant Vicardi bellowed. 'Get into formation!'

The soldiers scrambled to their places, a group of them rushing to form a ring around the mages barrelled forward on their horses. Wei charged across the plains together with them, sword in one hand and reins in the other.

The Oasis troops closed in with their spears. More were lying in wait for them up ahead. Their pre-emptive attack had worked; the Lettorians had most certainly been caught off guard. But what the Lettorians lacked in the element of surprise, they made up for in ferocity.

Blades clashed. The shriek of steel pierced through the cool morning air, and the ground shook under the thundering hooves of horses. Wei swerved and dodged the onslaught of swords and arrows, never lingering in one place long enough to become a target. The aim was to arrive at the gates of Oasis Kingdom, to break through its defences while the troops were busy with the Ferros and the mages so he could reach Han undetected.

Oasis soldiers, barely recognizing him under his armour, were relentless in their attacks. Wei threw a couple of them off their horses as they were about to attack the mages.

What would father say if he saw this? His rogue son abetting the enemy to tear down the Wall that his ancestors had erected to safeguard the kingdom from magic.

But was the Wall truly a form of defence or was it imprisonment? Did it protect the people from the magic that lay beyond it or keep them enslaved to those in power within? As with all change, the first step was the hardest.

Wei ducked a blade swinging straight at him and struck the offending soldier in the chest. Recognition bloomed in the soldier's eyes just before Wei shoved him off his horse, letting his voice get drowned out by the roar of hooves and clashing blades.

The Lettorian army approached the western wall, where a contingent of soldiers awaited. These were the Black Guards, the elite army specially trained to destroy foreign threats ranging from spies to assassins to whole battalions. But they were, after all, mortal. How would they defeat the special army King Falco had created?

With the help of the Iron Guards, who felled and destroyed anything in their path, the Lettorians cut through the melee, penetrating the Blue and Red Guards with ease. Wei stuck close to them; they were his best bet at making it into Oasis Kingdom.

While the Ferros swept out half the offensive troops, the mages, still surrounded by a nearly impenetrable ring of guards, huddled in a tight circle, now within range of the Wall. They raised their arms, palms directed at the invisible magic barrier, and began to chant.

It started as an almost imperceptible disturbance in the air, a ripple that grew into a whirlwind. Then a swirling vortex swept across the plains, the force emanating from the stone walls of Oasis Kingdom. The ground growled and shook beneath their feet, throwing half the guards and soldiers off balance. Wei's horse whinnied and reared, almost flinging him off its back until he gave up and hopped off.

Wei caught sight of his target at last, standing atop the highest watchtower, away from the reach of arrows and protected by at least twenty soldiers in a close circle around him. Han was dressed in a luxurious black silk robe that looked ridiculously inappropriate for the battlefield. He had always been a little vain.

The sight of his older brother stirred up all the grief and rage he had carried within him these few months. He let his emotions wash over him, consume him, and stoke the fire within him. His mother and Matron had died at his hands. He would seek justice for them today, even if it was the last thing he did.

He was so close now.

He pressed on, keeping his head low as an insistent wind whipped around the plains.

From the depths of the earth came a deafening crack, followed by a deep rumble that knocked everyone off their feet. Wei scrambled to right himself and leaned against a slain horse to secure his bearings.

Something shimmered in the distance. A translucent wall in front of Oasis Kingdom was revealing itself, stretching towards the sky and spanning across the entire length of the kingdom's borders. It rippled like silk, iridescent and almost hypnotic in the sunlight, until inch by inch it seemed to melt, eroding into the ground. Around him, Oasis soldiers cried out in shock; others were transfixed in horror.

It didn't take long for the Wall to disintegrate. When the last trace of it finally dissipated, the mages, still in their circle not ten feet away, lowered their arms.

They had done it. The Wall was gone for good. And Oasis Kingdom was officially under siege.

Han remained on the watchtower, surrounded by imperial guards and soldiers waving their spears as though that would in any way defend them against the onslaught of magic that could now enter the kingdom. He didn't seem the least bit bothered by the Wall being taken down. It was almost as though he had expected this.

On the ground, General Yue barked at the Black Guards to maintain their positions as the Ferros advanced towards them. The Iron Guards were unmatched in their speed, agility, and strength. With the added physical advantage, one Ferros could easily match three regular soldiers. Wei was almost mesmerized by the way they cleaved and smashed their way through, until the groan of a heavy metal gate caught his attention.

A tall, slim boy dressed in imperial armour stepped out, regarding the wreckage before him.

The boy from the bazaar.

Back then, he had loped next to Han, looking extra gangly next to Han's burly build. But now he strode with an assuredness that made him seem older than he was—especially with the ball of fire he was casually toying with in his palm.

The Fire Elemental. Of course, it was him. He must have been the one who had set the bazaar ablaze too.

With a flick of his wrist, he flung the ball of fire at a group of Ferros. The flames grew larger as they careened towards the soldiers and consumed all five of them before they could react.

The Fire Elemental lobbed another ball of fire through the fray, sending soldiers from both sides ducking and running helter-skelter for their lives. The flames hurtled around, rampant and merciless, setting several soldiers alight.

Wei was about to avert his eyes when someone flung out a metal spear.

The flames streamed away from it as though they had met a wall. Now more subdued, they went straight back into the palm of the Fire Elemental. The boy frowned.

'There he is,' said Ruslan, cutting through a group of regular soldiers, metal spear in hand. He plunged it into the ground and levelled a look at the Fire Elemental. 'I've heard a lot about you, my fiery brother.'

'I go by Lazar, actually,' the other boy replied. 'But you won't be living long enough to utter that name.'

Wei snorted. *Just destroy each other and be done with it.*

Lazar flung out his hands, blasting a jet of flames at Ruslan. But once more, the Metal Elemental held out his spear, clearly fortified and specially forged for this exact purpose. The flames came to a halt before the blade as though hitting an impenetrable wall.

Lazar only chuckled, unimpressed, before throwing out a pair of darts that were no doubt poisoned. But Ruslan dodged those cleanly, recovering himself just as Lazar whipped out twin streaks of fire at him. The first streak knocked Ruslan off balance, the second made him lose his grip on his weapon. It landed several feet away from him, just out of reach.

Now that Lazar was preoccupied with Ruslan, the Ferros resumed their attack, slashing through a herd of soldiers with near effortless ease. Meanwhile, a pair of Oasis soldiers charged at Wei. Recognition flashed in their eyes as soon as they got close enough, but they didn't go any easier on him.

A chilling scream cut through the din, almost lost in the mire of the battle.

Ruslan was aflame. Despite his specially forged armour that protected him from neck to toe, Lazar's unearthly fire had managed to burn through it. The Fire Elemental was straining too, his hands shaking as he blasted through Ruslan's armour.

Wei turned away as Ruslan sank to his knees. He sounded awfully mortal then, a mere boy rather than an all-powerful Elemental. His screams would live in Wei's head from that moment on. The Fire Elemental was far stronger than any of the other Elementals he had met. Desert Rose had only just managed to control her magic—how could she survive Lazar's?

He shook his head. First things first.

The soldiers were still distracted by Ruslan's slow death and the Ferros' destruction. Wei seized his moment to escape, slipping through the main gate that was left ajar after Lazar's grand appearance.

In a corner of the western wall, not five feet away from the main gates, was a door tucked behind a heavyset drum that entry guards would strike to announce important arrivals. Beyond that nondescript door were two flights of stairs, one that led to an underground pathway that would take him directly to the palace, and another that would take him up to the watchtower. Matron had shown him that door when he was younger. She knew all the secret passageways in and out of the kingdom and had imparted her knowledge to him on the sly many years ago, probably because she reckoned he would come to rely on it someday. Despite being a woman of few words, Matron had—apart from Yong and his mother—looked out for him more than anyone else in the palace.

He found the secret door behind the drum just as he remembered it. A pair of soldiers charged at him just as he pushed it open. He sidestepped them deftly, then aimed a kick at one of them and shoved the second soldier into the first. Together, they went stumbling into the fray and were soon kept busy with some Lettorian soldiers. *Probably not the best idea to have a battle right at your doorstep*, Wei thought. What was Han thinking?

He would find out soon enough. He ducked behind the door, then charged up the stone steps. His ragged breaths echoed in the empty tower, but outside the battle raged on.

Han was already waiting for him at the entrance. As soon as Wei pushed the metal door open, Han's sabre swooped towards his neck. It would have landed on its target had Wei not swung the door close in time. The blade slammed against the door.

Wei tightened his grip on the hilt of his sword before stepping out again, this time ducking low and aiming for Han's knees right away. He crashed into the older boy, sending them both rolling across the ground. Wei flipped to his feet hastily, ready for the guards that would rush to Han's defence, but none came. The watchtower was empty aside from the two of them.

Everything felt amiss. Warning bells clanged in Wei's head, but he couldn't pinpoint the reason for his growing unease. Why was Han not protected? Why was he unfazed by the Ferros, Lettoria's secret weapon? Who was the real enemy here?

'I've been waiting for you, little brother,' Han said, as though he had heard Wei's thoughts. His smile was a nasty grimace as he flung his sabre down at Wei.

On reflex, Wei raised his sword. Their blades screamed against each other when they met. With his hulking almost bear-like size, Han towered over him, pressing his weight against Wei's blade, unrelenting. But Wei pushed back with all his might. The sabre was thicker and heavier than Wei's, filed to a lethal edge that gleamed like a warning. One swoop and Wei's head would be rolling on the floor.

'I had to be here to throw you off the throne myself, didn't I?' Wei replied through gritted teeth.

Han sneered. 'Says the one who walked right into our trap.'

In a burst of strength, he shoved against Wei's blade, sending Wei staggering backwards before kicking him in the gut. Wei's sword clattered to the side and lay just beyond his reach. Wei barely managed to recover before Han pinned him to the ground with a knee on his chest.

Han leaned down to murmur into his ear. 'You've done a great service to the kingdom, little brother. I'll be sure to spread your good name far and wide.' He straightened with a smirk. 'I've heard about your desert friend—or should I say, your Elemental friend. Do you suppose my Fire Elemental has already done his job in killing them all?'

Despite himself, Wei faltered at the mention of Desert Rose. *He's distracting you, Wei. Stay present.* He raised his leg and rammed his knee into Han's groin. Han grunted and toppled forward, loosening his grip on Wei's arm, allowing Wei to roll out from underneath him and pick up his sword again.

But Han recovered with lightning speed, spinning back around with his sabre. The blade snagged on Wei's hemp bracelet and snapped it apart. It drifted off in the gentle breeze. Wei scrambled to reach for it, but Han yanked him back and slammed him against the ledge with such force that Wei almost tipped over. Wei wheezed, trying to regain his breath. Han brought his blade down again, this time coming dangerously close to Wei's neck.

Wei threw all his strength into his blade, flinging it aside along with Han's sabre. Without missing a beat, Han wrapped his fingers around Wei's throat. 'You know what I've learnt over the years? The best way to weaken your enemy is to take away everything and everyone they care about, make them have nothing to fight for or live for.'

Wei fought against his brother's grip. 'This is an elaborate setup, even for you, Han,' he choked out.

Han laughed and loosened his grip, as though to prove that he was the one in control. 'You overestimate your significance, bastard brother. You're just an inconvenience King Falco and I are happy to be rid of. We have bigger concerns than the likes of you.'

'So you didn't have us followed and ambushed at Ghost City? You didn't try to blow us all up?'

'Oh, that. I didn't even have to lift a finger, really. King Falco very generously offered to do it.'

Wei froze. 'What?'

'Well, we had to give you a reason to go to Lettoria, didn't we?' Han said. 'And what better reason than revenge? I'm sure you received a rather warm welcome in Lettoria. The king had been expecting you for a while.'

I have been waiting for the day you step through my doors. Those were King Falco's first words to him.

'Word on the street was that you were travelling with an Elemental. Did you know that Elemental essence is incredibly precious? Enough to wake an entire desert and even unlock a magical spring? So, naturally, King Falco had his sights set on her. We both did. Since we both want to unlock the spring, why not gather our resources, throw them all in a battlefield and let them fight it out? Their destiny is to kill each other or be killed—we're just giving them the stage to play out their destinies.'

'So you killed my mother just to make me desperate enough for revenge to seek Falco's support,' Wei said.

He had used him. Of course he had. Han had always had a knack for identifying his enemy's weakness and using it against him.

Han shrugged. 'We knew you're not going to join forces with me, so we had to make sure you and your Elemental friend went to Lettoria. You'd want King Falco's backing to defeat me.'

King Falco, too, had played him from the moment Wei entered the Grand Palace. He had orchestrated the whole setup and ordered the attack in Ghost City just to lure Wei to Lettoria and bring Desert Rose right into the tiger's den. He'd then put out the news of the Metal Elemental's whereabouts knowing that she would try to kill him, and had her poisoned knowing that Wei would do anything to save her life. Just like he knew Wei and Rose would walk right into this staged battle.

This was a game of chess, one that Han and Falco had played from the very beginning. This was why Han had been calm and confident since the start of the battle. Because it was never about Lettoria going to war with Oasis Kingdom; it was about exploiting the Elementals to gain access to the spring.

Rage surged through Wei, at Han and King Falco, but mostly at himself. How could he have not seen this coming? How could he have let himself be so misled by vengeance—and, if he were truly honest with himself, ambition—to be so thoroughly played by his enemies?

With a burst of strength, he shoved him away. Han keeled over, but rolled away and got to his feet with practised ease even before Wei could retrieve his sword.

A slow smile slid across Han's face as his attention shifted to something over Wei's shoulder. 'Here comes our Water Elemental.'

Wei spun around and scanned the plains. Indeed, there she was, a striking figure in red, riding hard across the plains on a brown steed. His brave, strong Rose. She cut through the skirmish, eyes fixed ahead and body pressed low, quick to employ her double knives against anyone who got too close. Arrows rained down from the Oasis guard posts, but somehow, she managed to dodge them all by a hair's breadth.

She had never looked more beautiful.

Wei had seen her fight before, when she was an assassin-in-training at the House of Night. He had also crossed blades with her when they first met in the Khuzar Desert last winter. But each time he watched her in action, he was still transfixed. She moved with strength and grace, sure-footed and determined. Her skills had only grown sharper in the last few months out on the road and in Lettoria.

A kick in the back sent him sprawling back to the edge of the watchtower. Han's sabre descended on him, aiming for his neck again. Wei swerved but just barely. A sharp sting made him wince and he looked down to find a long gash running down the length of his arm. Han wrenched Wei's arms behind him and pinned him against the ledge. Pain shot through his injured arm.

Upon a sharp whistle from Han, a pair of guards came running towards them. They clamped down on him, unyielding despite his fierce struggle.

'So brave, so foolish.' Han snickered. 'I can see why you're attracted to her. She looks heavenly in red.'

Wei strained against the guards' grip. The urge to knee him in the groin again was strong.

'If she manages to survive, perhaps I'll invite her into the palace again,' Han mused. 'Imagine the things we could do with all these Elementals. The things we could do to them.'

Rage clouded Wei's mind. He wanted to yell out to her, tell her to approach no further. There was still time for her to abandon this battle. She could still avoid this trap laid for her, avoid the same fate as Ruslan.

But she was already making her way towards the Metal Elemental who lay prone at Lazar's feet. She was heading towards Lazar despite having seen what he had done. What he could do.

Rose had gone to Ghost City in the hopes of getting the Ghost King's aid. Did returning alone mean she hadn't managed to persuade him? Would she now face off against the other Elementals alone with her defective magic? Every muscle in Wei ached to throw himself before her, to protect her from Lazar.

She came to a stop before the Fire Elemental and spoke to him with a strange calmness, as though ready to meet her end. Han's words echoed in his head. *So brave, so foolish.* Wei hoped she knew what she was doing.

She knelt before Ruslan and leaned close to him, as though listening to what he was saying with his dying breath. A subtle nod, then she got to her feet, picked up Ruslan's sword, and turned to face the Fire Elemental head-on.

TWENTY-EIGHT

Desert Rose

The midday sun was blinding. A monstrous heat seared through the land. By the time Desert Rose arrived at Danxi Plains, the battle was in full swing.

Bodies lay bloodied and inert all around her, and the smell of burning flesh attacked her senses. She averted her eyes from the sight, already feeling sick to her stomach. This was the first time she was surrounded by so much violence, bloodshed, and death. It was everything Papa had tried to protect her from when she grew up in the Dugur tribe, when he had forbidden her to hunt with the clan boys or venture to the frontier lands that often saw clashes between the western nations and desert tribes.

It was hard to tell which side was winning. Some Lettorian soldiers seemed to possess superhuman strength and speed, killing Oasis soldiers without breaking a sweat. Unnatural streams of fire seemed to target Lettorian soldiers everywhere they went.

The Fire Elemental. It had to be him. Windshadow had caught her up on the wrath-filled boy named Lazar who aspired to ascend to the heavens after he defeated all the Elementals.

She charged towards the source of the flames.

Amidst the sound of clanging blades, cries of slain men, and shrieking horses was the thundering of her own heart. There was no sign of Wei around. Had he managed to enter Oasis Kingdom? Had he found Han? She could feel Windshadow's presence on her shoulder, a gentle puff of wind that provided some reassurance.

She found Ruslan lying in an incinerated patch of grass, his body armour looking just as charred. His face was a brutal shade of crimson, as though he was being baked in his suit. He was still conscious, but his breaths came out feeble and shallow. She reached out to touch his sweat-drenched face, drawing her hand away almost as soon as it met his flushed, burning skin.

She looked up at the boy standing before them, watching them with a crooked smile. His casually extended hand, palm facing Ruslan, radiated undulating waves of heat. He appeared no older than her, but there was no trace of innocence in his eyes, only malice.

'You must be the Water Elemental,' he drawled.

She shot him a scathing glance, already despising the cocky arch of his brows. 'What makes you think that?'

'Well, no one has seen the Earth Elemental—though rumour has it he's hiding in the Yeli Mountains—and I've already had the pleasure of meeting our Air sister, so that leaves you.' He glanced around. 'Speaking of whom, where is our Air sister? I didn't think she would miss this battle of a lifetime.'

Ruslan let out an anguished moan.

'What are you doing to him?' Desert Rose demanded.

He cocked his head at her. 'Slowly cooking him to death, evidently. Don't look so aggrieved—it's all part of our destiny, after all. I'm just getting rid of one of our competitors.'

How did this boy have so much cruelty in his heart? What had he gone through in his life to be this cruel and twisted?

Ruslan seized her armoured arm, drawing her attention back to him. 'Tell my brother...' he rasped. 'Tell him ... not to wait for me.' There was more he seemed intent on saying, but the light disappeared from his eyes. His hand fell slack to the ground.

'Just you and me now, azzi,' said the Fire Elemental.

'I am not your sister,' she spat.

She picked up Ruslan's sword as she got to her feet. It was still warm to the touch. Could she even wield this thing? It wasn't her element, and this weapon would only obey its maker. But she couldn't call upon her own element now without hurting herself. This would have to do.

A sharp gust of wind whipped around the Fire Elemental, spinning him off balance. Windshadow revealed herself by the time he found his footing again, flashing her daggers and a wicked smile.

The Fire Elemental smirked. 'I was a little hurt you left so hurriedly the last time, azzi,' he said. 'You should have taken me up on my offer.'

Windshadow snorted. 'Unfortunately, I don't have delusions of grandeur. I'm not under the impression that we're destined to ascend to the heavens.'

'Then why? Why are you here? Why not just give up now, if you believe we're doomed to die for nothing?'

'Because there are things worth fighting for in the meantime, and you're in my way.' With that, she spun into a whirlwind and charged at him.

Desert Rose joined her, trying to get used to the weight of Ruslan's sword. It was heavier and more unyielding than regular steel ones, though the energy it carried imparted some strength to her, almost as though Ruslan was fighting alongside her.

But the Fire Elemental was possibly the strongest one she had met so far. He was quick and well-trained in combat, and his element was clearly meant for destruction. Even Windshadow, with all her speed and ruthlessness, was no match against him.

The only advantage they had was in numbers. They attacked in tandem, never giving him a moment to breathe. Windshadow darted around the Fire Elemental, lashing at him while Desert Rose combated his fiery whip with Ruslan's sword.

Around them, the roar of battle was relentless. The superhuman Lettorian soldiers seemed to be gaining the upper hand due to their obvious advantages. And with the Fire Elemental preoccupied here, the regular Oasis soldiers were left to fend for themselves.

But the Fire Elemental's energy seemed inexorable. Desert Rose wasn't sure if she was the one wearing him down so that Windshadow could go on the offensive, or if it was the other way round and he was expending their energy.

Stay focused, Rose. It was still early in the battle. She could not give in now.

As Windshadow sent him sprawling to the ground, Desert Rose lunged forward, aiming for his heart. The Fire Elemental flung out his whip at her and knocked the sword out of her hands. The whip looped around her waist, singeing her skin through her armour but not yet burning her.

He reeled her in and caught her in a chokehold. 'You seem a little preoccupied with me, azzi. Maybe you should worry about someone else instead.' He spun her around and pointed at something in the distance. She squinted against the sun's glare, making out a familiar silhouette.

Wei.

He was at the highest point of the watchtower with Han. A pair of soldiers had pinned him against the ledge, locking his arms behind his back. Bent over the stone wall, his position precarious enough for him to pitch over anytime the guards decided to let go.

Desert Rose cursed inwardly. She was too late. Wei had entered Oasis Kingdom before she could arrive with the Ghost Army, and now he was outmatched.

The Fire Elemental's whip continued to trap her, the heat reaching her through the armour. She strained against it, a low panic beginning up in her. Windshadow swooped towards the Fire Elemental, extinguishing his flames for a split moment, just enough for her to reach for Ruslan's sword and sever the whip. She broke free and rolled away before the Fire Elemental could capture her again.

'Go,' Windshadow yelled, slipping momentarily out of her elemental form. 'I'll take care of this one.'

Desert Rose spared only a moment's hesitation before taking off. She leapt up the nearest horse she could find and nudged it into action.

The distance to the watchtower felt like an eternity away. She rode like the wind, her heart thundering in her chest as she cut through the storm of the battle. But she blocked out every clang of a blade and cry of a soldier. Reaching Wei as fast as she could was all that mattered now.

Han was watching her. She could make out his still, burly form and dark, hooded eyes the closer she got. So was Wei. He was yelling at her as he strained hard against his captors. But whatever he was saying would not make her stop. She did not come here to watch him die.

Now would be a really good time for the Ghost Army to show up, she thought. Would they? Would the Ghost King keep his word? Or had he changed his mind and left her to fend for herself?

Han waved a hand, his expression still stoic.

In that instant, she knew what Han meant to do. And she was too late to stop it.

'No…' The word escaped from her in a breath.

Horror washed over her as the soldiers shoved Wei over the ledge. He plummeted through the air, catching her gaze for a fleeting moment before disappearing into the throng of soldiers fighting at the foot of the tower.

A scream tore out of her throat. She hurtled through the plain, abandoning all caution and thought.

The ground rumbled and shook, as though a creature was rousing from the earth. A wall of sand rose from the ground, churning and whirling, ripping up the plains from its roots. This was no ordinary sandstorm; it seemed to have a life of its own. Desert Rose struggled to stay on her feet, but like everyone else around her, she fell to all fours as a thick coat of sand swept through the plains.

The Ghost King. This had to be his doing. He couldn't come aboveground, but bringing the desert with him was within his control since this land was once part of the Hesui Kingdom.

The sandstorm wiped out all visibility. Nothing could be seen beyond three feet around her. She lay low, keeping her head dipped as she crawled in what she hoped was the right direction.

Out of the tumult, someone grabbed her arm. Windshadow's voice rang out near her ear. 'Let's go.' The other girl began tugging her in the opposite direction.

Desert Rose pulled out of her grasp without bothering to explain. The sandstorm made it nearly impossible to speak anyway. Was the Ghost King taking out all these centuries of his rage on everyone?

'What is wrong with you? Let's go!' Windshadow snapped. But Desert Rose continued straining towards the watchtower.

The ground issued another reverberating growl, a warning. It seemed as though it might swallow the earth whole. They were so small, so powerless against the elements, the gods. How were they ever to survive a fate already laid out by them?

Windshadow's hand was still in hers, thin and cold but strangely reassuring. She held on tightly, waiting for the storm to pass. If it ever would.

Another deafening roar. And then the world erupted in dust and fury.

TWENTY-NINE

Windshadow

Why am I even doing this? Windshadow thought as she attempted to drag Desert Rose out of the fray.

A voice in her head—the sane, rational voice—told her she should just leave the other desert girl here. She could. It would make perfect sense to. She was not beholden to her conscience. She was not meant to save the girl's life or protect her. They were enemies; their destinies dictated it. Windshadow had learned a long time ago that love and friendship were things that her heart had no room for, and momentary kindness and sentimentality could get her killed. She had a scar on her chest that served as a reminder every day.

Yet, she found herself unwilling to let go of Desert Rose.

'Rose, we have to go—*now.*' Desert Rose was still straining against her grip, tears streaming down her face. Windshadow gave her a hard shake. 'Rose. Remember your purpose, for the gods' sake. Do you intend to die out here?'

'Wei...'

'Is likely dead so there's nothing you can do. If you die on this battlefield, you will have no chance of saving your tribe.'

Where had this freak sandstorm originated? Was this some sort of divine help from the gods? Why would they bother?

Then she saw it, a pearly silhouette illuminating a spot in the ground. A spirit? Windshadow believed in a few things, but only those she could see and touch. Ghosts were neither of those. Besides, how could a ghost raise the desert like that? And why would it interfere in this battle?

Whatever it was, it was destroying everything in its path. The sooner she and Desert Rose got out of here, the better.

The storm raged on for gods knew how long. It was almost exhilarating, lying in the midst of this chaos. In fact, with Desert Rose— perhaps the first person in her life she could almost call a friend—lying next to her, it was the closest to happiness Windshadow had ever felt.

The plains plunged back into an eerie silence just as abruptly. The girls got to their feet, picking each other up. Apart from the faint rustling of wind, everything was still. Slain soldiers—and even a few of the freakishly superhuman Lettorian ones—lay all around them.

Lazar, however, was nowhere to be found. Did he survive?

Desert Rose's voice cut through the silence. 'Windshadow, behind you!'

Windshadow whipped around to find a devilish whirlwind of sand careening towards her. On instinct, she slipped into her element, barely skirting past the sand devil's grasp. It charged at her again, as though possessing a mind of its own. What sort of being could have such power?

'No, not her!' Desert Rose yelled. Who was she talking to?

'We had an agreement,' a deep male voice boomed from the earth, authoritative and unyielding. He spoke the old tongue like a native. No one spoke the Hesuian language anymore, much less sounded like a native speaker. Whomever Desert Rose was engaging with, he was ancient and he was powerful.

'You wanted my help and I provided it. Now, it is time to hold up your end of the bargain,' said the voice.

Desert Rose made a deal with some powerful ancient being to help her eliminate the other Elementals? Windshadow would have laughed if she weren't too busy trying to stay alive. Making under-the-table deals to advance her agenda was something she would do without any qualms. Who would have thought *Desert Rose*—whose conscience took up more room than Windshadow's—would have done this? Then again, desperation could make even the most righteous person do the unconscionable. And Windshadow had betrayed her desert sister before too.

Lucky for her, she knew what to do when someone stabbed her in the back.

She fled.

Collecting herself into a tight pocket of wind, she hurtled towards the watchtower before the sand devil could launch another attack on her. The Wall might be down and every manner of magic could now penetrate the kingdom, but the old sorcerers had put in place other barriers that might keep the desert's magic away.

Emperor Han had retreated. There wasn't a soldier or guard in sight at the northern wall of Oasis Kingdom. The sentry towers were empty, and everyone on the battlefield was dead—including, she presumed, Lazar. Everyone here today had been sacrificed.

A lone wind whipped through the plains towards Oasis Kingdom. Windshadow captured it in her palm and closed her fingers over it. Everything went still—not a single breath or ripple in the air. She flung the wind back out, letting it tear through the charred expanse before her so that anyone still alive in the plains would be torn apart. Just for good measure, in case Lazar or the sand devil were hiding among the dead bodies.

The unnatural silence crept under her skin. She couldn't shake the feeling that she was walking into a trap, stepping through the northern entrance of the most tightly guarded kingdom in the world with no one stopping her.

But when else would this opportunity come again? Now that the Fire Elemental was defeated and the Wall was taken down, Han no longer had the protection he once enjoyed. It would be the perfect time to assassinate him. With some subterfuge, she could bide her time, recuperate and plan her next move.

A voice behind her broke the silence, stopping her in her tracks. 'You made it out alive.'

THIRTY

Desert Rose

At last, the dust settled.

Desert Rose cracked open her eyes and found herself lying face-down on the ground. She picked herself up gingerly in case anything was broken, ignoring the ringing in her ears as she let her vision focus.

Everything was over. The fighting, the burning, the indiscriminate destruction by the superhuman Lettorian soldiers, the Ghost King's wrath. All that remained was scorched, flattened ground, strewn with the dead and their bloodstained weapons.

She broke into a run. Ruslan was dead. What about Wei? She had watched him fall from the watchtower, but she refused to believe he had met the same end. A thought came to mind, making her sick. Would she find Wei's body lying at the foot of the watchtower?

And what about Windshadow? Did she manage to survive the Ghost King's attack?

Every muscle screamed in protest as she dragged her battered body towards the kingdom walls. There was nothing left here on the battlefield. Ruslan and Lazar were gone, and Windshadow—

She spotted her shifting into human form at the Oasis gates. The other desert girl took a moment to survey her surroundings, as though waiting for someone to stop her. But no one did. The watchtower was as empty as the plains, with no guard or soldier in sight.

Desert Rose sped up the steps to join her. 'You made it out alive,' she said after catching her breath.

Windshadow whirled around with a smirk. 'So, who did you send to kill me?'

Her question caught her off guard. 'The Ghost King,' she blurted.

Windshadow looked impressed. 'You made a deal with the *Ghost King?*'

'He agreed to help me eliminate everyone else if I free him from his underground purgatory. My father is there too. If I win the race, I can save him and my tribe.'

Windshadow shrugged. 'Well, I'm still here. You should have left me there to die if you wanted to save them.'

'You didn't leave me there to die,' Desert Rose pointed out.

Something passed between them. The recollection of their conversation in the northwest tower.

'I contemplated leaving you behind,' Windshadow said. 'Would have been doing you a favour, letting you die with your beloved.'

A sharp pang struck her heart at the mention of Wei. She abandoned Windshadow without a word and combed the entire vicinity of the watchtower, even heading up to the highest point where he had fallen. But there was no body, no sign of Wei at all.

Did that mean he had escaped? But how could he have survived that fall?

Windshadow appeared next to her with a sigh, as though impatient for her to move on. 'He's dead, Rose. Gone. You're wasting your time.' She glanced around. 'And we're sitting ducks out here in plain sight.'

A part of her wished she had Windshadow's ability to pack up her emotions and stay true to her mission. But another part wouldn't have it any other way. She had laid bare the most tender part of herself, and there was no going back from that. Even in the absence of him now. She would carry a piece of him with her for as long as she lived.

'What happens now?'

For months now, her goal had been to find the Fire Elemental. Now that Wei was no longer by her side as a constant, an anchor, an ally with whom she could formulate plans, she found herself staring down a fork in the road. Should she return to find her tribe or continue her search for the remaining Elemental? Or should she continue searching for Wei? Was he even still alive? How could she move on from something that had no answers?

She hadn't realized she had asked the question aloud until she noticed Windshadow staring at her.

'I'm going this way, if you want to come with me,' Windshadow said, jabbing her finger over her shoulder. To Oasis Kingdom. 'I'm going to hunt down the last Elemental. Then we can finally get this over with.'

Rumour has it the Earth Elemental is hiding in the Yeli Mountains, the Fire Elemental had said. Was Windshadow really going to return to Oasis Kingdom based on the Fire Elemental's word alone?

'It's the only lead we have now, and I'm taking it,' Windshadow said, as though she could hear her thoughts. 'And it's only a matter of time before our Earth friend comes looking for us. I'm not sitting around waiting for him to kill us both.'

The battle at Danxi Plains might be over, but theirs was not. It would not be over until the last Elemental was found, until a clear winner emerged. And until then, they would always be hunted down and used by mortal men for their pithy wars.

A new path lay before her, one where she could not see beyond two feet ahead. But it was a direction, a goal to keep her going, keep her preoccupied. And she would continue moving forward for now. Staying still made her grief unbearable, large enough to consume her, something she could ill afford at this point.

She cast one last look at the plains behind her, then turned and headed back into Oasis Kingdom. Towards a new beginning and the ultimate end.

THIRTY-ONE

Wei

Wei roused to complete darkness and, for some reason, the smell of earth laced with myrrh.

Was he dead? Could dead people smell things?

It was a familiar smell, one that reminded him of Ghost City. He remembered its pungency when he was last here with Desert Rose.

Why was he here? How could he be here?

The last thing he had seen before everything went dark was the one image he held on to—Desert Rose riding towards him, steely determination in her eyes, courage in her face. They had been so close, but the distance between them ultimately proved uncrossable.

A bittersweet heaviness gathered behind his eyes. At least he got to see her one last time.

He pulled himself back to the present. The stillness here unnerved him after the chaos of the battle. One moment, he was crossing blades with Han and the next, he was trapped here in this stifling darkness. He raised the arm Han had slashed and felt no pain whatsoever. His sword was tucked in his waist belt, clean and polished, as though he hadn't just been on the battlefield.

An opalescent light appeared in the distance, illuminating the grim darkness. Wei squinted, making out the Ghost King's silhouette as he approached with his army of souls. This was Ghost City. That would mean he was … dead. The realization ran him over like a cartful of bricks.

He tried to come up with a plausible explanation for how he got here. The Wall had been torn down, so the Oasis Kingdom was now part of the old Hesui Empire again—which meant the desert could lay claim to him and his soul if he died. Which meant he was now one of the undead trapped in this purgatory until Desert Rose could set them all free. Assuming she was the last surviving Elemental.

Wei bowed, remembering his manners a beat later. 'We meet again, Your Majesty.'

'Men who come to Ghost City are those who died ignoble deaths or have unfinished business with the living,' said the Ghost King. 'They are either doomed to eternity in purgatory or choose to hold on until wrongs have been righted.' He stared Wei in the eye.

Wei forced himself not to look away, to hold his gaze. He had nothing to hide; his death was not dishonourable. But what was to be his fate?

'You do not belong here,' the Ghost King pronounced. 'You are not dead.'

Wei blinked. 'I—I'm not?' Hope flickered inside him. Had Zeyan and Beihe managed to save him somehow? Why, then, was he here? More importantly, did that mean he had a chance to return to the living?

He ached desperately to do so. There was still so much left to do. The battle at Danxi was only the beginning. Han had plans for the Elementals, and getting rid of Wei was just the first step.

His gaze landed on Desert Rose's father milling among the souls behind the Ghost King. His pearlescent light shone brighter than anyone else since he was, technically, here under different circumstances from everyone else. When their eyes met, he seemed to recognize Wei too, from their last encounter. Something unspoken passed between them, the understanding that they shared a common purpose.

'Your mortal body lies somewhere aboveground, and it is being maintained,' the Ghost King replied. 'I cannot claim your soul just yet.'

The spark of hope grew into a flame, enough to light up this chamber.

The shadow of an idea began brewing in his head. His business with the living was far from over; he would not give up until he settled every single one of them.

Han was no longer the fearsome big brother who toyed with his life when they were children, just a man with his own weaknesses and flaws. Someone who felt so threatened by his own brother he had to kill him personally. Someone who sought power through intimidation and cruelty.

Someone he could ultimately defeat.

Wei himself was no longer that sixteen-year-old who ran away from home and his father who had shunned him. He was not the outlawed prince who roamed the wilderness seeking a purpose and had nothing to fight or live for. A girl from the desert once told him that he was the maker of his own life, and he now knew what his destiny was.

Now, he would claw his way back to Oasis Kingdom if that was what it took. He would return from the dead and claim what was his. His kingdom, his title, and the girl he loved.

'I need your help, Your Majesty,' Wei said at last. 'To save the Elemental that can free us all.'

Acknowledgements

It takes a village to produce a book, and this one is no exception. I'm sure I'll miss out on many more people to thank, but here goes.

First, biggest thank you to the Penguin Random House SEA team—Nora, Garima, Chai, Alkesh et al—for helping realize this lifelong dream of mine of being an author. For your dedication and enthusiasm and support, for taking my suggestions into account, for replying to my emails and texts even on weekends. For your passionate championing of writers and their stories in this corner of the world, and your efforts in taking it to other parts. Thanks also to Thatchaa and Arpita for making the book the best version of itself!

Thank you to my scribe sisters Kayce Teo (Leslie W.), Catherine Dellosa, and Eva Wong Nava for the daily uplifting conversations on writing, life and everything in between. We'll leave the sappiness in our group chat but know that I cherish our affinity infinitely.

Thank you to the Muses, Meredith Crosbie and Nicole Evans, for being a constant source of support, kindness and encouragement ever since we found each other in 2016. Someday, we will make that Middle Earth trip together. Sending Hobbits hugs in the meantime!

Thank you to the authors I've made friends with on social media. We may be miles apart but I'm here rooting for you all—Amélie Wen Zhao for writing the kindest blurb and being a positive ray of sunshine in the community; Joan He, June C.L. Tan, Chloe Gong, and Sue Lynn

Tan for your stories that inspire me not just to up my writing game, but also to embrace my roots; Tanvi Berwah, Isabel Strychacz, Ann Liang, Axie Oh, and Robin Alvarez whose books I discovered on Instagram and immediately added to my TBR.

Thank you to authors I've made friends with offline, namely the PRH SEA writer fam, Lauren Ho, Vivian Teo and more for being such fun companions as we navigate the waters of publishing.

Thank you to readers and bookstagrammers like @maireadingparty, @wordwanderlust, @phuajieying, @nonsenseoctopods, @ levairereads, @houseofhikayat, @ohthathayley, @thefictionmagnet, @tanvisreadventures, @nofrigatelikeabookstagrammer, @dbookis hprincess, @bellainherlibrary, @yy.writes etc, and the team at The Publishing Post for doing what you do—shouting about your favourite books and authors, giving us a platform and a voice, for cheering us on and fangirling with me over books, drama series and 'hot, tragic male leads'. You have no idea how our interactions and your enthusiasm have motivated me to keep writing through the times I thought of giving up.

Thank you to every reader who picked up this book (and the ones before it) and gave it a chance. My stories might come from me, but they all end with you. Thank you for giving life to them too.

Thank you to my non-writing friends—Sook Han, Valerie, Prashanti, Triveni, Xinghua, Shoniah, Vivian, Jarrod, Leo, Meena, etc.—for your listening ears and quiet support over the years.

And last but not least, thank you to my dad—you are my rock.